JOHN WYNDHAM

FOUL PLAY
SUSPECTED

THE MODERN LIBRARY

NEW YORK

FOUL PLAY SUSPECTED

By John Wyndham

The Day of the Triffids
Foul Play Suspected
The Kraken Wakes
The Midwich Cuckoos
The Outward Urge
Plan for Chaos
Stowaway to Mars
Trouble with Lichen
Web

CONTENTS

FOUL PLAY SUSPECTED

I

PHYLLIDA COMES HOME

A large car, much battered and repainted in the course of a long and useful life, valiantly set about grinding its way up the slope of the South Downs. The driver eyed the road ahead with misgiving and listened uneasily to his stertorous engine. The old hack was still good enough for running round on the level, but she was getting past mountaineering; it was quite certain that she would never make the top.

His passenger picked up the speaking-tube and a sudden blast of air took him in the ear. He frowned; years of experience had not yet inured him to this method of opening communication; nevertheless, he leaned obediently closer to the diminutive trumpet.

"Straight on through the village, and it's the next turning to the right—about half a mile beyond the church," said a voice.

He nodded thankfully. They ought to be able to get that far.

Phyllida Shiffer hung up the tube and leaned back against the worn leather of the lumpy cushions. Her fingers fiddled unconsciously and impatiently with the leather strap of her handbag. The sense of apprehension which had been growing fast in the last few days had become acute, and now that the driver needed no further directions, it rushed to fill her mind.

For all the three years and a few weeks which had passed since she last saw this countryside she had longed to see it again, and now that it was all about her, she could scarcely notice it.

Her thoughts would dwell only on her urgent desire to know what had been happening at home.

A week ago she had not felt like that. Her anxiety had not sharpened to its present keenness and, moreover, she had been uplifted by a sense of merciful escape from a fate which might have held her for life. She had been more interested in the effect on herself of her homecoming than in what she would find. She had pictured three years stripping and clothing the downland country in placid, uneventful rotation while she was away in India. Only so many months, really—thirty-nine of them, to be exact—but what a deceptive way to measure time; mechanical, mere circuits of the moon, and not accurate at that, suitable for machines, but not for human beings. To her that period was either a lifetime or a night's bad dream, as her mood alternated. One moment she was a woman whose life had been spoiled, who could never recapture a simple vanished faith in men and motives; another, she was Phyllida Woodridge again, and Phyllida Shiffer's existence no more than an unpleasant fantasy. That was the mood she hoped to hold: Phyllida Woodridge taking up life again where she had left it. But at that, anxiety flooded in again. What had been happening in this interval? Would it really be possible to settle down again as if Ronald Shiffer had never existed? Above all, why had her father not written for so long?

The long gap in their correspondence was not unique. Professor Woodridge, at best an erratic and indifferent letter-writer, was apt when engaged upon work of particular interest to forget the outer world altogether; or it might be better put that time slipped away without his cognizance, so that were the question put to him, "When did you last write to your daughter?" he would reply, "Oh, a week ago," omitting several intervening months with perfect good faith. Phyllida, therefore, had at first taken the cessation of letters as the result of preoccupation. Not until a cable announcing her intention of returning home failed to extract a reply had she felt any anxiety. When a second cable, sent on the assumption that the first had miscarried, remained similarly unacknowledged, her misgivings increased. Surely no father, however absentminded, could have neglected both through sheer forgetfulness. Several radiograms from the boat had proved no more fruitful than had even the final announcement of her time of arrival at Newhaven from Dieppe. Yet, until the last she had hoped to find him waiting for her on the quay.

She had waited there awhile, unhappily forlorn, trying to deceive herself that any moment would see him arrive, breathless and repentantly affectionate; but it had been a flimsy pretense. Before long, she and her possessions had been in this hired car, traveling through Sussex toward West Heading.

She reproached herself with not having radioed long ago to Mr. Drawford, his solicitor, or her Aunt Malvina, or her Cousin Derek, but she had been held back by her father's dislike of interference. Moreover, had his silence been due to illness, one of the three would have let her know long before this. There was just a possibility that he might have gone away, have taken one of his periodical trips to Germany; but even so, her messages should have been forwarded.

The car chugged its way up the village street of West Heading and started on the steeper slope of the Downs. Phyllida leaned forward, ready to check the driver if he should miss the turning. But it was unnecessary. Only too thankful to be rid of the hill, he steered into the drive without hesitation. The car swept forward with a new energy, its wheels plowing through a mush of lately fallen leaves. For fifty yards or so it traveled through a dankly odorous tunnel roofed with leaves yet to fall until it emerged on the wider sweep before the house. With a crunching of pebbles it drew up at the front door.

The driver allowed himself a few moments' disapproving contemplation of the scene before turning to her. The garden wore a tousled, unkempt appearance; nature, free for a while, had plunged with abandon into slovenly habits, seemingly intent upon wiping out all signs of earlier gentility. Already ambitious growths had trespassed well beyond their beds. Weedy pioneers had set up vigorous colonies in the gravel. A green, greasy film had spread itself over the front steps.

The driver was a man of intuition.

"Don't look like there was anyone 'ere, miss. You're sure this is the right place?" he said, looking up dubiously at the house itself.

The Grange, even when cared for, was an unattractive mansion; deserted, its windows dirty and the blinds behind them drawn down, it became repellent. Among neighbors in the more polite suburbs of a manufacturing town it might have escaped comment, but set solitary in the country it demanded notice. It had an air of seeming oppressed by its own misplacement, and forever stared gloomily beneath supercilious gables across the pleasant countryside. The well-intentioned efforts of its builders to cheer it up by ornamental ridge tiles, wavy-edged bargeboards and an ingenious, crossword-like patterning of blue bricks among the red had been utterly wasted. It remained determinedly melancholy.

"Gorn away. That's what it is," was the chauffeur's considered opinion.

Phyllida nodded. The sight of the drawn blinds had given her a sudden pang of alarm. Certainly the house bore every sign of desertion, but she had to be sure. She jumped from the car and ran up the steps to press the bell-push. Far back in the house she could hear the bell itself clatter with an aggressive resonance, echoing so emptily that she scarcely hoped for any result. The front door was firmly bolted, and she turned back to the driver.

"Wait here a minute. The back may be open."

But it was not. She looked up at the blank windows with a

puzzled frown, and then walked slowly back along the neglected path.

"Looks as 'ow it might 'ave been shut up for quite a bit, them windows is that dirty," the driver greeted her, discouragingly, on her return to the drive.

She picked her way across a flower-bed beneath one of the windows. The blind had not been pulled quite to the bottom, and through the chink she was able dimly to make out the dust-sheeted shapes of furniture. Some of her alarm gave way to puzzlement. Evidently the house had been shut up with a view to a long absence. But why had she heard nothing of it? Her gaze traveled involuntarily toward the new laboratory wing added by her Cousin Derek. It was impossible to imagine her father parted for long from his work, yet the house would not be closed so thoroughly for a few weeks' absence. Moreover, the driver was right, it had not been a recent departure. A movement behind her attracted her attention. He was wondering what to do next. Of course, she must decide that now. Her plans had extended no farther than an intention to get home. She must find out what had happened.

"We'll put my luggage in one of the outhouses," she said. "It ought to be safe there."

But the outhouses, like the main buildings, proved to be locked.

"Then we'll have to open one of them. The garage will be the handiest."

The driver demurred. The situation was outside his experience. Opening a garage on strange premises seemed to him uncomfortably close to housebreaking—besides, how was he to know that the young lady had any right to be here, let alone to be forcing an entrance? Phyllida grew irritable; his stupid over-conscientiousness, coming on top of her other troubles, began to exasperate her.

"But what's wrong with my opening an empty garage and putting my things in there?" she demanded. "It isn't as though I were going to take anything out—though I should have a perfect right to if I wanted."

"Maybe, but how do I know it's empty?" he objected. "How do you, for the matter of that?"

Phyllida repressed an urgent desire to shake him.

"Now, look here. I've told you that Professor Woodridge, who lives here, is my father. Of course I can open the garage if I want to."

"Ah! But 'e ain't living 'ere, by the look of it," the man objected, not without reason. "Besides, it don't say Woodridge on yer bags; it says Shiffer."

"Of course it does. That's my married name."

"Ah!" repeated the driver, noncommittally.

Phyllida considered silently for a moment.

"Look here," she began again. "Anyone down in the village will tell you who I am. If we put the luggage in the garage, then you can drive me down there and get me identified. Come along now. We can go to the policeman if you like," she added, seeing that he still hesitated.

The man scratched his head. He still considered it fishy and he didn't like it, but the last suggestion disposed of any objections he could think of at the moment.

"All right, miss—er—mum," he consented grudgingly.

The tool-box yielded a serviceable-looking tire lever, but his first attack with it did no more than to remove a part of the weather board which guarded the joint of the two doors. He looked at the splintered wood gloomily. Almost visibly his mind registered the phrase, "Damage to property."

"Oh, go on!" Phyllida said impatiently.

In the ensuing period of activity his knuckles were barked and the tire lever seriously bent, but, at last, the lock tore free of its bolts and clattered on the concrete floor inside. The driver swung open the door and poked in an inquisitive head.

"You said as it was empty," he remarked, as he withdrew and turned an accusing look on her.

"Well, isn't it?"

"It ain't. Car in there, all covered up."

Phyllida was surprised; she had taken for granted that wherever he had gone, her father would have taken the car.

"Well, anyhow, it's open now, so let's put the things in," she suggested briskly.

The man obeyed almost without taking his eyes off her. He seemed to fear that she might vanish and leave him unsupported in this ambiguous situation. He was relieved to find that when the two large trunks and a pile of miscellaneous cases had been stacked neatly in a corner she was ready to re-enter his car without protest.

"The policeman's cottage is on the left as you go into the village," she told him with a slight smile. "We had better go there first and clear your conscience."

But it transpired that Constable Green was away from home.

"'Ad to go and give evidence about that Alf Rose what they've caught poachin' again—'e always makes a 'ole day of it," his wife explained, after greeting Phyllida.

"Oh, I see. In that case, Mrs. Green, perhaps you'd be kind enough to tell this young man who I am. I think he's got an idea that I'm an adventuress who wants to burgle the Grange."

Mrs. Green gave the driver a look of cold disapproval which caused him to shift uncomfortably.

"'Ave you been annoying this young lady?" she began aggressively.

"Wot, me? No, I only said—"

But the policeman's wife swept his words aside. In a short time he was regretting that he had ever required this identification and feeling that his very suspicion of Phyllida was verging upon a misdemeanor. Her conclusion left him in a state of humble apology.

"—but you see 'ow it was, miss?" he explained.

"Yes, of course. Actually, you were quite right to be careful. Now how much do I owe you?" Phyllida asked.

As he drove away, she turned back to the policeman's wife. Her expression was serious and worried.

"Mrs. Green, how long has my father been away? When I was up at the house just now I found it all shut up—and it looked as if it had been empty a long time."

"There now, and do you mean to say that 'e never let you know? But isn't that just like him? 'E always was a forgetful one, was Mr. Woodridge. Time and again I've said to Mr. Green, ''Arry,' I've said, 'there's Mr. Woodridge's car outside the post-office again; you better go up to the Grange and tell 'im.' And when 'e got there, 'e'd find that Mr. Woodridge 'ad just walked 'ome and forgotten all about the car. Terrible absentminded, 'e is, beggin' your pardon."

Phyllida repressed Mrs. Green's tendency to rattle on by firmly repeating her question, and the lady knitted her brows in memorial effort.

"Let me see now, when was it that 'e went? Somewhere about the time Lucy Drake was 'avin' 'er second. That'd be the middle of June, like. I couldn't say as to the exact day. You see, 'e never told anyone as 'e was going—and I 'aven't 'eard as anyone saw 'im acksherly go, as you might say. But I do know it was just about then."

"The middle of June?" Phyllida stared at her. "But that's nearly four months ago. You're sure it was then?"

"Yes, Miss Phyllida. I remember Mrs. Church couldn't go and clean up at the Grange just then on account of Lucy 'aving 'er trouble, and when it was all over the Grange was shut up and Mr.

Woodridge gone away. Yes, gettin' on for four months, Lucy's second is now: time do fly, miss—I should say, mum."

"And you've heard nothing of him since then?"

"Not a word." Mrs. Green shook her head emphatically.

"And you really can't tell me for sure which day he left?"

"No, Miss Phyllida, that I can't—not for sure."

"But surely somebody knows. Mrs. Church, for instance, he must have told her."

Mrs. Green looked doubtful. In view of Mrs. Church's well-known incapacity for keeping any piece of information, however trivial, to herself, she considered it very unlikely. Nevertheless, decided Phyllida, Mrs. Church must be interviewed.

But the charwoman proved quite unable to give any more details. One day was much like another to her, it seemed, with the exception of Sundays and paydays. But reference to that local fixed date, Lucy's trouble, enabled her to agree with Mrs. Green that it was about the middle of June. It had been while she was looking after Lucy that she had received an envelope containing her wages to date and a note to say that her services would not be required for some time as Mr. Woodridge was about to take a prolonged holiday.

"It was Mr. Tiller brought it down," she added. "'Im and that wife of 'is 'ave been up there since the Robertses left."

Phyllida nodded absently. She remembered hearing from her father of changes in his domestic staff some eighteen months ago.

"And you haven't seen him since?" she asked.

"'Aven't seen none of them," Mrs. Church declared.

There seemed no more to be learned from the charwoman, and Phyllida felt that it was due only to the coincidence of Lucy's reproductive activities that this minimum was ascertainable. She gave orders that certain of the rooms in the Grange should be made habitable by the following night, paid Mrs.

Church a small sum in advance and set out for the post-office as a possible further source of information.

As she entered the small shop and encountered its assortment of musty odors, dominated as ever by the scent of paraffin, a round, red face wearing a walrus mustache popped up and framed itself between rows of hanging brushes and jars of sticky-looking sweets.

"Well, if it isn't Miss Phyllida?" remarked its owner in a hearty voice.

"Good afternoon, Mr. Greaves," she answered, and began her inquiries hopefully. But a very few questions were enough to reveal that he could give little more help than the policeman's wife or the charwoman. He agreed that Mr. Woodridge must have left about the middle of June, but he was equally unable to fix the exact day.

"But what about his letters?" she asked. "Surely he must have left an address for forwarding them?"

"No. He didn't *leave* an address." The shopkeeper looked at her doubtfully. "Strictly speaking, I oughtn't to tell you, but I did get a letter later on, asking me to forward any letters—near the end of June, that would be."

"May I see it?" she asked.

"Well, I don't see as there's any harm in *your* knowing—"

He reached a cardboard file from under the counter and began to search it industriously. At length he smoothed it open with the palm of a large hand and reversed it so that she might read.

"That's it, miss, and that's all I know about it."

At the top of the sheet Phyllida read a typewritten address—"112a Tolley St., Paddington, N.W.," and the date, "28th June." Two more lines of type instructed Mr. Greaves to forward all letters to the above address until further notice, and then followed the signature, "Henry Woodridge."

"I see," Phyllida nodded. "And there has been nothing further since then?"

"Not a word, miss. I've just sent everything along there as he said."

She thanked him and left the shop. She walked back up the village street, returning the greetings of the inhabitants with an absentminded smile. Nevertheless, their welcomes did something to lighten the depression which the sight of the empty Grange had induced. She was pleased that most of them addressed her as "Miss" or "Miss Phyllida." Three years ago, from her newly-married status, she would not have cared for it—now, she was glad: it helped to deaden the memory of the time in between.

Once clear of the village, and toiling back up the hill, she was able to give her whole mind to the immediate problem. Evidently there was nothing more to be learned in West Heading. The next step seemed to be to follow the only clue to Tolley St., Paddington.

Back in the garage she pulled aside the sheet which covered the car. To her relief she found that the tank had been left undrained and the engine could be started with little trouble. With a small, shiny traveling case of necessities beside her and the rest of her luggage left to the care of providence in the unlocked garage, she drove back through the village and took the London road.

FIRST INQUIRIES

Barry Long stared at a page before him and muttered malevolently. Without consciousness he lit a cigarette and inhaled. He ran his hands through a clump of wirily perverse hair and scratched the scalp beneath. In fact, he displayed his usual symptoms of thwarted literary composition.

"Blast it," he growled resentfully. What the devil was wrong with it? In the firm tones of one determined to rout vacillation, he began to read aloud:

"JOYCLAD UNDERWEAR

"*The trim daintiness of Joyclad is created essentially for the modern woman who demands fashion with comfort. The idea of shapeless undies repels her. She insists on warmth, but no less does she demand fashion's line....*"

The figure in the easy-chair beside the fire stirred restively.

"Rot!" it said. "She does not insist on warmth, nor does she demand comfort."

"Well, according to the Joyclad people, she ought to," Barry responded. "Besides, my job is to please the manufacturers, not the buyers—don't be so thickheaded."

He continued to read:

"*She knows that to be Joyclad is to have both. Joyclad caresses the body...*"

He stopped abruptly. Thoughtfully he picked up his pen, scratched out the word "body" and substituted "figure." A silly slip: axiomatically advertisement readers did not possess anything as earthy as a body. And "caresses" ... a bit daring, suggestive ... might get away with it in the classy papers, but ... He sought among the scatter of papers and found a penciled list:

caress	*enfold*
cherish	*enshrine*
clasp	*embrace*
cleave to	*fondle*
cling to	*hug*
cuddle	*nestle to*

No. An interval of profound reflection determined that it would have to be "caresses." A pity. "Enshrines the body—er—figure" would have been pretty good and original, but ...

And what about "trim daintiness"? Mightn't "dainty trimness" read better?

He sighed. The copy showed signs, as copy will, of running to irreducible lengths. Nothing about health yet, and the Joyclad people were hot on health. And the awful phrase which they complacently called a slogan: "To be Joyclad is a Joy" (probably the inspired adage of a director's daughter), that must be brought in somewhere. And there would be trouble with the layout people, as usual. How they hated "Underwear" in the heading—it took up too much room and threw out the balance; furthermore, it sounded frowsty. But the Joyclad people were dead-set on it. It might be cut to "undies "in the copy, but there must be dignity in the heading. Yes, by some inconceivable mental process the directors had found that the word "underwear" was dignified. Now, where was he? Oh, yes ...

"Joyclad caresses the figure; knowledge of its chic soothes the mind. Perfect poise ..."

"For God's sake!" protested the voice from the chair. "Have you *got* to recite that drivel?"

Barry remained unperturbed.

"All right, you'll be rid of me soon. Got to go out. I say, how about 'enraptures' instead of 'soothes'?"

Derek Jameson, present occupant of the fireside chair, sat up.

"Look here," he began coldly, "this stuff may be bread and butter to you, but it's damn near prussic acid to me. Why can't you go and get yourself a decent, moral, respectable job—or at least hide your present one under a bushel?"

Barry raised a pained face.

"My dear chap, Advertising is an Honorable Profession—oil on the wheels of commerce, and all that."

"Well, you might at least keep your oil-cans in the workshop."

"You're wrong." Barry shook a reproachful head. "We must always be studying the psychology of appeal—in the street, in the home. You, Derek, represent the home. You are a potential customer. . . ."

"I do not want my figure caressed, and you are not enrapturing my mind."

"But if there were a woman here . . ."

"But there isn't, so try a shirt advertisement. That couldn't be quite as fatuous."

"Fatuous!" Barry's brow clouded momentarily, but he soon rallied. He looked at the other thoughtfully. "Well, talking about shirts, I can see you haven't changed to Soapydol."

"Now, look here . . ."

But a prolonged ringing of the flat's front doorbell cut Derek short. He rose.

"That'll be one of your pals re-discovering that free Beer is Best," he suggested as he left the room.

Barry picked up his pen and held it in pensive hesitation over the word "soothes." A pleasant voice at the door interrupted him by saying:

"Hullo, Barry."

He jumped up, staring. The blood rose in a fierce flush to his face and then drained away, leaving it paler than usual. An immense time seemed to pass before he spoke. When he did say her name, it was in an unsteady voice.

"Phyl!"

He recovered himself sufficiently to study her face intently, looking for changes in it, and he found them. No marks, no lines, nothing definable, but an indivisible factor which had somehow given it maturity and greater understanding. She was smiling slightly, a trifle nervously, perhaps. Her eyes rested on him in a friendly fashion—yes, he looked more deeply into them, just friendly, holding nothing of the look which he had last seen in them. They held his own steadily and calmly unkindled; their level gaze seemed a statement of policy, of intentions—or, should it be, of no intentions? Quite suddenly the tension which had held him relaxed. Normality came flowing back. He knew that a problem which, despite its seclusion in the far recesses of his mind, had been gnawing away, maggot-like, was scotched. The question which he had so rigorously repressed as never to have examined its detailed structure suddenly ceased to be. He smiled back into Phyllida's eyes and took her outstretched hand.

Derek came strolling back into the room with the air of one who has allowed a decent interval to elapse.

"Well, well, well! A bolt from the blue," he said.

"May I suggest an angel from the blue as a more tactful expression?" Barry offered.

Derek shrugged.

"Gallant—if a little hackneyed. I say, Phyl, isn't there some old saw about 'cousins may kiss'?"

She laughed and kissed him lightly on the cheek.

"A rather distant cousin," he commented, regretfully.

He helped her off with her hat and coat and dropped them on the divan while Barry dragged the largest and most comfortable armchair nearer to the fire.

"Thank you, Barry."

She sat down on its forward edge, holding her hands out to the flames, a slight figure against the cavernous leathern depths of the chair. For some moments none of the three spoke. An awkward sense of restraint suddenly invaded the room. They watched her as she gazed into the fire, noticing afresh her profile and the way her short, dark red hair fell in a rippled curtain half across her cheek as she leaned forward; seeing in her shadowed eyes quick darting reflections of the flames. It occurred to Barry, looking at the slender form in its close green dress, that, after all, "dainty trimness" and "trim daintiness" meant much the same thing.

But for one thing the hands of the clock might have been spun back through the circles of three years—but for one thing: a plain platinum ring which caught the firelight in dull gleams; a narrow thread of metal, but heavy with significance. Yes, an evening in the old days—but for the ring.

Phyllida turned her head. Without meeting their eyes her gaze roamed round the room. They saw her take in the ranks of books, linger on the ever-fresh beauty of the two Van Gogh prints, sweep past the desk with its untidy litter of underwear rhapsodies, pause a thoughtful moment on the divan and return to the fire. Still their eyes did not meet.

"The same cozy old room—I always liked it."

There was an odd, uncertain quality in her voice. "But there is one difference." She was looking at the mantelpiece.

"Yes. We put it away, Phyl. At least, I put it away. It—it—" Barry lapsed into awkward silence.

She nodded slowly, with a faraway look in her eyes. He had an impulse to fetch her photograph from the drawer where it was hidden, but he resisted it. Instead, he fell to wondering why she had arrived thus, suddenly and unannounced. She should have been in India with that husband of hers.

Derek took it upon himself to stir up a rapidly clotting situation.

"Now, Phyl, tell us all about it. Firstly, what the dickens do you mean by bursting in on us like this? It's not fair; no band, no flags, not even a postcard. And you know we would gladly have fatted a calf. How are you? How's Ronald? How's everything?"

"Ronald?" She looked at him curiously. "Oh, of course, you couldn't have heard. Ronald is dead, Derek."

They both looked at her stupidly.

"Dead?" Derek repeated.

"More than two months ago." Her voice was calm, unemotional.

Barry abruptly realized what was due.

"My dear, I'm so sorry. . . . You see, we didn't know."

She had been looking into the fire again, but now she turned and faced him.

"That's not honest, Barry. You detested him. Remember, you once told me what you thought of him."

"Please, Phyl. . . . I ought never to have said those things. I— I just lost control of myself and they all came out. It's been hell remembering it ever since."

She shook her head slowly.

"They were true, Barry."

He made no reply to that. He knew he had told her the truth—the very unpleasant truth. Not nice to remember. Pouring it all out on the man's intended wife. . . . A kind of cold-blooded brutality. . . . He had wanted to hurt her just then.

"Yes, they were true," she repeated. "I found it out later—too late. I thought at the time—oh, well, I told you what I thought. But just then I didn't care what happened. Even if I had believed you, it would have made no difference. . . ."

She broke off, changing the subject swiftly. With a rush of contrition she returned to the problem which had been haunting her all day.

"I cabled to Daddy, of course. I thought he would tell you."

"Not a word," Derek assured her. "He's in one of his silent spells again. Haven't heard from or of him for months."

"Nor has anyone else, Derek. He's disappeared, vanished."

Her cousin caught her tone and looked at her anxiously.

"What do you mean, Phyl? Is there something wrong?"

"There seems to be something very much wrong. Nobody has seen a sign of him since the middle of June. I hoped you might be able to tell me something about him. You've heard nothing at all?"

"Not a thing since I saw him last. That must have been, let me see, nearly the end of April. You mean that he left the Grange in June?"

"Apparently. And that's about all I've been able to find out."

"But I don't understand, Phyl. People don't disappear suddenly and completely like that—not people like Uncle Henry. Do you mean he just walked out of the house and hasn't been heard of since?"

"No. The house is all shut up and—look here, I'd better tell you it all from the beginning."

Barry broke in.

"Tell it all to him, Phyl, and he can hand it on to me. I'm afraid I'll have to go out for a bit."

"Oh, Barry. Must you?"

"Can't help it. Got to address a lot of youths on 'Truth in Advertising'—God help me—the thing's due for nine o'clock, and I'll be late as it is."

"Oh, put it off, damn it. Leave the lads with pure minds for a bit longer," said Derek.

"Wish I could, but it's one of a series—the whole thing will be thrown out if I cut it. By the way, any luck today, Derek?"

"Not an ounce. . . . Nobody wants architects any longer; they all employ engineers and jobbing builders, blast them."

"That's tough. I'm sorry. Look here, I'll be back in an hour and a half."

"I shall have to go before that," Phyllida said. "I've got to drive all the way home."

Barry paused in the act of struggling with his coat.

"Rot. You can't go all the way down there tonight. We can put you up here—can't we, Derek? Whole spare bedroom."

"No, really, I—"

"Nonsense. Look here, I simply must go now. You shove a little sense into her, Derek. Absolute foolery. Hold her by force if necessary."

He grabbed his hat and shot out of the door. They heard him go bounding down the stairs in a series of thunderous leaps.

Derek gave Phyllida a cigarette and took one himself. When they were both lighted, he went on:

"Now, Phyl, what is all this? Tell me about it."

"It's simply this. Daddy's gone, vanished, and absolutely no one can tell me where he's gone. He may be anywhere. I'll tell you exactly as much as I know. After Ronald died I sent him a cable telling him about it, and saying that I should be sailing for home as soon as I could get everything settled. . . ."

He listened patiently while she gave in detail an account of her unacknowledged messages and her subsequent discoveries at West Heading.

"After that," she went on, "the best thing to do seemed to be to follow up the only clue I had. Tolley Street turned out to be an awful place in the slums near Paddington station, and number

112a was one of those shops which sell cigarettes and racing papers and have a lot of nasty-looking magazines in the window. I didn't like the look of it at all, but I went in. There was a horrible fat creature behind the counter who looked at me queerly when I asked if she knew anything of Daddy.

"'We don't give no addresses, even if we 'ad them,' she told me, and she pointed to a card which said, 'Letters may be addressed here.' She added that 'some folks wants to do a bit of business private-like.'

"'But I must find out where Professor Woodridge is—he's my father,' I said to her.

"She seemed to think that was very funny and began to laugh. It was nasty, because she shook all over like a sloppy blancmange.

"'That's good, that is,' she said, but she didn't explain why. 'Any'ow,' she added, ''e 'asn't been 'ere for 'is letters for more than a couple of months now.' And she showed me a bundle of letters with some telegrams among them.

"Well, that really finished it. And as nobody had called for the letters, it explained why I had had no answers, but it didn't tell me any more about what had happened to Daddy. So then I went to Aunt Malvina's in Kensington."

"And she knows nothing about him?" Derek broke in.

"Nothing. But then, I had hardly expected that she would. You know how they avoid one another as a rule and always quarrel whenever they do meet. She wasn't very pleased to see me, and only politely puzzled over Daddy, as though she expected him to be unaccountable, anyway. However, she couldn't very well turn me out, so I spent the night there."

She went on to recount the events of the current day. The first had been a visit to Mr. Drawford, the family solicitor, known to her since infancy as Uncle Miles.

"But it wasn't any good," she went on. "He's just as puzzled about it all as I am. He saw him last in March, and heard from him in June, but none of his letters since then have been answered. He hadn't even heard that the house was shut up."

"Then he hasn't tried to let it?"

"Not through Uncle Miles, certainly. Not at all, I think. There were no boards up."

"But isn't it rather odd that old Drawford didn't make some inquiries when his letters weren't answered?"

"Not really. You see, there was nothing of vital importance. He says he did think once or twice of going down there, but you know what Daddy's like when he gets wrapped up in a piece of work—just hopeless, besides being very rude to people who interrupt him. So Uncle Miles decided that he was probably deep in something and had better be left alone. And we can hardly blame him for that. The only thing he could suggest at the moment was that we should go and see if Daddy's bank knew anything. So we did.

"The manager, Mr. Fisk, was awfully nice and sympathetic about it, but actually he couldn't help a bit. He hadn't heard from him since June, either, and the last letter he had had was to say that he was shutting up the Grange for a time and he would like the bank to store his silver. A few days later a box arrived and they sent off the receipt for it. Since then they've heard nothing at all."

"But hasn't he drawn any checks?" Derek asked.

"No, that makes it all the queerer. I asked about that because I thought it might at least give us some idea of what district he was in, but it wasn't any good."

"Then there's nothing to show whether he's in England or abroad, even?"

"No. He may be anywhere."

"That makes it much odder still—his not wanting any money, I mean. Unless, of course, he's lost his memory or something like that."

"But why should he?" Phyllida demanded.

"He might. I mean to say, people do, you know."

"And shut up their houses and store their silver? Don't be an idiot, Derek."

Derek considered for a moment in silence.

"What about the other people there—servants and things?"

"There was a man Tiller and his wife who looked after the housekeeping, and Daddy's assistant, Mr. Straker. I don't know any of them. Uncle Miles is going to try and get hold of them, but nobody seems to know which day they left or where they went to."

"Oh, I've met them when I've been down there. The Tillers seemed quite a decent couple—efficient and all that. Straker's a bit of a queer bird, frightfully earnest about his work—in fact, all work and no play. Made him a bit one-sided, but he's a good sort, all the same. Tremendous admiration for Uncle Henry. Queer that he should have gone too."

He frowned in a puzzled fashion and returned to the pecuniary aspect of the problem. Surely, wherever he was, Professor Woodridge must have had some need of money in four months.

"He didn't cash a big check just before he went?"

"No. Nothing big. In fact, for years he doesn't seem to have drawn a check to 'Self' for much more than ten pounds at a time."

Derek temporarily relinquished that angle.

"And what after that?"

"Well, Uncle Miles asked the manager a lot of questions, but we didn't get any farther, so he took me out to lunch—Uncle Miles, not the manager—and we made a list of all the people who were likely to know anything about it. There was Daddy's old friend, Sir Seymour Franks, who lives somewhere in St. John's Wood. And Dr. Fessler, a funny old German he stays with when he goes to Berlin, and who stays with us when he comes over here. And one or two others. After lunch we sent a telegram to Dr. Fessler and rang up Sir Seymour. He was annoyed with Daddy and rather short with me at first. It seems that they had been in the middle of a correspondence about something bio-chemical which I didn't understand at all, and just as they were reaching a decisive stage (as old Sir Seymour put it), it had all stopped and he hadn't heard a word since. He said some very blunt things about Daddy's manners, but even when we ex-plained that something must be wrong, he couldn't tell us any more."

"And the Berlin man?"

"No. He wasn't any good. We got an answer about tea-time. He hasn't seen him since last year. Before that we'd been on the telephone to every likely person—except you and Barry, who were out all the time—and simply nobody knows anything at all. It frightens me, Derek. How can somebody vanish utterly and completely, like that?"

III

ANOTHER DISAPPEARANCE

Barry returned to the Gordon Square flat soon after half-past ten to find it with a single occupant. Derek, sunk almost out of sight into the chair which Phyllida had occupied, was staring thoughtfully into the dwindling fire. He roused himself from contemplation and stretched out his hand for a conveniently placed tankard.

"Hullo! How did it go? Tell the little boys a lot of pretty lies?" he inquired.

"I lectured," Barry replied severely, "upon Truth in Advertising."

"Quite. You know it's high time that phrase was amended— I suggest 'The Place of Truth in Advertising.'"

Barry looked round the room.

"Where's Phyl?"

"Gone. Dashed off. I did my best to persuade, but no."

"But hang it all—"

"I know. I know. Short of applying force, as suggested, I did all I could, but go she would. Filial instinct in full command, and all that. She thinks there might be some news waiting for her down there."

"Damned silly." Barry dropped into another chair. After a short pause:

"Queer about the man Shiffer," he said.

"How queer? Best thing that could have happened."

"Quite, but it so seldom does happen to the out-and-out bad eggs. And he was one all right."

Derek lit a cigarette and returned to his contemplation of the fire.

"Yes, he was," he agreed. "Now he's gone, we are back in the *status quo*. And if you go and mess it up again, Barry, I'll never forgive you."

"That," Barry said to himself, "is where you are wrong. No *status* is ever quite *quo*." Aloud he said nothing. Derek went on:

"If you'd just stuck around quietly, she'd have broken off that engagement. But when you flew off the handle, abused the man left and right and accused him of pretty well every known crime, you just drove her to him. No woman likes to be told that she's backed a loser and, in effect, that she has neither sense nor taste—particularly when she's none too sure about it herself. There was one obviously wrong road to take and you had to go charging up it like a stampeding buffalo."

"But the man was a swine."

"I know he was—we all knew it. And she probably would have found it out in time, too, if you hadn't put yourself in wrong and twisted everything up. Phyl's my cousin, I'm damned fond of her and I want to see her happy. You've got a second chance now—though it's more than you deserve. For God's sake, don't go and mess it up again."

For some seconds indignation and a slightly bitter amusement struggled inside Barry, but he contented himself with saying:

"You're quite wrong."

"Not if you play your cards right. But don't go slanging her friends again. All women are convinced that they can tell swine from heroes on sight, and an average of seventy-five percent errors doesn't shake them a bit."

"Dear me," said Barry thoughtfully. "You know, there's a suggestion of the second-hand about that. You've not been taking a correspondence course on 'How to Manage Women,' by any chance? Never mind, as I said before, you're quite off the rails. Did you ever hear a little yarn about motes and beams and things?"

"I don't see—"

"Oh, well. Have another beer and think it over."

He crossed to the cupboard, returning with two bottles and another tankard. Derek refilled his own and raised it.

"Luck," he said.

"—and tact," Barry added, with a fleeting grin.

He half-emptied his tankard at a draft, set it down and lit a cigarette. His flutter of irritation at Derek's presumption in dressing him down had subsided, and he was left with a sensation of slight amusement. Besides, Derek had been right to a point. There was no doubt that his blackguarding of Ronald Shiffer had helped to drive Phyllida into his arms. Where he was hopelessly at sea was in his idea that with Ronald out of the way, Barry himself and Phyl would have made a match of it. Not that he had not been blindly in love with her in those days, and with the memory of her ever since, but he had been sufficiently blind to miss the real direction of her attractions. Seeing her again he had found in a flash that he was no longer in love with her, simultaneously he had been smitten with a sudden understanding of her. He was aware of a curiously paternal, head-patting attitude toward her. The type of his affection had changed rather than diminished— perhaps increased, now that she had lost the power to disturb and hurt him. Curious that a thing like that could happen in a moment—or had it been happening subconsciously for some time; unsuspected until her appearance had toppled over his usual mental scenery? Difficult to tell. Certainly until this evening he had thought himself still in love with her; equally certainly Derek still thought so—would continue to think so. Derek's mind was like that. An idea once grafted into it required a devil of a lot of removal, not to be achieved in a day. Time for that later. He broke the silence:

"I say, what is all this about your uncle?"

Derek looked up, emerging with apparent difficulty from a maze of private thoughts.

"It's odd," he said, "very odd." He gave a résumé of Phyllida's inquiries and discoveries. "Can't think what the old boy can be playing at," he concluded. "Not like him at all. Mind you, it's easy enough to understand his doing odd things out of sheer absentmindedness—he's like that—but there doesn't seem to be much absence of mind about this. Now, if it were some other old buffers I know; my late un-respected employer, for instance, I'd say that he'd gone off for a spree with a piece."

"Spree with a piece?"

"Sure. Quaint, old-fashioned term meaning razzle with a bit, or whoopee with a skoit. But as far as Uncle Henry is concerned, that's a washout. For one thing, he only gets bored with sprees, and, for another, he's never shown the faintest symptom of an interest in pieces."

"The tougher they are, the sloppier they melt. You never know—"

"But I *do* know. None of that kind of melting about him, nor guile, either. One of these great brains, and all that. Downright and appallingly straightforward. Whenever he can be dragged down from the heights to talk about ordinary life, he always says just what he thinks—pretty disastrous as a rule. That's one of the reasons why Aunt Malvina stopped asking him to parties; if he did turn up, he was usually far too biological. Embarrassed the entire assembly, and then couldn't see why. No, the razzle idea is altogether out."

Barry nodded. "All right. Though further, and to my mind, more convincing: pieces must cost money and he doesn't seem to have any."

"Quite. In fact, to judge from experience—my late employer's experience, that is, and it was considerable—they're hellish expensive. He liked talking about it: he used to say to me, 'My boy, avoid women if you can. If you can't, get married; it's cheaper.' Though I can't say he seemed to pay much attention to his own advice."

For a short while both lay back in their chairs, pleasantly employed in calculating the probable details of the necessary outlay. Derek's voice dragged Barry back from the invention of a touchingly glamorous episode.

"And this accommodation address business! Why on earth should he want to do a thing like that?"

"Well, that certainly looks like a deliberate attempt to hide himself," Barry said.

Derek tossed an end into the fire and lit another cigarette.

"Let's try to look at it logically. Now, when a man shuts up his house, dust-sheets his furniture and stores his silver, it means that he intends to be away for some time; with the place so thoroughly closed, it could scarcely mean anything else. Now then, question one: why does a man go away for several months at least? We've ruled out Paris with pieces (and anyway, that would be a shorter jaunt). We can be quite certain that he hasn't bought another house. Obviously, he isn't staying with relations, or there would be no mystery—besides, beyond Phyl and myself, there's only Aunt Malvina, and they're spitting at one another on sight, lately. He isn't the kind of man to commit a crime which makes disappearance necessary (further objection: he would scarcely delay to close up his house if he had). Phyl's inquiries pretty well show that he hasn't gone to bury himself in research in Germany. Add to all this his disdain of correspondence, his lack of money—and the answer's a lemon."

Both were silent awhile.

"Isn't it possible," Barry suggested at last, "that he did mean to write and say where he was, but was somehow prevented?"

"I wonder? Yes, I see what you mean. He might have shut up the house, intending to let old Drawford know all about it, and then—"

"—Have lost his memory? So many people do since the wireless."

"No. I tried the loss of memory one on Phyl."

"She didn't cotton?"

"She told me not to be an idiot."

"Oh."

"But an accident—that's feasible. He shuts the place, gets mixed up with a bus or something and can't be identified. When he comes to, he can't remember who he is. That might fit."

Barry dissented slightly.

"Bit filmish, isn't it? Besides, it doesn't explain why he shut it up to begin with."

"True, but we may find that out tomorrow."

"Tomorrow?"

"Well, Phyl suggested our going down there and looking through his papers on the chance of a clue, so I said we would."

Barry frowned. "That's all right for you, but I'm not one of the great unemployed."

"Tomorrow's Saturday. You get half the day anyhow. Ring 'em up and tell 'em you can't come in the morning. Important family business, and all that."

"But—"

"My dear chap, what's the good of being a trained advertiser if you can't put across a simple lie like that?"

"Look here, Derek. Advertising is—"

Derek raised a hand for peace.

"I know. I've heard it all."

"Oh, well, perhaps I could phone them that copy. All the same, I don't—"

"Good. That's that, then." Derek drained his tankard and yawned. "Time for the chief nourisher in life's feast, I think."

"What?"

"That's Shakespeare—a man of ideas. You probably only think of sleep in terms of night starvation."

At Liphook Derek managed to shed the gloom which, as usual, had wrapped him ever since they had left London. From Hammersmith to Guildford he had held forth uninterruptedly upon the eczema of speculative building marring the fair face of England—with notes and special reference to those builders who had dispensed with the services of architects. The prospect as they climbed the road to Hindhead had begun to dissolve his disaffection, the run down the other side had further raised his spirits, and now that they were heading south, leaving the hustle of the Portsmouth Road behind, he had returned to normal.

The village of West Heading lies at the very foot of the Downs. And though from any elevated spot in it—say the church tower—it is almost possible to throw a stone into either Sussex or Hampshire, yet it belongs to neither. It is exactly here that a narrow tongue of Winshire runs up to separate the two larger counties. Geographical error in this matter is not taken kindly by the natives; they will correct you firmly. They are Winshire men, and proud of it. You will receive the impression that you have done that which is not done. Upon proper apology you will find that they are good fellows who drink good beer.

A representative gathering was so engaged before the *Hand in*

Hand when Barry's car rattled by and began its stertorous climb of the hill. Their heads turned as one and they gazed musingly at its back.

"Goings on at the Grange," observed an ancient.

The rest nodded.

"It be queer as she don't know where Mr. Woodridge be," he continued. "My daughter says as Miss Phyllida was fair 'mazed when she came back and found 'e were gone away."

They nodded again, save for one purist.

"She be Missus now, not Miss," he objected.

"Don't make no difference," the ancient growled, without covert intention. "Don't so 'appen as you'll be goin' by the Grange in a bit, Alfred?" he asked, guilelessly, of one of the younger men.

"Likely I shall."

"There be goings on there, all right," the ancient repeated dreamily.

Barry's car panted its way up the hill and turned into the neglected drive. Clumps of bushes among the trees cut off their view of the house, and it was not until they reached the wider sweep of gravel that they became aware of the presence of another visitor.

A handsome black saloon car, not yet entirely bereft of its showroom shimmer, stood before the front door. Beyond it, a darkly-clad figure could be seen standing in an attitude of some dejection upon the top step. The squeal of Barry's brakes as he came to rest was a painful sound and one impossible to ignore. The visitor turned a pained and disapproving face, but at the sight of them his expression changed. He waved a welcoming hand and trotted down the steps toward them. His build was slightly stout, with a length of torso intended for a six-foot frame. Nature, however, in one of her less balanced moments, had given him an overall height of only five feet six, with the unhappy result that he appeared either to waddle or to trot, or even, upon occasions of extreme dignity, to strut. As a consolation, perhaps, she had endowed him with a slightly tanned face, friendly and pleasant-featured. In his eyes was a kindly expression, and at their corners small wrinkles suggested that they could, and frequently did, twinkle. His only facial adornment was a mustache, gray and trimmed, like his hair, to a nice balance between political exuberance and military restraint. He nodded to them both and held out his hand to Derek.

"Ah! Glad you've come, my boy."

Derek shook the hand.

"You know Barry Long, of course?"

"Yes, indeed. Mr. Long and I have met several times."

A moment later he turned back to address Derek again.

"Phyllida gave me to understand that she had seen you yesterday evening, so I suppose you know all about this extraordinary business?"

"Most of it, I think. But she forgot to tell me that we should see you here this morning."

"That was settled later. She rang me up last night after she had left you, and told me of the arrangement. When I heard that she proposed to go through her father's papers I suggested that it might be as well if I were present—just a formality, you understand. In case of later controversy the fact that a solicitor had been present would tell."

Derek nodded agreeably in spite of his inability to see what kind of controversy was in the least likely to arise.

"And you've just arrived?" he asked.

"Ten minutes ago, but no one has deigned to answer the door yet. It seems a little odd. I understood her to say that a Mrs. Church from the village was going to look after her, but there seems to be nobody here at all. I suppose she did come back last night?"

"She certainly intended to. We did our best to persuade her to stay in London, but she was set on coming down here."

Derek crossed the drive and ran up the steps. He kept his finger on the bell-push while he pounded the knocker. The ringing and the hammering resounded through the house, but they roused no other response than echoes. After a while he descended the steps and joined the others. All three regarded the unimposing elevation thoughtfully.

Derek's gaze wandered momentarily to the laboratory wing which he had added. The sight of it irritated him, as always. Not that the work wasn't good in itself, but because this appalling house killed it; it would kill anything. He returned to contemplation of the front. Drifts of dead leaves silting up against the walls, weeds impertinently flourishing among the gravel, untended plants sprawling rankly, all assisted in the depressing effect of the whole. Every window save for a pair on the ground floor and a pair immediately above them was blinded behind dirty glass, and even the two unobscured pairs looked out with a discouraging starkness.

"She must be here," murmured the solicitor uneasily.

"Somebody's been here, anyhow," Barry said. "She told us that all the blinds were down—they would be, of course."

"Let's have a look at the garage," Derek suggested.

He led the way to the left of the house and pulled open the unfastened doors. The place was empty save for a few battered cans and worn-out tires.

"Strange," said the solicitor. "She must have gone away again this morning, but it isn't like her to be inconsiderate."

"And what's become of the heavy luggage? She left that here. She can hardly have carried the trunks indoors by herself," Barry put in.

Derek was making a close inspection of the tracks on the gravel.

"Well, she certainly came back last night—in fact, it looks as if she had been in and out a number of times by the amount of tracks here."

"Perhaps she found she hadn't enough food to give us all lunch. She may have run over to Paulsacre for something."

Mr. Drawford brightened slightly at the suggestion.

"Yes, very probably, Mr. Long. That's a good idea."

"In that case she may have left the back door open," Derek said, again leading the way.

But the immobility of the back door was such as to suggest that not only was it locked, but also bolted top and bottom. Derek began to feel genuinely worried. As the solicitor had said, it was unlike Phyllida to be inconsiderate of her visitors. She had known approximately the time of their arrival. Had it been necessary to fetch supplies, she would surely have left a note of explanation in case she should be delayed. Barry, too, upon further reflection seemed to become dissatisfied with his solution of the matter. He tested the window beside the back door and found it no less firmly fastened.

Mr. Drawford, watching him, nodded.

"Yes," he said. "I think that in the circumstances we might consider ourselves justified in forcing an entrance."

Together, they made a circuit of the entire house and laboratory wing, testing every window without success.

"There's only one thing for it," Derek said, as they came back to the front drive. "We'll have to smash a pane."

He took a rug from Barry's car and with it pushed in the glass close to the catch of one of the front windows; a moment later he had raised the sash and was over the sill.

"I'll open the front door for you," he called back.

They heard him clatter from the bare boards of the room on to the tiles of the hall; after an interval a muffled voice emerged from the letter box.

"There's no key, damn it. You'll have to come in through the window, too."

Mr. Drawford stood among the shapeless mounds of dust-sheeted furniture. He was breathing a little heavily from an unaccustomed form of exertion. It was a long time, he reflected, since he had last clambered into a house over the window-sill.

"And what do we do now?" he inquired.

"Search the premises," Derek directed.

They began a tour of the ground floor. Empty houses can in themselves be eerie; even in daylight dust-sheets covering the unknown appear suggestive, and when, in addition, there is a suspicion that something not quite straightforward has taken, or is taking, place, uneasiness is unattractively amplified.

"I'm hanged if I can understand why Phyl was so keen on getting back to this," Barry observed as they peered into one room after another, each full of dim, amorphous shapes. "I can think of plenty of places where I would sooner spend the night. Spooky, isn't it?"

Only two of the ground-floor rooms showed signs of recent occupation: the front sitting-room and the kitchen. In the former the carpet had been rolled out and the furniture uncovered. A gate-leg table set near the fireplace still held the remains of a meal; close to it stood a chair, carelessly pushed back as though the diner had risen hurriedly. Derek inspected a congealed mass on the plate.

"Bacon and eggs. Might mean either breakfast or a snack after the drive. But I doubt if breakfast could contrive to look so horrible so soon."

The kitchen showed a grate half full of cold ashes.

"That settles it. It was supper—" He broke off as he caught sight of an oil-stove, and crossed the room to examine it carefully. "No, this hasn't been used for months—it was supper, all right."

They looked at one another. Mr. Drawford spoke for all three.

"I am beginning to dislike this very much. Why should she go off when she had only just started her meal?"

"I suppose there isn't a gas ring or a stove?" Barry inquired, hopefully. "I mean, she couldn't have made breakfast on that perhaps . . . ?"

"No. No gas. And no electric cooker, although they do make their own light."

"Isn't it time we looked upstairs?" suggested the solicitor, moving toward the door.

The bed in the one habitable bedroom had been made up ready for its occupant, but the sheets still awaited her, smooth and uncreased. A pair of blue silk pajamas carelessly tossed upon the dark eiderdown made two vivid dabs of color. A brush, a comb, a bottle or two and a pot of cream adorned the dressing-table. A shiny black blouse case from which a silken something half overflowed stood on an occasional table against the wall. Derek lifted the lid and let it drop again; only immediate necessities had been unpacked. The rest of the room, save for the fireplace where a half-burned lump of coal stood upon a little ash, told them nothing. Derek sat down on the side of the bed, lit a cigarette and looked up at the others.

"Well, what do you make of it?"

"I don't like it," Mr. Drawford repeated. "What can have happened?"

"Let's see what we do know. Now, after she left the flat, she telephoned to you. What time was that?"

The solicitor considered doubtfully, then his face cleared.

"Almost exactly half-past nine. I was just waiting for the wireless news and I missed the weather-forecast in answering her call."

"Right. We will assume she made it from a public call-box—"

"Why?" Barry objected.

"Because she didn't make it from the flat. Obviously the idea occurred to her just as she had started. It's ten to one she got out of the car, made the call and then drove straight on. Now, she could scarcely have taken less than two hours and ten minutes to get down here, and (washing out for the moment the possibility of a breakdown) she isn't likely to have taken more than two hours and a half. That puts her arrival here at somewhere between a quarter to and five past midnight. How's that?"

Both the others nodded.

"Then she puts the car away—say three or four minutes. Comes indoors and up to this room, chucks out her pajamas, lays out the things on the dressing-table, runs a comb through her hair, lights the fire—ten minutes or so, do you think? Then she's feeling a bit cold and peckish. The fire in the kitchen is still alight, she cooks herself bacon and eggs, makes herself some tea and carries the lot off to the sitting-room where the table is already laid."

"Why?" Barry inquired again. "I mean, how do you know the table was already laid?"

Derek regarded him sadly.

"Because," he said, patiently, "if it hadn't been that the bread and butter and implements were laid out there, she would have eaten more or less out of the frying pan, or, anyhow, in the kitchen where it would have been less trouble. Well, that might take her a quarter of an hour or a bit longer—it rather depends on the condition of the fire and how handy the things were. She has now been home something just over half an hour, so that somewhere between a quarter-past twelve and five-and-twenty to one she gets up from a meal she has scarcely touched, and flies off into the unknown. Why?"

"Telephone message," offered Barry promptly.

Derek shook his head. "No go. Instrument's gone. Why go on paying half a crown a week for keeping it in an empty house?"

"A personal message. Perhaps something from Henry Wood-ridge?" asked the solicitor.

"Exactly. There's not much else that would be likely to take her out so suddenly at that time of night. Someone must have brought news of him."

"But wouldn't she have left us a note?" Barry looked dubious.

"In the excitement of the moment?"

"You may be right." But he sounded far from convinced by Derek's reasoning. "What about asking in the village? They might know something there."

The solicitor rose from his seat on the slender-legged dressing stool.

"A good idea, Mr. Long. It certainly doesn't look as if we are likely to learn much more here. Yes, we'd better go down there at once."

The usual delay in starting Barry's car allowed the saloon to get away well ahead of them, but a very short distance outside the gates they caught it up again. It stood stationary in the middle of the road, interestedly surrounded by a small body of local men. As Barry drew up behind, a policeman detached himself from the party and advanced heavily.

"Now, what——?" he began.

"Oh, hullo, Green. What seems to be the trouble?" Derek inquired.

The policeman's face lost much of its official severity.

"Oh, it's you, Mr. Jameson! Didn't know as you was in this."

"What's the matter?" Derek repeated.

"Well, sir, it's like this. Alfred 'ere"——he indicated an undistinguished member of the group about the saloon——"Alfred 'appened to be passing the Grange, and 'e seen people gettin' in by one of the winders——"

"I see——though 'happened to be passing' is good," said Derek, thinking of the quantity of greenery which shielded the house upon its three approachable sides.

"That's as may be, sir. But very rightly 'e comes and tells me about it. Us, knowing as the 'ouse was shut up——"

"Just what we want to talk to you about, Green. In fact we were coming to see you. If we can continue in your office, I'm sure Mr. Drawford will give you a lift."

"Well, yes, sir. It would be quieter there."

The small crowd, visibly disappointed that it was not to be called on to assist at the arrest of dangerous criminals, was waved back with an authoritative air and the policeman climbed ponderously into the leading car.

The three seated themselves in a small room, half office, half parlor, and Constable Green addressed himself to Derek.

"Now, sir, I'd be much obliged if you would tell me what it is all about."

Derek began by introducing his companions. He went on:

"The trouble is, Green, that we hardly know ourselves. You see, Mrs. Shiffer asked all of us to come down here today, and now we're here, we find she's not. Do you know where we can find her?"

"I don't, sir." Constable Green shook his head. "She went up to London the day before yesterday."

"Yes. She came to see us. But she was to come back last night—in fact, she came back. Her things are there now, but she didn't sleep there. And the car is gone."

"That's queer, sir." He paused, fingering a ginger mustache thoughtfully before he added: "Strikes me there's been too many queer things goin' on at the Grange lately."

"Queer things?"

"Well, perhaps not queer, so much as one thing after another."

"Such as?"

Green thought for a moment.

"Well, first of all there was the burglary."

"Burglary! I never heard anything about that?"

"Yes, about four months ago, when Mr. Woodridge was still at 'ome. The 'ouse was broke into one night—leastways, not the 'ouse itself, but the labbertery."

"Was it? What did they take?"

"Nothing, sir. That is, Mr. Woodridge couldn't find that nothing was missing. Queer, it was, especially as there was some of that there platinum there—very valuable stuff that is, I'm told—and they never touched it. Must've been several of 'em on the job, too, judging by the marks."

"And then?"

"Well, the next thing was Mr. Woodridge's goin' away so sudden. Never told nobody 'e was goin', and nobody never sawr 'im go. First thing we knew about it, the 'ouse was all shut up like it is now, and 'e'd gorn."

"And the servants?"

"Tiller and 'is missus, they'd gorn too. And Mr. Straker 'oo was living there. Then there was nothing until the day before yesterday when Miss Phyllida—Mrs. Shiffer, I should say—came in and asked my missus where 'er father was. Well, she didn't know, and she knew as I didn't know, and nobody else 'ere didn't know. Fair amazed, we were, to think of 'im going off like that and tellin' 'er nothing about it. Anyway, she told Mrs. Church to get some of the rooms ready for 'er last night."

"And she came back right enough."

"And now she's gone again. That's what I meant by things being queer."

"Do you think we could see Mrs. Church?"

The charwoman was speedily fetched from her cottage a few doors away, but her story did little to clear up the matter. She had gone up to the Grange and carried out her instructions. Set a sitting-room and a bedroom to rights, lit fires in both rooms and the kitchen, run the electric-light engine for a bit, laid the table, brushed up a bit here and there and then gone home. Derek interrupted to ask if she had used the back door.

"No, the front, sir."

"And the key?"

"Left it on a 'ook in the garage, ready for Miss Phyllida when she came back."

"No. I mean, where did you get the key?"

"Borrowed a box of old keys from Mr. Wicker, the blacksmith. Them old-fashioned locks ain't per-tickler what key you uses, 's long as it's about the right size."

This morning she had returned about half-past seven to find the garage still empty, but the key gone from the hook. Barry slipped in a question about the trunks. No, they hadn't been there this morning, the woman admitted, though they had been when she had hung up the key yesterday. She had just thought that they had been taken inside—though it did strike her as strange that the car was not there, but she had not given any great thought to that at the time. She had knocked and rung at the front door, but at last, finding there was no answer, she had gone away again.

"And all that," Derek summed up, when the charwoman had been dismissed, "leaves us just about where we were before. You didn't happen to hear a car pass here somewhere between a quarter-past twelve and a quarter to one, Green?"

"I was asleep, sir, but I'll ask my wife—she may 'ave heard one." He rose and disappeared toward the kitchen.

"Well, so far your detection seems to have been all right—apart from the matter of the bedroom fire," said the solicitor, seeking to relieve the silence.

"Have you considered the possibility of an accident to my

uncle?" Derek asked, and went on to put forward the theory which he and Barry had talked over the previous evening.

"It had occurred to me," Mr. Drawford admitted, "but I was unwilling to distress Phyllida, perhaps quite unnecessarily, by mentioning it. After all, one would scarcely be justified yet in suggesting fears that he may be dead."

"You think he is?"

"No. I see no real reason to suspect that. A great many persons may be missing though undeceased. I meant merely that the possibility had crossed my mind, just as it crossed yours, so I put my clerk, Micken, on to finding out whether any of the unidentified persons who had lost their lives within a week or two of his disappearance could have been him. I am happy to say that the descriptions were all utterly unlike him."

"And so far as you know, he hadn't been mentally—er—he hadn't been showing any signs of overwork? Suppose he had had a breakdown—people like him do sometimes."

The solicitor shook his head.

"Straker would have let me know of such a thing at once."

"Straker! Yes, I keep on forgetting that he's missing too. Mightn't it be wise to advertise for him and see what he may be able to tell us? Anyhow," he reverted to the earlier question, "we might try to get hold of his doctor. . . ."

He broke off as the constable returned triumphantly.

"She did," he announced. "A bit earlier than the time you said, she 'eard a car goin' up the 'ill, and then a bit later, another, and then, later still, two cars came down close together."

"Two?"

"Yes, sir."

"Might be a coincidence."

"'Ardly likely, sir. I'd say they was together. Nobody much uses this road by night—it only runs on to a farm or two—as you know."

A short time later the group broke up. There was little to be gained by further discussion. Leaving the policeman with instructions to pass on at once any information of Professor Woodridge or his daughter, the three adjourned in the direction of the *Hand in Hand* and a stiff drink.

"It will be all right," the solicitor attempted to reassure them with an optimism he was far from feeling. "Quite likely we shall soon get news with some simple explanation we have overlooked."

"You think so?" Derek's expression brightened for a moment. Then he shook his head. "No, I see you don't really. Hang it all, people don't disappear like that for no reason. . . ."

IV

PHYLLIDA IS MORE MYSTIFIED

The sound of a rapping on the door percolated slowly into Phyllida's deep sleep. Still less than half awake she called:

"Come in."

Not until she saw by the dim light filtering past the drawn blinds the entry of a large, unfamiliar figure preceded by a tray did her memory suddenly revive. She sat up abruptly. A half-alarmed exclamation escaped her, and then as the full realization of her position came back to her, she relaxed and, leaning back upon her pillows, watched in silence. The bulky manservant advanced sedately to place the tray on the bedside table. Then, seeming not to give her so much as a glance, he moved with dignity to the windows and occupied himself for some little time in raising the blinds and adjusting them carefully to an even height. On the point of leaving he paused and spoke for the first time.

"There is nothing further you require, madam?"

The question itself was a mockery, but there was none in the voice which asked it. His manner was entirely formal. Phyllida shook her head. He bowed. As he closed the door behind him, she heard the key turn in the lock.

She turned to the tray, suddenly aware that she was extremely hungry. It was now, she found from the small clock beside her, half-past eleven. She had eaten nothing since dinner the previous night, and had indulged in a great deal of activity. She took the glass grapefruit cup, and while she dug at its contents with the spoon, began to review her present situation and the events which had led to it with more calmness than she had been able to achieve during the night.

Half-past eleven on Saturday morning. . . . That meant that Derek and Barry and Uncle Miles (by which name she had thought of Mr. Drawford for as long as she could remember) would soon be arriving at the Grange—to discover that she was no longer there. What, she wondered, would they do? What, in fact, could they do? Was there any possible chance of their finding out what had happened and following her here? It seemed most uncomfortably unlikely. She herself had no idea where she was; what clues could they possibly find? Unhappily she searched her memory for any indication which might have been left at the Grange, and reluctantly she was forced to the conclusion that there would be none.

Her thoughts left the probable reactions of the three men and returned to a bewildered review of the events of the night. They seemed to take on a dreamlike quality, unreasonably detached from ordinary life—from all life, as she knew it. Pervading everything was a sense of confusion and irrationality. There must, she supposed, be some kind of link to connect the things which had been happening to her with normal, everyday existence, but what was it? What were these people doing? It was difficult to believe that she had not dreamed herself into one of those film comedies where everyone was completely mad. But it was not a dream. The bed in which she lay was large, solid and comfortably real. There had been nothing in the least ethereal about the massive butler, and the breakfast he had brought was both appetizing and satisfying. She went back over last night's happenings, looking for a purpose.

The deductions which Derek was to make would lie close to the truth—to begin with.

Phyllida had indeed, in response to a sudden impulse, stopped her car by a telephone kiosk in order to inform Mr. Drawford of her plans, and it had been with a comforting feeling that his participation would put the affair on a proper footing that she had continued her drive. Nevertheless, even the sense of having done the right thing proved a poor armor against the prospect of an empty—a suspiciously empty—house by night, and sharp misgivings found chinks widened by chilliness and growing appetite.

Her first reaction when the Grange loomed before her, slightly blacker than the night itself, was to regret her refusal of the spare room in Derek's flat. Her second, an impulse to return to the village and knock up Mr. Hawkins of the *Hand in Hand*. He and his wife were old friends of hers; they would be pleased to see her even though it was almost midnight. Her hand was on the gear lever to slip it into reverse when she changed her mind again. It was in a mood of stubborn refusal to be frightened away from her own home that she drove into the garage.

The trunks still stood where her reluctant driver had placed them. Evidence of Mrs. Church's activities was present in the shape of a key hanging from a rusty hook. She reached for it somewhat reassured; a part, at least, of the house had been made ready for her. Once she had safely reached her own room, she would be able to shut out the rest until morning.

Discovery that the lights were in working order gave her further encouragement; she blessed Mrs. Church for having had the sense to run the engine awhile. The bright electric lamps had the effect of making the place, if not homely, at least less mysterious; it was mostly due to their influence that she amended her original plan of going to bed hungry. Investigation of the big sitting-room—the "drawing-room" when her mother had been alive—revealed a table ready laid, and bacon and eggs had been put handy for her in the kitchen. She felt that the food, in addition to filling a void, might instill a degree of fortitude—the lights had not entirely succeeded in dispelling a sense of eeriness. Her meal was quickly cooked, and then, just as she had sat down to eat it, came the sound of a car on the drive. A few moments later followed the ringing of the bell, and the din of the knocker clattering frighteningly in the empty hall.

Phyllida hesitated. The Grange had got on her nerves more than she would admit. For a second she had thought of staying where she was; sitting tight and pretending that the house was still empty—then she realized that the caller—whoever he might be—must have seen the chinks of light. . . . She jumped violently as the knocker began to pound again. Then, filled with the idea that it might mean news of her father, she had jumped up and run to the door.

A man wearing a light raincoat and carrying a rug over his arm faced her on the step. He smiled pleasantly.

"Please excuse me for troubling you at this hour," he apologized, "but I am looking for a Mrs. Shiffer. Perhaps—"

Phyllida opened the door wide.

"I am Mrs. Shiffer," she began. "Is it about—?"

But he had given her no time to finish. In a flash he had snatched the rug from his arm and flung it over her head. Before she realized that it was happening, his arms were round her, pinning her own to her sides. She heard him call out. Other hands slipped a cord on her ankles and tied them tightly together. A second was wound about her waist, holding the rug firmly in place, and then the arms about her relaxed. Two pairs of hands picked her up and carried her down the steps.

Phyllida paused in the act of munching toast spread with excellent marmalade. It was difficult to remember in detail just what had happened after that. Perhaps if she had been less surprised, her memory would have been clearer. She could recall that she had been hustled into the backseat of a car, and that one of the men had followed to make sure that she did not get rid of the stifling rug. There had been a lot of talking by several voices; sounds of feet hurrying to and fro and a fuss which sounded like an argument, though she had been unable to distinguish any of the words. Then the sound of a heavy door slamming—the front door, she guessed, for its thud was followed by a sharp rap as if the knocker were dropping back; the noise of another car starting up; finally, a lurch as two more men got aboard the car she was in. They slammed the doors behind them and the engine started.

On the ride her several surreptitious efforts to remove the rug had been forcibly discouraged by the man who sat beside her. He must, it seemed, have kept his eyes fixed upon her the whole time. As a result of the fifth or sixth attempt he had grown impatient and bound her wrists with something which felt like a pocket handkerchief. After that, nothing could be done, and she had been forced to resign herself—insofar as the word might be applied to one who was in a state of semi-suffocation from close wrapping and surging indignation—to her helplessness.

Of the journey itself she could remember little but her own discomfort. Her judgment of the passing of time was entirely upset: it was impossible to tell whether one or several hours passed. She knew only that while the air beneath the rug grew hotter and stuffier, she herself became uncomfortably colder. And with increasing chilliness her first furious anger underwent a change. It was not diminished, but alloyed with determination and some apprehension; it set into a mold of bitter resentment. In this new mood she tried to catch any sounds which might suggest the route, but such as penetrated the enveloping rug were for the most part mechanical noises from the car itself, and the knowledge that they were now making a long climb and now rushing down hill could give no certainty to her speculations.

Only when they slowed down considerably and began to take frequent corners was she sure that they had entered a town of considerable size. Then, finally, had come a slow, deliberate bump, and hands grasping her again as the car came to a stop.

A few moments later she stood in the large hall of an unfamiliar house, unbound, and free at last of the stifling rug. She started to look about her, but the two men with her were in a hurry. One of them crossed the hall and held open a door; the other urged her forward.

Her first impression of the room she entered was its glitter of plated metal. Chairs of several types, but all with skeletons of convoluted tubes, vaguely suggesting bicycles which had lost their wheels, were disposed about a carpet resembling a diagrammatic explanation of the atomic theory. Here and there stood occasional tables, also metal framed, but topped with plate glass. The two men directed her toward the largest piece of furniture in the room; a desk with a surface of black glass. Behind it sat a darkly handsome individual of late middle age. One of her escort dragged forward a chair for her and looked questioningly at the man beyond the desk. He nodded.

"You can go," he told them.

As they left he turned to fix Phyllida with an unremitting stare. She knew without being told that he expected her to break into hysterical accusations, to make violent threats. More than that, she felt that he hoped that such would be her reaction. The unwavering examination was intended to have a disquieting effect, to frighten her, and in that way dispose of her first defenses. Undoubtedly, had she been given less time to prepare herself, had the drive been shorter, she would have obliged him involuntarily, but enough time had elapsed since the assault at the Grange to give her an attitude of cool, controlled animosity. She determined to disappoint him.

"Was it necessary to suffocate me?" she inquired.

For a fleeting moment he looked surprised, a little thrown out; then his expression changed as he shifted his mental stance.

"You must excuse their lack of consideration for your comfort on the grounds of over-anxiety for your safety," he said, seriously.

There was a further short pause. He seemed uncertain how to proceed. At last, in the tone of one going through a formal, unnecessary preamble, he asked:

"You are Mrs. Shiffer?"

"I am," Phyllida said shortly. There seemed to be little use in withholding the fact.

"The daughter of Professor Woodridge?"

"It is true—though I don't know what business it is of yours."

The man behind the desk continued calmly.

"Do you know anything of your father's work since he left the University?"

Phyllida frowned. She wished she could see what he was getting at. However, since the answer was almost entirely negative, nothing could be lost by replying.

"Hardly anything. For one thing, I have practically no knowledge of either chemistry or biology, and, for another, I have been away from home for the last three years. In any case, I cannot see what business it is of yours, Mr. . . . ?"

He chose to ignore her request for his name.

"It is very much our business, Mrs. Shiffer. We have good reasons for believing that Professor Woodridge made some very interesting discoveries in the course of the last year. Unfortunately his present whereabouts is a complete mystery. His house is—or was, until your return—closed, and we have been unable to get into touch with him. It is, however, extremely important that we learn the results of some of his experiments. It is possible that you will be able to help us."

Phyllida all but let fly. The cool cheek of the man took her breath, and it was only by a severe effort that she managed to keep control of her tongue. When she did answer, it was in a hard, sharp tone.

"My replies to that are, firstly, that my father is not an inventor of patent medicines: he is a scientist and when he has proved his results, he publishes them. Secondly, that if he does withhold a result, it means that he is dissatisfied with it and does not wish others to know of it. In any case, I have no authority to speak of his work and, lastly, do you think that in the circumstances I should be likely to give you the slightest help—even if I could?"

He looked at her steadily for some seconds. When he replied, it was in answer to her last question.

"I think that if you can, Mrs. Shiffer, you probably will."

Phyllida shrugged her shoulders.

"As I cannot, the question does not arise," she told him.

Her voice was steadier than her feelings. There had been an unpleasant suggestion of threat behind his last words. He nodded slowly.

"I see that I must be blunt. I am afraid that you do not quite appreciate the situation."

"I assure you I do—and I know that abduction involves heavy penalties."

"If the abductee is found and able to lay information," he agreed. "But what if she is not? You are in my house. Your friends do not know where you are, and they have no means of finding out. I think if you face the position squarely you will agree that it would be as well to answer my questions at once—it may save so much unpleasantness."

"I have told you that I know nothing of my father's work," Phyllida repeated.

The man behind the desk sighed with a suspicion of theatricality.

"I see that you are determined to make things difficult for yourself, Mrs. Shiffer."

"I think they will be still more difficult for you," she said. "I have made appointments to meet friends today, including my solicitor. When they find that I am missing, there will be inquiries." Her words were braver than her hopes. She did not see what possible means there could be of tracing her, but it was a gallant determination to put the best face on things and to keep fright at bay.

"Your solicitor?" He referred to a piece of paper on the desk. "Ah, yes, Mr. Miles Drawford of Bedford Row. I wonder . . ." He thought in silence for some minutes, seeming entirely to forget Phyllida's presence, though his eyes were still on her. When he did speak again, it was to impress upon her that there was no chance of her rescue.

"We have taken the precaution to bring your car away. That will not deceive them for long, of course, but it will help to delay the alarm, and then—if you will excuse a hackneyed phrase—the scent will be cold."

He paused again, looking down at his desk, playing absent-mindedly with a small plated paperweight in the shape of a sphinx. At last he seemed to come to a decision. When he looked up his face was harder and his voice harsher.

"Look here, there's been enough of this nonsense. We want—we intend to have—some information of extreme importance to us—much too important to allow any squeamishness to stand in our way, you understand? I have good reason for believing that you can give us this information, and I mean to have it—at any cost." His brows lowered as he looked at her. From lids narrowed beneath the frown his dark eyes stared into hers, measuring her strength. "Why not tell me at once?"

"Because I do not know? Isn't that reason enough?"

She attempted to answer in the same calm tones she had used

before, but even to her own ears it sounded scarcely successful. His change of manner, the coldness of the gaze drilling into her, produced a wavering in her mind, the vanguard of panic. A frightening sensation of unsupported emptiness swept her. How far he understood her mood it was impossible to tell. He went on:

"Your life, Mrs. Shiffer, probably has some value for you. For me it has none."

The tone of voice was so calmly level, the statement made so cold-bloodedly, that panic rushed all her defenses. She lost her head, knowing only that she must do something, however futile. She jumped forward and, snatching the plated sphinx from the desk, flung it full in the man's face.

It glanced from his forehead and crashed through the lower pane of the window. Her hands were on the telephone when the door burst open, and the two men who had escorted her dashed in. One wrenched the instrument from her while the other, standing behind her, grasped both her arms above the elbows. The man at the desk pulled a handkerchief from his pocket to wipe his forehead. He looked thoughtfully at the little stain upon it, and then glanced up at her.

"First blood to you, Mrs. Shiffer. But not last, unless, of course, you change your mind."

Phyllida said nothing. She had reached a point where the choice lay between silence and crazy tears. The man nodded. "We shall see," he said.

The two men led her across the hall and up several flights of stairs, stopping before a cream-painted door. One of them released her arm to take a key from his pocket and open it while the other urged her on. The door closed sharply behind her and the lock clicked across. Phyllida put out a hand in the darkness, groping for a switch beside the door. She found it, and a moment later was surveying a large, airy bedroom. The room was dominated by the bed itself—a big, comfortable-looking, inviting bed.

A clock on the small table beside it showed her that it was almost five a.m. Twenty-one and a half hours since she had last got out of bed in her aunt's Kensington house. And this bed looked tempting and restful. . . . Well, why not? What else was there to do? Anyhow, she would feel the better for some sleep.

She was hardly able to remember getting herself to bed. She must have fallen asleep at once.

Still feeling only partly awake, she sipped her coffee. Alice, she reflected, must have felt a quite similar bemusement in Wonderland. The apparition of a butler who brought one an excellent breakfast and asked, "There is nothing further you require, madam?" was not a sensible corollary to last night's happenings. Far more logical would have been an entire absence of food—an attempt to starve her into telling them what they wanted. A sudden hope sprang up—they must have realized that she could tell them nothing. . . . But the hope withered almost as it sprouted. The man behind the black glass desk had been convinced that she did know—nothing could have occurred in this short time to change his mind. He had threatened . . . Abruptly the meal lost its flavor. An insidious notion which would not be expelled suggested that something even less pleasant than starvation might be in store. She recalled the pair of hard, callous eyes which had bored into her own and a mouth set into firm, relentless determination.

She pushed the tray away. She did not so much give herself up to thought, as strive to prevent the invasion of her mind by successions of unpleasant pictures.

She was not very successful. Fight as she would to direct her reflections upon more welcome or, at least, less frightening subjects, the trend of her own mind defied her. Unpleasant forebodings, kept in check for a few moments, rallied and returned to shoulder out her conscious choices of thought, to substitute

themselves in increasingly gruesome forms. Nothing would help but action of some kind within the limits her captors allowed.

She got up, dressed herself, and began an aimless wandering of the room. The furnishings were modern and good. Bed, wardrobe, dressing-table, chairs, a small chest of drawers and a few other pieces were all designed in admirable proportions and carried out in a variety of unfamiliar woods. They showed taste and restraint and their modernism had nothing in common with the *outré* furnishing of the study downstairs. The lighting was by two windows, both on the front of the house. With more curiosity than hope she raised the sash of one and prospected. The ground was a discouraging distance below. A drop from the first floor she might have risked, but they were taking no chances; to drop from this, the second floor, was out of the question. And the walls were smooth, without even a drainpipe to serve as a precarious ladder. The large front garden was screened from the road by a wall and a tall evergreen hedge; beyond it she could see an empty house with "To Let" notices in the windows. On the lawn, close beneath her, a small woolly dog was tethered by a chain to a peg. It was evidently his nature to take an inquiring interest in everything about him, but, prevented at present by the chain from making close investigations, he had to be content with uttering short, interrogative barks. He directed a volley of these at Phyllida's head protruding from the window.

A sound in the room behind her caused her to turn. A man whom she did not recall seeing on the previous evening had entered and was relocking the door. He looked across at her and the open window beyond, and shook his head.

"No, Mrs. Shiffer. It is a long way down."

"I'd decided that for myself," she said.

She had a better view of him as he advanced toward the light and laid several books upon a table. A tall man of twenty-nine or thirty, with a pleasant, intelligent face. Less good-looking, she reflected, than her questioner of the night before, but more wholesome. He was dressed in a gray suit, irreproachable save for a bulge in the right-hand jacket pocket. The blemish was removed when he withdrew a box of cigarettes and extended it to her. She hesitated a moment, and then took them. A dignified or melodramatic refusal would have been at variance with the attitude she had decided to adopt—moreover, she felt the need of a cigarette. She opened the box, took out one for herself, and offered it to him. Both smoked for the first few puffs in silence, indulging in mutual covert study. At last:

"I have been sent to ask you if you have changed your mind," he said.

"I can only repeat what I said last night; that I know nothing about it, and if I did I should not tell you. By now," she added, "my friends will have arrived at West Heading and have informed the police of my disappearance."

He remained unmoved by the information and continued to talk calmly, asking questions in a smooth, even kindly voice. Phyllida began to feel that he had some sympathy with her predicament. She answered many of the questions which she would have ignored had they come from the other man. After all, it did not seem to matter—she had nothing to hide. At last he finished. He lit a fresh cigarette and gazed at her through the smoke with an expression she failed to understand.

"I see that you know nothing about it. He is a fool—I told him you wouldn't."

"I'm glad someone believes me. Does 'he' refer to your friend downstairs?"

"My dear Mrs. Shiffer, one's business associates are not necessarily one's friends. I hope you don't think that I approve of his methods?"

"Why not? Aren't you aiding and abetting?"

"We wanted certain information. He was certain that you could supply it; I was doubtful, more than doubtful. I could have made certain in a little time by my own methods, but he was in a hurry, and it is he, not I, who gives orders. He believes in what he calls 'direct action'—so many people who cannot be bothered to think things out believe in 'direct action,' don't you think? His handling of this affair is a sample. You will believe me when I say that I shall always despise myself for having been in any way connected with it?"

There was a solemnity in the question which set a panicky apprehension rising again in Phyllida's mind. There had been an uncomfortable emphasis on the word "always."

"But he'll let me go now, won't he? Now that you are convinced that I can tell him nothing about it?"

The man hesitated. He seemed to be finding the reply difficult.

"You *knew* nothing, but now you no longer know nothing. You see, because of his stupid, melodramatic methods, you now know two things. One, that he wants your father's secret, and, two, that this is his house—which means that you can discover his identity. He can't afford to let you go now."

Phyllida was weakening. She began to slip out of her chosen part. The panicky feeling increased as she asked:

"But if I promise not to tell? If you took me away in a car as I was brought? I don't even know where I am now. There was a rug over my head all the way here."

He shook his head.

"Now you are lying, Mrs. Shiffer. You saw the empty house opposite; you saw the agent's name and his address. That has given you a good enough clue."

"I couldn't read it—it's too far away," she cried desperately.

"No. That's not true. Honest people like you make bad liars."

Phyllida changed her line.

"But what will he do? He can't keep me here always."

The man frowned. His eyes did not meet hers as he spoke.

"No. He will not want you here. You will have to disappear."

Phyllida, still half detached from reality, found herself asking in a queerly objective way:

"Do you mean he'll kill me?" It seemed absurd as she said it for her to speak in this calm voice. The truth was that she could not realize it—he couldn't really mean that. But the man downstairs had threatened . . .

"Kill you? Oh no, I don't mean that, but—well, young women are frequently disappearing, you know where they go to."

She stared at him with widening eyes.

"Not . . . ?"

The man nodded. He was looking out of the window when he spoke again.

"It might even be better to try that . . ." he said, slowly.

V

DESPERATE REMEDY

Phyllida was given ample time to review her situation. Whatever plans might be made for her future, there was no sign of any attempt to put them into immediate operation. Such arrangements, she supposed, must by their natures be delicately complicated. It had not been until the departure of man Number 2—as she had mentally classified the gray-suited visitor—that she had been able to restore any degree of order and clarity to her mind. When she did succeed, it was only to plunge herself into a blacker hopelessness as the implications became plainer.

By kidnapping her (an action clearly disapproved by Number 2 on several grounds) Number 1 had encumbered, not to say endangered, himself uselessly, and she must be got rid of. It was not impossible that the real object of Number 2's visit had been to tempt her to try an escape by the window, but she considered it unlikely. In spite of the company he kept, she found herself inclined to believe him. Moreover, it would hardly be less awkward for them to have a suicidal captive, than to kill her themselves. At that point her thoughts turned back into familiarly disturbing channels. Suppose Number 1 still refused to believe in her ignorance? Would he try force to make her speak? She was entirely at his mercy. . . .

The more she considered it, the more frightening the aspect. The affair took on a hard reality at last. Until then, although she had been kidnapped, carried off and threatened, it seemed to her that she had been treating the whole thing objectively. It had been too fantastic to be a part of real life. She had had a dream-like sense that such things could not indeed be happening—as though it were all part of a queerly distorted play. Then, with a rough jar, it swept over her that it was serious—the horrible thing was actually happening to her. A man had just seriously suggested that she should kill herself. . . .

It shocked her. The idea of death made her feel more vitally alive than ever before. Being alive abruptly ceased to be a state taken for granted; it became a force in itself, active and driving. It was difficult to explain to herself what she had actually felt in that moment. The nearest she had come to such an emotion before had been after a smash which had wrecked her car, leaving her miraculously uninjured. She had wanted to shout and sing with the sheer thrill of finding herself still alive. It had been an amazingly beautiful world at that moment.

And so it was now.

She crossed to the window and looked out into the wintry sunshine. No, she was damned if she would go that way. If the worst came to the worst, there was always that, but this was too soon to give in.

Not bravado, but a harsh, bitter stubbornness was behind her thoughts, goading her with a sense of outrage. For a man, she guessed, it would have been different; he could not have been upset by the same sense of shock which shifted all her standards. She had been snatched from the human, civilized world and told that she must disappear—shown that she was a saleable com-modity; that she had a trade value, and as a result she found herself more frightened than she had been in the whole of her life. Frightened not so much by the concrete dangers—the pros-pect of being shipped to South America was too remote for that as yet—but by finding that she herself did not count in the scheme. Her body could be sold like any other piece of furniture; what went on inside her, what she thought about it, would trouble no one. She, that part of her which made her Phyllida and nobody else, was reduced in the scheme of things to complete and utter unimportance. Possibly it would have shocked her less to know that he intended to silence her by killing her. She had never known before the full meaning of the word "indignity." She paused in her thoughts; they had been running away with her, piling on the agony, but not without cause. Somehow her whole conception of the order of things was altered. She had thought that marriage to Ronald had taught her a lot. Life had been wretched enough with him, but she had still been herself, not utterly abased; she had never been regarded as a piece of indifferent livestock. . . .

It was a long time before she was able to concentrate upon immediate practicalities, and still longer before the nebulous idea of escape could be contracted into even the most rarefied form of plan. The primary certainty was that if an escape were to be made at all, it must be made at the first attempt. Failure would assuredly entail fettering or some similar form of restraint. But into the details of its accomplishment, her mind steadily refused to be driven.

By evening she had reached a stage contiguous with hopelessness. Nothing but her own action could help her. Long ago Derek, Barry and Uncle Miles must have discovered her absence, but it would be impossible for them even to make a guess at her plight; there was no chance whatever of outside help. She alone could help herself, and only that if a plan would offer. Her sole consolation for the present was that the quantity of books brought by Number 2 indicated no intention of her immediate removal.

In the evening she retired to bed, not to sleep, but to lie there in the dark creating and destroying impossible schemes. In desperation she tried to call to mind all the thrillers she had ever read—and to wish that she had read them more carefully. But thrillers had been thrillers, and there had been no reason to expect that they would suddenly overlap real life. Then, too, they all seemed to have dealt with special cases rather than the incarceration of an ordinary person in an ordinary room. She began a mental tabulation of answers to the question, "How did the heroine escape from the locked room?":

1. She is rescued by the hero.—No good at all in the present case.
2. She vamps the jailer.—But the butler who had brought her her meals appeared unvampable, a peripatetic ice-box. And man Number 2 had not paid a second visit.
3. She stands behind the opening door and hits whoever enters with something heavy.—Not practicable for several reasons, the best being that the door was set in the corner and opened back against the wall.
4. She throws a faint and escapes while the jailer fetches brandy.—A bit obvious; besides, any jailer of sense would shout for someone else to fetch the brandy.
5. She ties her bedclothes into a rope and climbs down from the window.—Yes, but not if a yapping dog is tethered below to give the alarm.
6. She flings pepper into the jailer's face.—Quite, but after that—?
7. She suddenly produces a weapon concealed in her garter.—Certainly, if she has one.

There were plenty more. With a little effort it was surprising how many one could remember in rough outline, but not one of them seemed quite as workable as it had in the books. And then, at last, the idea came. An old one, a simple one—with a slight variation. Phyllida sighed thankfully and turned over on her side.

Next day it became clear that Phyllida's spirit was broken. During Saturday she had put up a brave show which secretly impressed the butler, but he entered on Sunday morning to find a figure of weeping dejection huddled in the bed. When he returned to remove the tray, she pleaded with him so brokenly that even his schooled exterior showed a flicker of distress at her misery. Nor, it seemed, did the passing of the day increase her self-control. The man she had called Number 2 looked in once during the morning, but his visit was brief, and his manner as he left was one of barely concealed disgust at her collapse.

She had decided not to try anything before night. There was a risk that she might be removed during the day, but it was a risk which must be taken; daylight set all the odds against her. Not until shortly after dark, therefore, did she begin the business of tying sheets and blankets together by their corners to form a rope.

The number of times she had read of this operation was beyond her counting; it was, in fact, the old-established method of leaving upper windows. Nevertheless, as she regarded her handiwork, she was relieved to think that her life did not depend on its security. However, it would serve.

The corner of the last sheet was firmly knotted to the leg of the bed, and the business of paying out the rope began. Its lowering was an occupation requiring extreme care lest the dog below should become alarmed; to her relief it was carried through without raising so much as a single yap. Then she turned her attention to the bed. As quietly as possible she moved it across the room until its foot was against the wall below the sash, taking care that the way to the window itself was not blocked. After that there was little to do but wait. She squeezed herself close to the wardrobe on the side hidden from the doorway, and hoped that the butler would bring her dinner before long.

But he was later than he had been the previous evening. She had overlooked the fact that this was Sunday. She was forced to stay in her hiding-place, watching the luminous hands of the clock crawl round the dial in so dilatory a fashion that several times she thought it had stopped. They showed just after nine o'clock when there came a rattle of the key in the lock, followed by a tap on the panel. She shrank back in her corner as the door opened. A moment later the lights flashed on. An exclamation broke from the butler as he caught sight of the bed skewed out of place. He set down the tray with a sharp jangle and ran, as she had hoped, to the window.

In a flash she was out of her corner, running across the room. He stood with his head and shoulders out of the window, looking down the improvised rope. She flung herself at him with all her strength, and her shoulder took him in the middle of his broad black back.

His feet slipped on the polished boards of the surround. He gave a cry, clawing wildly at the sill to save himself, but it was too late. He toppled headfirst out and vanished into the darkness. Only by clutching at the bed foot did Phyllida save herself from following him.

A heavy thud came from below; the small dog began barking in a frenzied fury; voices shouted at one another somewhere in the lower rooms. A second later Phyllida was out of the bedroom and running for the back of the house. As she turned the corner of the passage she heard a babble of voices in the hall and a pounding of feet on the front stairs.

Her immediate fear was that she might be unable to find the back stairs, or that having found them, she would encounter other investigators of the alarm in the act of climbing them. But her luck held. To judge from the sounds of shouts and running feet, she had succeeded in attracting everyone to the front of the house. She discovered and tore headlong down two flights of back stairs. At the bottom of the second she was faced with a choice of three doors. The baize-covered one on the right she judged to lead to the main part of the house. That on the left was ajar, giving a glimpse of the kitchen. The one before was paneled in the upper half with obscured glass; it looked as if it should lead out of doors. It did. In a rush she was through it, across a small yard, through another door and running down the back garden.

From the front of the house proceeded a medley of raised voices with an obbligato of continuous yapping. The sounds spurred her into running as she had never run before. But the garden ended in a brick wall too high for her to climb. Desperately she swerved, making for the side, and there she had better luck. Only a flimsy fence separated her from the next-door garden. She scrambled over it and landed in a clump of bushes. Beyond them was a tennis lawn, and on the farther side of it, more bushes.

After that, followed a nightmare of running and scrambling. She lost count of the number of gardens she must have crossed before she was forced to stop and rest. So far the noise of her own progress had made it impossible for her to listen for sounds of pursuit, but now, crouching among shielding laurel bushes, she strained her ears. Comfortingly far away the small woolly dog was still yapping, that was all.

She wondered what had happened to the butler. Had the unfortunate man broken his neck? Not at all unlikely, falling from such a height. But what else could she have done? She might have run out of the door while he was looking out of the window, but he would have heard her and have given the alarm at once. By his fall he had attracted everyone to the front. Because he would certainly be in no condition to answer their questions, she had hoped that they would think for at least a few necessary minutes that she had gone down the rope, and that he, in attempting to follow her, had slipped. It had been essential for everyone to be at the front while she escaped by the back. At the time she had been frightened enough not to mind whether she killed one or all of them. . . . She began to feel the reaction as she crouched and recovered her breath. It was quite impossible for her to control the trembling of her limbs.

Some minutes passed before she forced herself to go on. Before her a lawn led up to a large house, dotted here and there with lighted windows. She approached it with caution, avoiding the pools of light, and made her way beside it to the front garden. There she hesitated again. Would she be safe even in the road? Men who had kidnapped her like that would not easily be put off. She decided to lie low a little longer.

When at last she took courage to leave the shadows, it was to emerge upon a road entirely deserted. Thankfully she started along it, half running. Her luck had held.

Within a hundred yards her road debouched at right angles into another. She hesitated again on the corner, wondering which side to take. To the right it stretched away, empty; some little distance to the left a knot of men stood beneath a lamp-post. As the light fell on the face of one, she caught her breath. She drew back, but too late; the man whom she had faced on the steps of the Grange had caught sight of her. She turned and fled blindly down the road to the right.

VI

A REAPPEARANCE

The best Monday breakfast is apt to be an overcast business: this Monday's was an orgy of gloom. Derek surveyed the food before him with an absent intensity sufficient to wither the goodness out of all it touched. Barry stood it for a while in silence. At length, he suggested:

"Look here, pull yourself together, old boy. Going off your food isn't going to do anyone any good."

Derek's reply to the truism was not couched in words: it was close to a snarl.

"Have some bacon and eggs. They're good," Barry mumbled, from a full mouth.

Derek helped himself vaguely and stared at them lying on his plate as if in doubt as to their proper function.

"But, damn it all," he muttered for the thousandth time since Saturday, "what can have happened to her? She may have crashed, been assaulted by bandits—anything."

"No, you can wash out the crash at least," Barry said, shaking his head. "Old Drawford had the number of the car circulated. We should have heard if it had been seen."

"That only makes it worse. We haven't a clue of any kind."

Barry looked at him curiously. Seldom, indeed, in all the years he had known him had Derek allowed anything to get on top of him. He had cultivated an air of detachment in the face of surprises, good and bad, with such success that it came as a shock to see it broken down. Had he ever visualized such a situation as this he would have predicted that he himself would have been unable to hide his distraction, while Derek would be the one to maintain a calm front. Somehow, their usual roles had reversed themselves.

"She'll soon turn up all right," he said.

"Don't be a fool. Do you think I'm an idiot who needs humoring?" Derek snapped. A moment later he seemed ashamed of his tone. "Sorry. This damned business has got me down," he said, and relapsed into a silence which remained unbroken until Barry was on the point of leaving. He paused at the door.

"I say, Derek, if you do get any news, you'll let me know at once?"

"Of course. The moment I hear anything."

The door banged. Derek lit a cigarette and slumped moodily into an armchair. There was the devil of a lot to be said for having a job on a day like this if only to take one's mind off things: Barry was lucky—though his job did lie in one of the more immoral callings. Queer how he was taking it—how did he manage it? If he had been in Barry's position he'd have been off his head with worry. When he had lost Phyl to Ronald three years ago he had been nearly demented, and yet now, when she had come back only to disappear again, he could control himself as though ... Oh, who could predict, anyhow?

He began to wonder how he would occupy the day. The problem of Phyl had been debated *ad nauseam* all Sunday—he must somehow stop himself stewing over it all today as well. He dragged himself out of his chair. A bath seemed a good beginning. The moment he was fully immersed the telephone bell rang. In two seconds he was back in the sitting-room, dripping and clad only in a towel. Damn the thing, of course it was in the bedroom—these plug-in telephones were always somewhere else. He streaked back along the passage.

"Hullo? Yes?"

Miles Drawford's voice answered him.

"Is that you, Derek?"

"Yes, is it news about either of them?"

"Phyllida's been found. The police have got her."

"Thank God for that. But what do you mean, 'got her'?"

"I don't know. I've just had a message to say that she is being brought up at Golders Green police-court this morning."

"Good Lord! But why? Do you mean . . . ?"

"Yes. Assaulting the police or something of the kind. I couldn't make head or tail of it over the telephone. Anyhow, she seems to want me there. Can you meet me at the court?"

"Of course. What time?"

"As near ten as you can manage."

Derek glanced at the clock. It showed almost half-past nine.

"Right you are, but I may be a bit late."

He replaced the receiver and waited a moment before lifting it to dial Barry's office number.

"I want to speak to Mr. Long."

An adenoidal voice announced that Mr. Long had not yet arrived. Derek looked at the clock again and swore.

"Hullo. Well, look here, can you take a message for him?— Good. Listen. Will you tell him the moment he arrives that Mrs. Shiffer—no, not Fisher, Shiffer—S-H-I-F-F-E-R, got it?— What?—Yes, I know it's a funny name. Now, get this straight. Mrs. Shiffer has been found and Mr. Jameson—J-A-M-E-S-O-N— will phone through the details as soon as he knows them. Got that? Just read it back, will you?"

He listened.

"No, no, no! Good God, man, don't tell him that. It's *found*, not *drowned.* F-O-U-N-D, found.—Yes, that's right, and be sure to let him have it the moment he comes in. It's very important."

He dropped the receiver back on its hook and dived for the wardrobe.

Police-constable Pennywise was giving evidence. He was one of those large and placidly genial men who give the impression of being *in loco parentis* to the whole fussy world which circulates about them. His nickname of "Foolish" was the result of a very obvious derivation, and its general use in "Q" Division was traditional rather than derogatory. He understood it and did not resent it; if he had in his official capacity a fault, it might be that he was sometimes a shade too tolerant; the troubles which certain classes of society contrived for themselves could distress him to the point of making allowances, but he was not foolish. Moreover, he had the distinction, rare in policemen, of sustaining the full dignity of the law minus a helmet. His manner even toward the Bench was slightly protective.

"On Sunday, the fifteenth of October, I was on duty in Gaydon Road. At approximately ten-fifteen p.m. I saw the lady come round the corner from Knight's Road. She looked first up one way and then the other, as if she couldn't make up 'er mind which to go. Then she sees me and comes running."

"Just a moment, Constable. You say she saw you, and came running. Are we to understand that she required your assistance?"

"I thought so at the time, sir. Looking distraught, she was, sir, very distraught."

"Ah, distraught. Thank you. And then?"

"Well, I started walking toward 'er. And before I'd got more than a few yards, a lot of people comes running out of Knight's Road."

"A lot, Constable?"

"Well, three, sir. Men, sir."

"Yes?"

"Then she looked back over 'er shoulder and began to run faster. I got the impression—"

P.C. Pennywise hesitated. There are courts which allow impressions and others which frown upon them.

"You received the impression that she was running away from these men?"

"Yes, sir."

"Continue, Constable."

"Well, sir, she came on until she was about half a dozen yards away, then she stopped and picked up something from the road and threw it at me."

"She did not say anything?"

"Not a word, sir."

"And she threw something at you?"

"Yes, sir."

"And what was it she threw?"

"Something lying in the road, sir."

"Quite, but what we want to know is what was this something which was lying in the road?"

"Er—manure, sir. Horse manure."

A titter in court was swiftly withered by official frowns. Phyllida gazed intently at the floor.

"Oh, I see. And after that?"

"I took 'er by the arm, sir, and started talking to 'er very severe. Then the three men what 'ad been following 'er came up and began apologizing. They gave me to understand that she wasn't responsible for 'er actions and had given them the slip—er—heluded them. They were very sorry such a thing should've 'appened and they would take good care it didn't 'appen—happen again. Then they asked me 'ow much it was going to cost me to get my coat cleaned. I wasn't sure what to make of it—the lady didn't seem very friendly with them, though they were pleasant spoken enough."

"Quite, Constable. But what we want to hear is what you did—er—make of it?"

"The lady 'erself decided that, sir. While we was talking close by Messrs. Goldfisch and Richstein, the tobacconists, she offed with 'er shoe and did in the window. That settled it, sir. I 'ad to take 'er along to the station then. The men became habusive, but I told them they'd have to come along and settle it with the sergeant. At that they grumbled a bit and then went off."

"Leaving the prisoner with you?"

"Yes, sir."

"It struck you as odd that they did not accompany you?"

"Very odd, sir."

After a number of questions which failed to shed any further light on the matter, Constable Pennywise was instructed to stand down.

The prisoner herself, when questioned, was found to have raised reticence to the status of an art. In the Bench's private opinion her recollection was fogged more by circumstances than intent, and, in consequence, there were magisterial views and foibles to be aired. He assumed an attitude of admonishment.

"Young lady," he began severely. "I do not know what you had been doing immediately prior to this disgraceful incident, but it was obviously something of which you are not proud. Had it not been that the medical evidence has expressly stated that no traces of alcoholic influence were observable when you were brought to the police-station, I should have suspected as the cause of your surprising behavior one of those all too frequent cocktail parties which have become such potent instruments for degrading the youth of the nation. These pernicious gatherings, where young men and women congregate upon terms of loose familiarity, are one of the crying scandals of the age. They utterly destroy that sense of modesty which makes our gently nurtured ladies aware that theirs is the finest type in the world: they are, in a word, un-English. I repeat that, but for the medical evidence, I should have been driven to the suspicion that you had been attending one of these disgraceful orgies. As it is, I am forced to the conclusion that you were concerned in some other form of amusement which may or may not have been harmless, but of which you see fit to be ashamed.

"From the constable's evidence, I deduce that you wished to rid yourself of the friends with whom you had been spending the evening, while they were so loath to let you go as to misrepresent your mental condition. In my view, you are well rid of such, but you have chosen an expensive method of severing your friendship. You will have to pay for the damage you have done, and I trust it will serve as a warning. . . ."

The three congregated outside the court.

"Well, it might have been worse," said Derek. "The price of Goldfisch and Richstein's window and two recognizances of five pounds, but mind you keep the peace henceforth. What on earth were you up to?"

Phyllida, hatless (the object lent her to place upon her head in court had been duly reclaimed) and wearing a dress which was far from presentable, shook her head.

"Give me some lunch. I'm starving. Then I'll tell you all about it."

"An explanation of how you came to be heaping such indignities on the law in the middle of the night should make good hearing," Mr. Drawford said, "but as far as I am concerned, I am afraid it will have to be postponed."

Phyllida looked disappointed.

"Oh, Uncle Miles, I thought you would be interested enough."

"My dear, you've nearly succeeded in driving three men crazy with worry over the weekend. That should be enough guarantee of interest."

"Is it really so frightfully important?"

"It is, and I'll pay you the compliment of admitting that only you and your misdeeds could have got me away this morning. The office was broken into over the weekend—it's like a pigsty."

"Burglars? What did they take?"

"We don't know yet. It'll probably take us days to get it all straight and find out what's missing. Allbright and Micken are at it now, and I must help them; so the story will have to wait."

He hailed a taxi as they reached the street. They watched it disappear.

"Dash the old boy. So worked up he even forgets to offer us a lift. Look here, I'll phone Barry and get him to meet us for lunch. Won't be a minute."

He turned suddenly and collided with a burly figure in blue, apologizing hastily and dashing on. Phyllida smiled at the policeman; he grinned back at her.

"I'm sorry, Mr. Pennywise, but there really wasn't anything else to throw."

"Might 'ave been worse, miss—mum. Sorry I 'ad to take you up, but duty's duty, you know."

"Of course it is; besides, I wanted you to take me up."

Constable Pennywise shook his head.

"I don't know what it's all about, mum, but I 'ope it'll be all right."

"I hope so, too." Phyllida nodded. "Perhaps when I've found out what it's all about myself, I'll tell you. By the way, Mr. Pennywise, how much *does* it cost to get a tunic cleaned?"

"—And they saw me and I turned and ran away as hard as I could—luckily it wasn't far to the main road. You heard the rest from the policeman."

Phyllida ground out another cigarette-end. Gray ash dribbled from the overfull tray on to the tablecloth. A waiter hovered suggestively closer. He received a curt demand for more coffee. She sipped at that which had cooled in her cup.

"That's a most amazing story," Derek said, "but why didn't you tell it to the policeman or to the magistrate?"

She drew another cigarette from the packet on the table and tapped it thoughtfully.

"Really because I was so afraid that if I did, they might think I actually was mad. Those men almost convinced the policeman, as it was. If I hadn't broken the window, I believe he'd have let them take me back."

"But in court?"

"On my own unsupported word, without a scrap of evidence? Don't be silly, Derek, I should have got myself into an awful mess." After a pause, she added, "Do you know what really shocks me most about the whole thing? It's that it is so easy—so frightfully easy. I wonder how many girls are snatched up just like that and don't have the chance to escape?"

Barry broke in:

"Do you know the address of this house?"

She shook her head.

"No, but I could easily find it again. It's in one of the turnings off Knight's Road which runs into Gaydon Road."

"Anything distinctive about it?"

"Lots. The house itself has been fairly recently painted cream on the front, and the window frames are a kind of bluey-green. There's a wall and a hedge which almost hide it from the road, and the gates in the wall are the same bluey-green. And, of course, there's the empty house right opposite. But what's the good?"

"Well, I think you ought to tell the police," Barry looked questioningly at Derek, who frowned.

"Yes—probably they ought to know." Derek sounded a shade doubtful.

"Of course they ought. Damn it, we don't want to withhold information about white-slavers, do we?"

"That's not quite the point. They themselves obviously aren't white-slavers; that part of it was only subsidiary—their method of ridding themselves of the embarrassment of Phyl's presence; the alternative, to be quite brutal, to knocking her on the head. At least, that's how it strikes me." He looked questioningly at the girl, and she nodded.

"Yes, that was how it struck me."

"And their real purpose was to get hold of this information. Why? That's what I want to know."

He poured himself some fresh coffee.

"Yes. Why?" Phyllida echoed. "As far as I remember, Daddy always used to keep his notes in the lab, where they would naturally be handiest when he wanted them."

"In that case," Derek suggested, "either these particular notes were so very important that he hid them somewhere safe, or else they saw them and didn't recognize them."

"I don't quite follow that." Barry looked puzzled.

"Don't you remember, the village bobby told us of a burglary at the Grange shortly before Uncle Henry left?"

"You think that they were after the notes, then?"

"Of course I do. There's just a possibility of its being a coincidence, but, after all, it was a queer kind of burglary. Nothing was taken, as far as we know. It looks pretty fishy to me."

"But there's a third possibility," Phyllida interrupted. "I mean that the notes are imaginary—that these people have got hold of some wrong idea altogether. It's so unlike Daddy to be secretive about his work—he's just a straightforward research worker. Suppose they are after some notes which may not really exist at all?"

"A bit thin. They sound like a pretty efficient crowd to me," Derek thought.

Barry broke in:

"Look here, we can go into all this later. I think Phyl ought to rest and try to sleep a bit after all she's been through. She's looking dead-tired."

Derek ceased to draw patterns on the tablecloth with a fork and looked up at her.

"Yes, I'm sorry. At the risk of being considered as uncomplimentary as Barry, I endorse that. Bed for you, Phyl. Come along."

It was too true for Phyllida to protest. They pushed back their chairs. The waiter's gloom of an hour's standing was replaced by a scenic smile as he hurried forward to assist.

VII

LITTLE PROGRESS

Miles Drawford reclined in a posture which he considered less becoming than comfortable. He had never entirely succeeded in disabusing his mind of the idea that armchairs such as Derek's, with their long, low seats, were, in some undefined way, indecent, but he could not deny their restful qualities. Indeed, had it not been for the voice proceeding from the similar, though slightly smaller, chair on the other side of the fireplace, he could have slept. But the voice did not permit. It went steadily on telling its astonishing tale, so that he all but forgot the weariness induced by the hours which he and his partner and his clerk had spent in putting their office to rights. He lay back, watching the play of the firelight on the ceiling, noticing unaware, how the molding of the cornice now jumped into clarity and now receded into shadow. And all the time Phyllida's voice continued to tell a story which had no relation to his own experience of life. From anyone else the tale would have strained his credulity; he would have made reservations; but Phyllida, well, he knew her— had known her since she was a small bundle in her mother's arms. At least, he had thought he knew her, though he was at present learning of a more resourceful Phyllida than he had known before. He heard her through almost without an interruption, which, considering his legal mind, was one of her minor triumphs. At last she stopped, leaving him with a great deal to say, and nowhere to begin.

"When we left the police-court, I don't think you'd quite given up the idea that I was drunk and disorderly, had you, Uncle Miles?" she added.

He sat up a little in order to shake his head emphatically.

"My dear, after the fright we'd all had I was so glad to find you unharmed that I wouldn't have minded if you had been found drunk and incapable, but I did not think that. For one thing, it's not like you. And, for another, the police definitely said that there was no suggestion of alcoholic excess; and they've a pretty fair experience, you know. But I must admit that, like the magistrate, I was convinced that something very odd had occurred. However, I never suspected anything like this."

"You think I ought to have told them all about it?"

"No. I should say that in the circumstances you took the wiser course. Unsupported allegations, you know. Excitement in court. Evening papers making the most of it. People you know only slightly saying to one another: 'It sounds a queer kind of story to me—I wonder what really happened?' And then going on to suppose this and that. It would have been most unpleasant for you. But that does not mean that the police ought not to know. Of course, it is really for you to decide, but I think that out of— well, call it public duty, if you like, you ought to tell them."

Phyllida frowned slightly. Obviously the idea did not appeal to her.

"But they won't be able to do anything. Those men will just deny it."

"True. They may not be able to do anything directly, but information of that kind is useful. It's a case of 'little drops of water, little grains of sand.' They go on quietly and patiently building up and fitting together. You may be quite sure, for instance, that after they have heard your story they will find out whether anything else is known against the men and who they really are. Quite likely something will come of that."

"All right then, Uncle Miles. If you feel I ought to, I'll go round to the police-station in the morning, but only on condition that you come with me."

"I think we can do better than that. In a practice like mine one doesn't often come up against criminal matters, but it has happened once or twice that I have met one of the Scotland Yard men—a Detective-Inspector Jordan. I fancy that if you tell him, he'll know what to do about it. You see, for all we know, it may be just the link they are waiting for."

"I don't see how—?" Phyllida began, doubtfully.

"Nor do I. But it will surprise me if it doesn't fit in somewhere. There was an organization behind their methods which suggests practice. Besides, you remember the threat of the man you call Number 2? If it was not said just to frighten you, it presupposes wide collections. Such a transaction would need a lot of handling; one would have to know where to go and how to set about it."

"Yes, I see that now. I didn't quite realize it before. When shall we go, Uncle Miles? Tomorrow morning?"

"The afternoon would suit me better, if you don't mind. I've still a great deal to get straight at the office."

"Of course. Just when you like."

Miles Drawford looked across at her. The light of the fire softened the lines of her face. Only when the flames leaped momentarily higher was it possible to see the details of worry upon it. There had been little sign of that this morning; she had still been sustained by excitement then. Now that activity no longer kept worry at bay, the reaction had set in.

And his own mind was far from easy. Not only was the mystery of Henry Woodridge's disappearance intensified, but there was this matter of the injured butler. From her tone as she related the incident he could tell that it was getting on her nerves. Even though the circumstance had demanded it, it could scarcely be a pleasant recollection. He was, he had gathered, a heavy man, and he had fallen from the second floor. . . . It might be only a broken leg or arm, but it might equally well be a broken neck. . . . It was hard to see how trouble might come of it for Phyllida, but it was safer to be prepared. For this reason, as much as for any other, he wanted her to tell the police. He looked at her again, wondering whether to raise the point. He decided that no useful purpose could be served by that at present—better try to get some information on the man's condition first.

A key rattling in the front door interrupted his thoughts. Derek and Barry entered together.

"We're sorry we're late," Derek announced. "Not only because we have been without your delightful company, but also because we're damned hungry. How now, fair coz? I hope you took a glass of Vitaltine and ensured restful sleep. Wonderful stuff, Vitaltine, as Barry will tell you—transatlantic flyers take it to keep them awake; stay-at-homes take it to send them to sleep."

Phyllida looked up. Her introspective gloom vanished.

"How many times, Derek, have I told you that I will not be referred to as 'fair coz'? It's a revolting phrase. I loathe it."

"So much for the Bard. I take it he was wrong, too, in supposing that sleep would knit the ravell'd sleeve, or perchance you dreamed, was that the rub?"

"On the contrary, I slept very well. Probably I should be sleeping now but for the telephone."

"Oh. Who?"

"Old Sir Seymour ringing up to know if there was any news of Daddy yet. He was awfully sweet about it and apologized for being so grumpy the other day."

"Nice old boy, Sir Seymour. Rang up yesterday, too. To hear him and Uncle Henry debating some higher scientific point which no one else can understand at all, you'd think they'd nothing in common but mutual contempt. When you really get down to it, you find that they are as attached to one another as two old chaps can be."

"If you don't mind," put in the solicitor, "a little less of this 'old chap' business. Seymour Franks is only a year or two senior to me."

Phyllida intervened.

"What's the matter with you, Barry?" she asked.

He was wearing a despondent expression, and had not spoken since he entered the room. Derek answered for him.

"He's had a sad disappointment, poor lad. Went out looking for a fight and only found a raspberry. He'll be better after food. So shall I. So will you. Put on your things, and ho! for Charlotte Street."

———

Miles Drawford swept unenthusiastic eyes across Gustave's. He was a solicitor, his office was in Bedford Row, his house in Four Horses' Lane, Hampstead. Upon the exceedingly rare occasion when he found himself in Soho, it was at one of the southern restaurants which boasts a commissionaire: one of the places which has 'got on,' runs a table d'hôte dinner and has built up a reputation known even as far away as Hendon. This northern Soho he knew not at all, and was prepared to like but little more.

"You must not," admonished Derek's voice in his ear. "You must not sniff at the way we poor live—have a look at the menu first." Mr. Drawford looked. It cheered him slightly. Derek produced a wine list. That was even better reading; parts of it were almost literature. Gustave himself bustled up to the table and began a high-speed recitation of comestibles. The effect was confusing.

"Don't mind him," Derek advised. "It's his great parlor trick. We all admire it, but nobody listens."

They ordered. Gustave produced an excellent sherry. Mr. Drawford sat back and began to take fresh stock of the place. The small restaurant was blue with more smoke than appeared compatible with the power to breathe. From the surrounding tables arose fountains of chatter and still more smoke. Vehement arguments were in full swing at several tables or between groups at different tables. He compared it with some of the more polite restaurants he knew, not entirely to the latter's advantage. This might be a trifle too noisy and boisterous, but it was preferable to a number of the haunts of self-conscious solemnity, and at least there was no need of second-rate music to cover patrons' conversational poverty.

"That's Grost, over there." Derek indicated a big man who wore a dark beard. Mr. Drawford observed him. The man was laying down principles in a booming voice which accorded with his frame.

"And who is Grost?"

Derek looked a little shocked.

"Don't you ever read *New Politics*? He writes articles for them in favor of dictatorship."

"H'm. That doesn't sound very new. Does he want a dictator for England?"

"He certainly does. The only trouble is that he can't decide who it should be."

The solicitor looked again at the vociferous Grost.

"He looks like a man with convictions," he admitted.

"Oh, he is—only they change so often. A year ago they were Communistic convictions—now all his red comrades regard him as a backslider, while he thinks they are back numbers."

Derek went on to point out several notable Bloomsbury dwellers, and to enlarge upon their peculiarities. Of a few the solicitor had heard; the fame of the majority was purely local. Phyllida and Barry began to interest themselves in a conversation of their own.

"Thank God," Barry contrived to yell confidentially above

the surrounding babel, "that you're back safely with us. Phyl, my dear, we've been more scared this weekend than you will ever know. If it had gone on any longer, I think old Derek would have gone potty."

"Gone what?" Phyllida demanded, as Grost's booming carried away the last word.

"Potty," shouted Barry.

The bearded Grost, who had just delivered himself of a triumphant climax, turned to glare. There was a light of misunderstanding in his eye.

"He'd have gone mad," Barry amplified, hastily.

Grost changed his mind and turned back to his party with a shrug. Barry went on:

"It was that awful feeling of helplessness—being sure that you were in some kind of trouble and not being able to do a thing about it."

Phyllida looked at him curiously.

"You or Derek?"

"Both of us."

"He seems cheerful enough now."

"Yes, now. He's the normal Derek again now—just as if it had never happened—to look at. But over the weekend—well, it was a side of him that I've never seen before. He felt—we both felt that we had let you down. You had just come back, we'd barely seen you again, and then the very first time you wanted some help, we couldn't give it. We..."

He caught Derek's eye on him with an expression he did not quite understand, and stopped on the word.

"What?" said Phyllida.

"Oh, what does it matter now?" Barry raised his voice again to compete with the surrounding chatter. "You're safe and you're back. It's over now, thank God." Nevertheless, a frown inconsistent with such sentiments made its appearance. "All the same, if

I ever meet that swine Draymond again, I'll push his bloody face in."

He spoke with ferocity and determination. The last half of his sentence unhappily coincided with one of those unanimous pauses in conversation which are apt to fall upon a room full of people. Somebody chuckled audibly. Grost's head went back to emit a booming laugh. Barry, coloring, glared at the amused faces about him. He seemed to be on the point of taking out his wrath on any convenient person.

"What's all this? Whose bloody face?" inquired Derek.

"Who is Draymond?" Phyllida asked, with the evident intention of calming him.

Derek frowned. "Barry, what did I tell you? The woman, my cousin, the female escapologist, kept us waiting all through lunch for her story, now she can wait all through dinner for ours."

"What is it? What have you two been doing?" Phyllida demanded. "If it's anything to do with me, I think I ought to know at once."

Derek groaned.

"There now. See what you've done, blast you, Barry. She won't be happy till she gets it, and I shall have to eat and talk at the same time—which means that both operations will be conducted indifferently."

"What is it?" Phyllida repeated, unrelenting.

"Oh, all right, I'll tell you. And if I get indigestion, it'll be your fault—however, no doubt Barry can get me some Minsoda tablets, 'The Sentries of the Stomach,' at trade price." He reflected a moment.

"We will call it *The Case of the Bland Householder* or *All at Golders is not Green.*" He helped himself despondently from one of the dishes of *hors-d'œuvres*. "You know, I shan't enjoy this stuff half as much as I ought to, and I'm devoted to raw cabbage."

"Go on," Phyllida insisted.

"Now, where was I? Oh, yes, that was the title. Well, after we'd left you, Barry was all of a sweat. Nothing would satisfy him but that we go sleuthing. I don't know what his firm thinks about it. He wasn't there on Saturday; I gather that he did no work this morning, and he played truant this afternoon. Probably, quite a serious number of persons has failed to have its taste corrupted and various firms will go bankrupt as a direct result.

"I must admit that I wasn't over-keen. My own view of sleuthing is the conservative one, that it should be done mentally, preferably while wearing a dressing-gown, and at a respectful distance from the sleuthed. Barry's idea of a bit of subtle detective work is to open the conversation with some sort of pleasantry such as: 'Ha, ha, you swine! We meet at last.' He has no patience with that school of thought which works, deeply cunning, until the final coup."

"I was damned angry," Barry put in.

"You're telling me? Anyhow, it's no proper frame of mind for a detective. My great fear," he explained to the others, "was that he might find a pistol and try to shoot people up. He might, at that moment, have been described as righteous revenge incarnate."

Barry snorted. "Look here, if you can't tell this properly, let me."

"All right. All right. Just getting the atmosphere of the thing; the noble spirit in which we started, and all that. I admit frankly that my own attitude was less heroic. In fact, it was that of one who was going to see the show, and possibly clear up the bits afterward.

"Anyhow, off we went to Golders Beastly Green, where we found Knight's Road without any difficulty." He turned to the solicitor. "You've never seen Knight's Road? You ought to, it's such a thoroughly *nice* place—though funny things do seem to go on inside some of the houses. We started examining all the side roads for *The House with the Bluey-Green Gates*. It was dreadful. Every house had what I believe is called 'character.' There was a sort of horrid fascination about them which put me in a kind of stupor, so that it was Barry who actually found the bluey-green gates, and clutched me by the arm. There was no doubt that it was the right place, for there were the optimistic 'To Let' bills in the windows of the unspeakable house opposite. Barry was all for direct, frontal methods, but there I struck. I admit that, as things turned out, they would have been just as productive as the course we took, but it seemed a pity not to get right inside the house now that we had come so far. We had a bit of an argument before he could be dragged away from the spot, but finally we went off in search of a directory.

"'"The Laurels," Catalan Road, Golders Green, is the residence of Ferris Draymond, Esquire. He . . .'"

"Ferris Draymond?" asked the solicitor, suddenly.

"Yes. Do you know him?"

Mr. Drawford shook his head.

"No, but I've heard of him in the City."

"Any details?"

"Nothing I can call to mind—just a pretty well-known figure."

"Well, after that we got his telephone number and found out that he had just come home. It was getting on, for six o'clock by this time, and I thought that tomorrow might do for an interview. But Barry didn't. He was full of Vim and Vigger, so back we went to Catalan Road and presented one of my professional cards at 'The Laurels.' I scribbled something about urgent business on the back, but I was doubtful if it would fetch him. So, apparently, was the man who opened the door. His tone was most discouraging when he said: 'I will see if Mr. Draymond is at home.'

"However, a couple of minutes later we were shown into his study. Phyl had already prepared us for something of the kind when she described it, but, with all deference, I don't think she did it justice. There were at least eight of those bent steel chairs which were intended for German tenements until the intelligent said: 'Why shouldn't we call them smart and sell 'em to poor goops at two pounds ten each instead of six bob?' We looked at the black glass desk: it made me think of a snack bar. The carpet was a crime committed in the name of modernism. The whole room was neo this and neo that. I've never encountered such determined neoism in my life. After the silver panels and the dark walls and the green tinge of the ceiling, I expected the man behind the desk to look like one of those dummies in Jaeger's windows. It was quite a shock to find a normal-looking human being asking what he could do for us. Barry started like Winter Shell:

"'You may explain, if you can, your treatment of Mrs. Shiffer,' he said.

"The man's eyebrows rose inches and then descended below normal.

"'I'm afraid I don't quite understand you,' he said, stiffly. 'I gathered that you wished to see me on business, Mr.—'—he looked at my card again—'Mr. Jameson.'"

"'I am Jameson,' I said, 'and—'

"'And this gentleman?' he interrupted.

"'Mr. Long, a friend of Mrs. Shiffer's. I am her cousin.'

"It was then that he adopted the air of the bland householder.

"'Doubtless your business with me would be made clearer if the identity of the lady to whom reference has twice been made could be further explained. I am afraid that I do not recall anyone of that name.'

"'Your memory must be remarkably short,' I said. 'I am referring to the lady who threw that paperweight'—I pointed to the little sphinx on his desk—'through your window early on Saturday morning.'

"'The lady you kidnapped and kept prisoner here,' Barry added.

"The man looked from one of us to the other. His air of bewilderment was well done.

"'My dear sir, this is a most extraordinary accusation. I assure you that I am holding no lady prisoner here.'

"'That's only because she was lucky enough to escape,' said Barry.

"The man turned to me with a puzzled expression.

"'Am I to understand that your friend seriously thinks that I—?'

"'You are to understand, Mr. Draymond,' I told him, with a feeling that this kind of thing might go on for hours, 'that we are both aware that you seized Mrs. Shiffer from her home on Friday night, and held her here by force until she made her escape on Sunday evening. We should like an explanation of your action.'

"He looked at me steadily; after a time he gave a slow smile and shook his head.

"'No, Mr. Jameson, not a penny.'

"We both goggled at him.

"'What do you mean?' Barry asked.

"'I mean that it won't work. Not a single penny are you two going to get out of me.'

"'If you think—' I began.

"'But I do. I certainly do. Consider a moment. If what you suggest had actually occurred, you would not be here interviewing me, you would be with the police, doing your duty as good citizens. Instead, you have come here to threaten, but threats don't work with me, Mr. Jameson; you've picked the wrong man to try and frighten.'

"'We shall certainly go straight to the police when we leave here,' I told him.

"That irritating smile of his grew broader.

"'Bluff, Mr. Jameson. Useless, I assure you. I have not the pleasure of your cousin's acquaintance, but I am sure she is well grounded in her story. Fortunately, however, all menservants—save for my butler, who is unlucky enough to be in hospital just now—will be able to testify that the whole story is a fabrication—not a very ingenious fabrication, I may add. I do not know off-hand what penalties are inflicted on those who try to obtain money in this way, but I should imagine that the sentences are unpleasantly heavy. It is such an old trick, my dear Mr. Jameson—if that is, indeed, your name—the police are, as the Americans say, "wise to it." You will have to get up earlier in future.'

"And there we stuck. Not only did he meet all our accusations with a flat denial, but he even went as far as to threaten calling in the police himself to give us in charge for demanding money with threats. We knew, of course, that that was bluff, but it didn't help. We argued and blustered for a bit. Barry ran verbally amok and told the man a few things about himself. But he just sat there at his ridiculous desk and smiled at us. He must have had a bell concealed somewhere, because two men came in to cut short as comprehensive a piece of vituperation as ever I did hear. Very firmly they 'gave us the gate,' and that was completely that."

He laughed a little ruefully.

"You ought to have seen us just then. Two chivalrous knights gallantly out to avenge the insults put upon a lady, reduced to standing on the pavement and wondering what to do next. Modern life is just a chain of anti-climaxes. I've come to that conclusion a lot of times, but I keep on forgetting it in the intervals. In the end we decided that there was nothing to be done, so we came home."

There was a pause. Phyllida said:

"It was sweet of you both to try. But what did you really mean to do?"

Derek shook his head. "Quite honestly, I don't know. I fancy Barry went with some idea of beating the man up, didn't you?"

"I don't think I knew, either," Barry admitted. "I just felt wild at the way you'd been treated, and I wanted to do something about it. It does seem a bit silly, I suppose, when one looks at it afterward."

"You're sure," Drawford put in, "that it was the same man?"

Barry stared. Derek chuckled.

"Ha! the legal mind looking for loopholes. I'm sorry to be prosaic, but I'm afraid it was. Phyl told us that the man she called Number 1 was a dark, good-looking fellow. Ferris Draymond is undoubtedly that. Also, he is clean-shaven, parts his hair in the middle, has brown eyes, broad, surgeon-like hands and wears a platinum signet ring on the left little finger. How's that?"

"Yes. That fits. I remember his eyes—a kind of rich brown."

"I took particular note of them. Why do women always manage to remember the color of eyes? I could tell you, but I won't. Anyhow, taking into account a recent small bruise and scar on the forehead, I think we can consider identity established."

"You mean that we assume that this man, Draymond, was responsible for the crime?" Drawford said.

"We do: we had already. Though if I were Phyl, I should kick at my adventure being sordidly described as 'the crime.'"

"And yet, to me, it is quite incredible that a respectable City man should behave in such a fashion."

"Why? Why is it more incredible in a City man than in anyone else?"

"Well—er—well, it just is," the solicitor said, lamely.

"Prejudice, Drawford: Class bias. Just think of the respectable City men who embarrass small schoolgirls in suburban railway trains. Dark horses are bred in City stables, Drawford."

The solicitor paid no attention; he had known Derek long enough not to rise.

"I must make some inquiries. There is undoubtedly more than we thought about this. I wonder if Henry—" He trailed off into silence, pursuing his own private line of thought.

"What's this?" Derek leaned forward. "Do you think he might know more about this Uncle Henry business?"

But the solicitor did not explain. His professional caution asserted itself, but his speculations had led him, apparently, on to interesting ground.

"Suppose," Barry suggested to the other two, "that that is the explanation of his disappearance. I mean, that Mr. Woodridge had certain information which he knew that Draymond wanted—and that he knew Draymond to be pretty unscrupulous. Might it not be his safest course to disappear and continue his work in peace?"

"It might," Derek said, but doubtfully.

"You think that's what Daddy's done?" Phyllida asked.

"Well, it's plausible."

"Only just," Derek qualified. "I don't want to be a wet blanket, but if his only reason for leaving the Grange was to avoid Draymond, why vanish totally? Surely he could safely have told Phyl and Mr. Drawford where he was. This complete secrecy doesn't strike me as natural or necessary."

He glanced at Phyllida to see if she grasped the possible application of his last words, but she had taken up a line of her own.

"For all we know, Draymond may really have got hold of Daddy. Don't you think he may have found him in spite of his shutting up the Grange and going away?"

"Certainly not."

"You sound very definite," Barry objected.

"Well, look at it," Derek said. "It isn't a nice suggestion to make, but I'm sure that if Draymond had got hold of Uncle Henry he would have had the information somehow. Friend Draymond isn't squeamish—at least, if we judge by his treatment and intended treatment of Phyl. It may be that all his threats were bluff, but Phyl doesn't seem to think so."

"I'm sure they weren't—he wouldn't stick at anything," she endorsed.

"Which seems to me to make it pretty certain that Draymond has not got him."

"And leaves us just where we were before: asking, 'Where is he?'" Barry said.

For a time there was silence at the table. The room had thinned, but bursts of laughter still came from other parties. Gustave came hustling up. It was, he felt, scarcely complimentary of his patrons to look so gravely thoughtful after the meal.

"It is good, yes?" with some concern.

Derek nodded. "I have no doubt, Gustave, that it was good, but who can judge if he is forced to be a raconteur throughout dinner?"

"Ah! So!" said Gustave, with tact.

They began to collect their belongings.

"Can I drop you anywhere?" Drawford suggested, as he helped Phyllida on with her coat. Her reply that she would be staying at the Gordon Square flat caused a slight shadow to cross his face. Derek laughed.

"Come, come, Drawford. Don't forget the status of the married woman. There's a different standard for her. Lord knows why. Perhaps she is supposed to be better qualified to avert any possible consequences."

Mr. Drawford looked pained. He demurred.

"Your aunt—" he began.

"Nonsense, Drawford. Stand by your conventions. Don't you know that married women are less human than unmarried? You can't go back on your generation's teaching like that."

The solicitor turned his appeal to Barry, who shook his head.

"He can't help it. His mind works like a corkscrew. But, honestly, I think we shall all sleep the sounder for knowing that Phyl is where Draymond can't get her without braining us."

"I suppose it is all right, nowadays," Mr. Drawford conceded, but in a voice which supposed the opposite. He turned to Phyllida.

"Let me know at once if there is any news, my dear."

"Of course. Good night, Uncle Miles."

They stood on the pavement and watched the black saloon depart northwards.

"You know," said Derek, thoughtfully, "I may be wrong, but I fancy the old boy could give us some ideas about all this—if only his legal caution would let up for a bit."

Phyllida nodded.

"He does seem to be keeping something dark. I'll try to get it out of him when I see him tomorrow afternoon."

VIII

A NOTE FOR PHYLLIDA

The room looked gray and cold. Phyllida pulled the clothes closer to exclude a chilly draft which was fingering her spine. Five minutes of semi-coma ensued. A small clock on the bedside table was ticking fussily, making a noise symbolic of irritated efficiency, as if it said: "You ought to be doing this; you ought to be doing that. I am the great Ought."

She opened one eye to take in the great Ought's instructions, but for the moment its face was obscured. She extended an arm and removed the note propped up before it. By the simple process of showing hands at a quarter to eleven, it said: "You ought to have been up two hours ago." She yawned in its face and unfolded the note:

Good morning. Barry has already dashed off to distort Truth into Advertising, and I am one of a thousand applicants for a tenth-rate job. Mrs. Roberts will bring you breakfast if you shout. There is one beautiful sight you will never see—yourself asleep.

Derek.

She smiled, dropped the note back on the table, stared at the foot of the bed for a few reflective moments, and then glanced out of the window. Something misty, too thin to be tasted and smelled, and therefore unclassifiable as fog, defiled the air. Not cheering; perhaps some food would lend a brighter prospect. She summoned breakfast in the manner suggested.

Mrs. Roberts maneuvered the tray and her own rotund person into the room with difficulty. She beamed upon Phyllida.

"Good morning, miss—er—mum, I should say now. It's good to see you 'ere again. Quite like old times."

"Thank you, Mrs. Roberts. That's nice of you, but you better not let Mr. Drawford hear you say anything like that. He doesn't think I ought to be here even now."

Mrs. Roberts snorted.

"Oh, 'im. 'E's an old fusty, that's what 'e is. A bit nasty minded, as you might say. Not that it's 'is fault, mind you. Just comes of 'is being a lawyer and forever thinking of divorces and what not. They can't 'elp getting like that. Why, I ain't never known a nicer pair of young gentlemen than Mr. Jameson and Mr. Long—and there ain't much I don't know about them after doing for them for close on six years. 'Ow did you like them foreign parts, mum—not-as much as your 'ome, I'll be bound?"

She rattled on. Phyllida contrived to slip in questions concerning Mr. Roberts' permanently unsatisfactory health and his equally permanent and unsatisfactory search for employment. She managed, too, to remember the names and natures of most of the Roberts brood. The replies were voluble, detailed and discursive. Moreover, since Phyllida's married state had rendered her eligible for a kind of Freemasonry of Misfortune, there was much intimate information upon matters of health to be imparted. Half an hour was swept away in the torrent of recital before either realized it. It was checked at last by a sight of the clock. Lawks, was Mrs. Roberts' reaction, there was the morning nearly done, and she had to get out for the shopping yet, if Phyllida would excuse her. She withdrew. A few moments later her behatted head was thrust into the room to give assurance that she would be back within the hour. Then the flat door slammed and she was gone.

Phyllida slipped out of bed and fetched the telephone from the sitting-room. Having plugged it in, she slid back into warm comfort and dialed Mr. Drawford's office number. No, she was told, Mr. Drawford was at the Law Courts; would she like to speak to his partner, Mr. Allbright? She decided that it would be a waste of time; if there had been any news, there would have been a message. When, she asked, would Mr. Drawford return? The voice at the other end regretted its inability to be definite, but, it thought, soon. She hung up and placed the instrument on the table.

"It's time you got up," said the hands of the great Ought.

She yawned once more and reached for the large, rather scratchy male dressing-gown. It felt as if one were putting on a tent. Her feet were sliding into slippers like small canoes when there came a clatter from the doorbell.

Damn! Probably some poor devil wanting to demonstrate a vacuum cleaner or a water softener.

A fresh-faced young man, dressed in a neat dark gray suit, stood on the mat. He removed a gray felt hat to expose smooth fair hair, and smiled pleasantly.

"Mrs. Shiffer?"

Phyllida was surprised.

"Yes?" A little doubtfully.

"I have a message for you."

From an inside pocket he extracted an envelope with her name on the front. She seized it with a sudden, sharp excitement. Tearing it open, she read the few lines written in a familiar, angular style.

My Dearest Phyllida,
I cannot say how sorry I am to have caused you such anxiety, but
circumstances of which I can give no details here have forced me into
a peculiar position. I am sending this by young Straker of whom I
have told you before. If you will come with him, all this mystery will
be explained to you by your loving

Father.

Phyllida looked up to meet the blue eyes of the young man watching her.

"You are Mr. Straker?"

"I am."

"Tell me, where is my father?"

"Do you mind if I come in? It might be wiser not to talk here on the stairs."

"Of course." She led the way into the sitting-room and turned to him again.

"Where is he?"

"I am afraid I am not at liberty to tell you that, Mrs. Shiffer. You must understand that Professor Woodridge has gone to a great deal of trouble to keep his present whereabouts a secret."

"Even from me?"

"Particularly from you. He considers it much safer both for yourself and for us if you do not know where he is to be found."

Phyllida stared at the young man; an angry flush began to spread across her cheeks.

"Do you mean to say that I—?"

"Please do not misunderstand me. We have heard that you have already suffered one unpleasant experience. Mr. Draymond, as you will have guessed, has few scruples where his interests are at stake. If he were to know that you could give him your father's address, it would put you into danger."

"But you are to take me to him?"

"Yes, but not to his present address—to a common meeting-place."

Phyllida frowned in bewilderment.

"What is it all about? It's so confusing."

"I'm sure he will tell you as much as he wants you to know when you see him. He is waiting for us now," he added, pointedly.

"Yes, of course. I must get some clothes on. I'll be back in a few minutes."

She crumpled the note into her dressing-gown pocket and ran back to the bedroom. She was half dressed when the telephone bell rang.

"Yes?" She lifted the receiver impatiently.

"Is that you, my dear?" The voice was deep and avuncular.

"Who do you want?" she demanded irritably.

"I want Mrs. Shiffer. Aren't you she?"

"Yes, but who are you?"

"Seymour Franks." The tone was slightly reproving. "I want to know if there is any news yet of—"

"Yes. Yes, there is. I've just had a note from him, and I'm going to see him."

"Has he been hurt?"

"I don't think so—there was nothing about it in the note."

"Well, that's splendid. Where is he now? I should like to give him a piece of my mind for alarming us all."

"I don't know where he is. You see, he just sent the note round by his assistant, Straker, telling me to go with him."

"Straker?" the voice repeated reflectively. "Oh, yes, I remember. Lanky fellow, looks as if he didn't wash overmuch—good man at his job all the same, I believe. Well, that's the best news I've—"

"Wait—wait a minute," Phyllida interrupted urgently. "Lanky fellow, looks as if he didn't wash overmuch"—? That didn't fit at all.

"Quickly, this man Straker. Can you describe him?"

"But you said he was—"

"Never mind. What does he look like?"

"Oh, tall, you know. Slight stoop, wears glasses, gold-rimmed, I think."

"What colored hair?"

"Just a sort of nondescript brown. Too long, trails on his collar. Good man all the same, so your father says."

"And his face? Is it rather red?"

"Oh, dear me no. No, no one could call it red. Is there anything wrong, you sound—"

"No, it's quite all right, thank you."

Phyllida hung up. She hesitated for a second, her finger on the dial. Then she lifted the receiver again and dialed "0." Speaking quietly and close up to the mouthpiece:

"Police, quickly," she said.

———

Had he heard the telephone? she wondered. Had he taken fright and gone already? She thrust her head out of the bedroom and called experimentally:

"He's sure to wait for us?"

"Yes, but we mustn't be long." The young man's voice sounded calmly unsuspicious.

"All right, I'll only be a few minutes now."

She closed the door. He must have heard the bell ring. Perhaps he had thought it was in the next flat. There was a bolt on the door; she slid it to reinforce the lock and then retreated to sit on the bed and look at it apprehensively. It was not a very good door; it did not seem capable of withstanding much force—and he was a very muscular-looking young man. Suddenly she recalled that she was still only half dressed. How long, she wondered, would it be before the policeman could get here?

She finished dressing and began to walk the room, aimlessly fidgeting. Eight minutes since they had said that the man would be round at once: it felt like eight hours. There was a tap on the door: she jumped as violently as if it had been an explosion.

"Aren't you ready yet, Mrs. Shiffer? We shall be late."

Did he sound suspicious? She thought not. But there was a slight change in the quality of his voice—uneasiness, perhaps.

"I've torn my stocking. I shan't be a moment."

Why couldn't that policeman hurry? One would have thought that after her message he would have come running. Only policemen never did run, did they? She must keep the man here. He must be arrested for them to get something out of him. So far this mystery had been all smooth—they hadn't been able to catch hold of anything. If the man should take fright and run away, they might never get any farther. He must be wondering at her delay. Once she let him smell a rat . . .

On an impulse she went to the door and slid the bolt back silently. She went out into the passage, still wearing the canoe-like bedroom slippers. The man appeared at the sitting-room door, an unmistakable expression of relief upon his face.

"I can't find my shoes," she said.

Mrs. Roberts had cleaned them. They stood, unfortunately obvious, close to the front door.

"They're here," observed the young man, with restraint. She felt that in other circumstances he would have delivered some scorching remarks upon her dilatoriness. His self-control was marked when she succeeded in breaking a lace.

"Damn!" she murmured, looking at it helplessly. "I wonder if there is another pair anywhere?"

"Let me do it."

He took the shoe from her and joined the broken ends of the lace in a large, inelegant knot.

She looked at it. "Oh, but I couldn't—"

"Come on," he snapped. Evidently the command sounded too abrupt even to his own ears; to soften it he added:

"It's getting late."

Phyllida was bending down to tie the bow when a ponderous clamor on the door caused her to straighten in a flash. Her hand went to the knob. The young man lifted his arm, but she was too quick for him. She turned back the latch. Through the opening door a classic phrase rolled weightily:

"Nah then! Wot's all this?"

IX

MISADVENTURE OF A CONSTABLE

Number 156, "O" Division, or, less impersonally, Police-constable Grayling, had covered the distance between the station and the flat with dispatch. The word is applied advisedly, for while he did not saunter, neither did he run. And there were three good reasons why he did not run. One, which Phyllida had recalled, that it is untraditional in the force; two, it might have left him without enough breath to meet an emergency as it should be met and, three, the sensation attendant upon such athleticism would have brought him to the door in company with a crowd of idle and troublesome persons bent on seeing the fun. Nevertheless, he flattered himself that he had made good speed, and much of the indignation he had felt at being dragged from a comfortable canteen and sent off to assist a woman who was probably culpable for whatever mess she had got herself into, had worn off by the time he was climbing the stairs. He paused before the ultimate door ("It would be the top," he told himself; "it always is"), and verified the number. Then he made his resounding assault.

Force of habit drew the words of omen from him as the door opened. He had a glimpse of a gray-suited young man whose face was in the act of replacing irritation by astonishment. Then things happened too quickly for the dignity of the law. The young man's head went down and he shot through the open doorway like a firework.

"Ugh," grunted Constable Grayling, as the head took him in the middle.

He staggered. Something astonishingly hard jolted him under the chin. He reeled. The landing seemed to tip up. His last awareness was a flash of sizzling white against a background of whirling black. . . .

Phyllida emerged. A mountainous blue-clad body lay on the floor. A clatter of racing feet was receding down the stairs. She looked over the banisters. The only visible part of her late visitor was a hand slithering at astonishing speed down the stair-rail. She turned back, gazing with a stupid helplessness at the very inactive Constable Grayling. Hitherto, she had been one of the many who have never seen a policeman laid out; there was an improbability about the sight; so must the spectators have felt when David's stone accounted for Goliath. Faced by fifteen and a half stone of inert embodiment of law, she was singularly shocked. Moreover, and more annoying, the fugitive had clattered out of earshot; however, there was a new sound of feet on the stairs. These were ascending.

"Hi," she called, experimentally.

"Hullo. What's the matter?" Derek's voice floated up.

"Oh, good. It's you. Come here quickly."

Derek ran up the last two flights.

"What is—?" he was beginning, when he observed the unfortunate policeman. He stared.

"What, again? Really, Phyl! What have you done to this one?"

"Don't be silly. He's unconscious."

"So I see. How did you do it?"

"I didn't, you idiot. A man did. He's run away."

Derek's face cleared. "Young chap; highly active?"

"Yes. Did you stop him?"

"My dear girl, why should I? Besides, he nearly bowled me over."

Phyllida looked upon the fallen.

"Come on. We must *do* something," she insisted.

Between them they succeeded in getting P.C. Grayling on to the sitting-room divan. Phyllida fetched a basin of cold water while Derek sought the brandy. The man did not appear to be seriously injured. A large bump was swelling at the back of his head, but the skin was unbroken. After a few minutes' ministrations with a damp cloth he stirred.

"Here." Derek offered the glass. The brandy had swift effect. Constable Grayling put up his hand and felt the back of his head with tender care. He looked at Phyllida in rueful apology.

"Sorry I let 'im get away, miss."

"Never mind. It wasn't your fault—he was too quick," she assured him.

"What—?" Derek began once more, but again he was interrupted. The sound of a key in the lock told of Mrs. Roberts' return. Through the open door of the sitting-room they could see her enter, a bulging string bag and a policeman's helmet dangling from one hand.

"I don't know—" she started. Then she caught sight of the figure on the divan. "Why, if it isn't Mr. Grayling!"

"It is," he agreed, mournfully. He had hoped that an account of this unfortunate incident would be for official ears only. Now that Mrs. Roberts knew, it would be all over the district by evening.

"Well, I never did. Whatever 'ave you been doin' to yerself?"

He snorted indignantly and sat up. Red-hot daggers shot through his head and he groaned. Mrs. Roberts advanced and laid the helmet beside him.

"You been and left it on the stairs," she said, with reproof.

Derek looked around. "Will somebody," he repeated, "kindly explain to me what the devil this is all about?"

Phyllida went to her bedroom and fetched the crumpled note from the dressing-gown pocket. Derek read it.

"Well?" he asked, frowning. "Why didn't you go?"

"Because, although it looks like Daddy's writing, it can't be. Did the man whom you just met running downstairs look like Straker?"

"Not a bit."

"Well, he said he was Straker. So when I found out that he wasn't like the real Straker at all, I guessed that it was another trap, and sent for the police."

The police groaned again. Its interests were still more personal than general.

"And you don't know who this man was? He wasn't one of those you saw at Draymond's, for instance?"

"My dear Derek, do you think they would be such fools as to send a man I had seen before?"

"I suppose he did come from them."

"Where else could he have come from?"

Derek shook his head. If only they knew more about what was going on, and how many people were wanting what, he would feel much happier. He felt as if he were wandering in a fog full of mysterious figures which came into sight and disappeared, leaving him to guess whether there was any or no connection between them. Probably the man had been an agent of Draymond. If so, it meant that they still thought that she might know something of her father's results; and that they had unlimited determination to learn them.

"How did you find out that he wasn't Straker. You've never seen him."

Phyllida explained Sir Seymour's opportune telephone call. He thanked God for the luck of it. They would have been more careful of her a second time. It wouldn't have been Ferris Draymond's house this time, but somewhere safer and well hidden.

Constable Grayling, somewhat recovered, began to take a

more active part. He produced a fat, shiny notebook, licked the stub of an unclean pencil and announced a thirst for particulars. He received only as much as Phyllida chose to give him, which was an account solely of the morning's events. He requested the note and, if possible, an authentic specimen of Professor Wood-ridge's writing for comparison by experts. Phyllida handed it over, and Derek, after rummaging in his desk, produced an old letter from his uncle.

"And you say you saw the man, sir?" the constable added.

"He nearly knocked me down on the doorstep."

"And you could identify him, if need be?"

"I don't think so. I'm afraid I didn't notice him well enough for that. You see, he bounded out of the house and jumped into a car outside. It all happened so quickly."

P.C. Grayling's memory stirred. He, too, had seen a car out-side. An elderly saloon. He had made a mental note of its num-ber from force of habit. Now, what the deuce had it been? Blimey, what a headache to try to think with. He got it at last:

"PRT 430," he announced, triumphantly.

"But that's my car," Phyllida said, in astonishment.

"Ah, then 'e stole your car to make 'is getaway."

He made a further note, moving his lips as he wrote with la-borious care.

"But it was stolen before," she objected.

"Then what was it doing outside 'ere?"

"I don't know."

Constable Grayling looked puzzled. Phyllida began to ex-plain and then changed her mind. It would mean telling the whole story of the kidnapping. There was no need to mix the local police up in that now that she had decided to go to Scot-land Yard with Miles Drawford this afternoon.

"I suppose they must have brought it back," she said, feebly.

"Bit queer, that. 'Owever, it's likely it was only took for a bit of a ride. And, anyway, it won't be the first car to be stolen twice." He continued his industrious writing.

"Of course, it wasn't really my car," Phyllida added, as an afterthought.

The pencil paused. Its owner looked up suspiciously.

"Well, first you say it is, and then you say it ain't. Which is it?"

"I mean, it's actually my father's, but he's—he's away at present."

"Oh, ah!" said Constable Grayling, and demanded more details of the car's appearance.

They got rid of him at last, and at the same time went Mrs. Roberts, intent on "seein' after" her husband's dinner. Phyllida and Derek were left alone.

"A drink each, and then some lunch," he suggested. "What time have you got to meet old Drawford?"

Phyllida frowned. In the excitement of events she had forgotten her promise to ring up and fix the time of meeting.

"It's getting late. Better ring him now," Derek advised. He fetched the telephone from her bedroom and plugged it into the sitting-room socket again.

"I want to speak to Mr. Drawford. It's Mrs. Shiffer."

An expression of surprise came over her face as she listened. She replied incredulously:

"But I—Are you sure?"

She turned and stared at Derek.

"What's the matter?" he asked.

"They say he left the moment he got my note."

"Well?"

"But I haven't written him any note."

X

ENTER INSPECTOR JORDAN

For the second time in one day the police called at the Gordon Square flat. But while their first representative had appeared in full daylight, looking every inch (and Constable Grayling had many inches in both directions) a policeman, their second came less obtrusively and by night.

He did not wear a blue uniform, he was not bulky, nor did his boots clump the stairs with massive dignity. He looked, in fact, like many another, a man of indeterminate, but probably respectable occupation, and it was not out of character that his home should be situated in Putney. His dark suit was covered by a gray overcoat having better aim at warmth than at style, his gray felt hat was just a necessary head covering. However much he might have wished them to do so, his light black shoes could never have mimicked the tramp of the official boot.

His was a face which gave little clue to its owner's potentialities. Just a face, pleasant enough, but not memorable. Only in the eyes was there distinction: they looked at one as though they really saw. Detective-Inspector Jordan's face was a piece of carefully controlled, noncommittal scenery. His voice in ordinary conversation suited his face. It was quiet, pleasant, almost diffident, and most misleading. In its time it had lulled many wrongdoers into the belief that life was just a bed of pansies, then, to their unhappy confusion, it had grown hard, hectoring, incisive, coming from a face which had disconcertingly put on a mask of unrelenting officialdom.

He was as unlike Constable Grayling as a man in the same profession could well be, yet, had he known it, he was asking himself an identical question as he rang the doorbell: "Why must one's objective invariably live on the top floor?"

His reception, however, was more kindly than that of the unfortunate constable. A young man opened the door.

"Mr. Jameson?"

"He's inside. You're Inspector Jordan? Come in," said Barry.

In the sitting-room he encountered three more persons. The thin, gray-haired, carefully dressed individual who would have been a safe bet as a lawyer at a hundred yards, he had met once before. He recognized him as Samuel Allbright, Drawford's partner. The solicitor introduced him to the others.

The girl whose dark red hair shot out little points of light as she turned her head was Mrs. Shiffer. Her eyes met his with a faithful trust which would take a deal of justification. Then a slight clouding of doubt crept into them. Was she disappointed by his harmless appearance, or was it the background of worry obtruding? A little of both, probably. Jordan was aware that he seldom inspired confidence at first sight.

The tall young man with untidy limbs in elderly flannel trousers, a blue shirt worn with a red tie and a tweed coat elbowed with leather, proved to be Derek Jameson. And the man in the dark blue suit who had admitted him was Barry Long.

Derek produced a box of cigarettes and pointed to an armchair.

"Whisky or beer, Inspector? I warn you it looks like being a lengthy sitting."

"Beer," Jordan decided, sinking into the chair.

"Splendid. That means we shall have plenty of whisky for Mr. Allbright."

The solicitor smiled with a detached tolerance. He had found it the best way of treating such remarks. He said:

"It is extremely good of you to come round here, Inspector. I, for one, feel guilty that we should be intruding upon your own time like this."

"Not at all. I owe a debt of gratitude to Mr. Drawford. I was sorry not to be able to keep his appointment this afternoon, but I was called out of London. When I got back I was told that you had been ringing me up, and that you seemed very alarmed for Mr. Drawford's sake." He accepted a glass from Derek. "Now, if you will tell me just what has happened?" he suggested.

Mr. Allbright hesitated. "It is a little difficult to know just where to begin," he admitted.

"The beginning, then. Why not?"

"Well, to be honest"—he glanced across at Derek—"we have had a difference of opinion on that very point. Mr. Jameson refuses to regard Mr. Drawford's disappearance as an isolated incident. He insists on connecting it with various curious occurrences of the last few days—and weeks."

"Quite right," Derek agreed, "though I should call 'curious occurrences' a little mild."

"But there is no proof—"

"I know, but look here. When in a comparatively short space of time one disappearance, followed by one abduction, followed by one attempted abduction are, in turn, followed by another disappearance, and all these occur within a small circle of people, it seems reasonable to assume a link somewhere, doesn't it?"

"Perhaps, but I don't see—"

"None of us do. That's why the inspector's here."

"Wouldn't it be better," Jordan put in, "if you started from what you consider the earliest possible point. Afterward we can sort it out and see which parts we may consider irrelevant."

"The logical mind," agreed Derek. Mr. Allbright assented

without enthusiasm. For the moment he was concerned only that his partner should be restored to Bedford Row with the least possible publicity. Connections with the lurid events to which Derek referred could do a steady, respectable firm no good. However, let it not be said that he was unwilling to give help where help was necessary. . . .

"You start, Phyl. Right from zero," Derek said.

Phyllida obeyed. She began from the moment of her first unacknowledged cable to her father. She gave an account of her arrival at the Grange and of her subsequent fruitless inquiries in London. Jordan listened patiently, occasionally watching her, but for the most part exploring the glowing caverns of the fire. His only movements were made to throw away a finished cigarette and to light a fresh one. She went on to her abduction on Friday night—or, more accurately, in the small hours of Saturday morning. Repeating it for the third time, it began to sound unlikely even in her own ears, but she forced herself to recall every possible detail. He smiled slightly at her account of her meeting with Constable Pennywise in Gaydon Road, but for that, not even his expression passed comment until he had done.

". . . And then when he began to march me off, the three men just melted away," she finished.

"You've seen none of them since? You've no reason to think that they are watching you?" he asked.

"I've not seen them, but they must have been watching me— at least, I suppose it was they; I don't see who else it could have been."

"Tell me."

She gave an account of the morning's adventure and the narrowly avoided trap.

"Have you still got that note?"

She explained that the constable had taken it to the police-station for examination. He nodded. She continued to the point where they learned that Mr. Drawford had left his office hurriedly in answer to a note purporting to be written by herself.

There was a pause when she had finished. Jordan broke the silence:

"He would, of course, be familiar with your writing?"

"Oh, yes. I've known him always, and I wrote him quite a lot of letters while I was away."

"I see." He turned to the solicitor, who was still looking a little incredulous over the story which he had now heard in full detail for the first time. "And did you see this note, Mr. Allbright?"

"I? No, I was out at the time."

"Did anyone, apart, of course, from Mr. Drawford himself?"

"My clerk, Micken, who told me about it. He did not read it, you understand, but he handed him the envelope. He told me that he became very excited when he had read it, and put it in his pocket. He gave instructions that if Mr. Jameson or Mr. Long rang up they were to be informed that he was seeing Mrs. Shiffer and would communicate with them shortly. Then he left in a hurry."

"Then it is not really certain that the note purported to come from Mrs. Shiffer herself?"

"I think so. Micken, who also knows Mrs. Shiffer's writing, says that the address was written in a hand like hers—that semi-printing script which is taught so much nowadays—and that, taken in conjunction with the instructions seems to prove—"

"Yes, I see. And what time was this?"

"About twenty to twelve, according to Micken. He had just returned from the Courts, and the letter had been delivered by hand a few minutes earlier."

Jordan was silent for a few minutes. When he looked up he

seemed to have shelved Mr. Drawford's plight for the moment; it was of Phyllida he asked:

"Now, this place at Golders Green, could you find it again?"

Derek cleared his throat.

"May I join in the story?"

"About this house?"

Derek nodded. "You see, I asked Mrs. Shiffer the same question, and Mr. Long and I went there hand in hand and got thrown out for our trouble. The dwelling is 'The Laurels,' Catalan Road, Golders Green: its occupant, a Mr. Ferris Draymond."

The inspector allowed a trace of surprise to show.

"Ferris Draymond? Are you sure?"

"We are. Moreover, he was the gentleman who interviewed Mrs. Shiffer when she was taken there. Who and what is this Ferris?"

But the inspector had no precise information to give on this point. Draymond, it appeared, was well known in the City.

"That's just what old Drawford said. I think I must go into the City one of these days and get well known for doing something that nobody knows anything about," Derek said, thoughtfully.

"What happened?" prompted the inspector.

Derek gave a detailed account of their abortive visit to "The Laurels."

"He didn't say which hospital the butler was in?" Jordan asked.

"No."

"H'm. Well, if it's true we ought to be able to find out easily enough." He produced a notebook. "Would you mind describing the man again, Mrs. Shiffer, as fully as possible, please?"

Allbright turned to Derek. "Do you mean that the man you saw completely denied everything?"

"*In toto*, as you might say."

"You didn't happen to look in the garage?"

"Good lord, no. Why should we?"

"I thought perhaps Mrs. Shiffer's car might have been there. If it had been—"

Derek sat up. "I say, Phyl, you forgot to tell the inspector about that."

"What's this?" Jordan inquired.

"Why, her car, the one they took from the garage, was the one in which the man bolted from here this morning. It seems to make it pretty certain that he was one of the same lot."

"But why should he bring that car?" Phyllida objected. "Of course, I should have suspected him at once if I had seen it."

"Well, it's an established practice nowadays to use pinched cars for dirty deeds. There must be quite a gang of people in with Draymond. It looks as if someone blundered somewhere," Derek suggested.

"I think we can let that wait for the moment," the inspector broke in. "What I would like to do now, if you don't mind, is to run through the chief points of what you have told me and get you to correct me when I make a slip."

The others nodded, save for Derek who got up and crossed to the cupboard. He returned and mutely dealt out bottles of beer.

"The center of all this," the inspector began, "seems to me to be the disappearance of Professor Woodridge. I don't think we are assuming too much if we say that all our strands must lead directly or indirectly to that. Now let us suppose first that to escape the attentions of certain persons he chose to vanish of his own free will. To support this we can cite the condition in which the house was left, but against it we have to put his failure to communicate with Mrs. Shiffer, Mr. Drawford, his bank manager or any other person known to us.

"If, on the other hand, we suppose him to have been removed

by force, we can support it by his failure to communicate, but against it we must quote the careful closing of his house and the storage of his valuables."

"Which brings us to where we took off," commented Derek. "And don't forget Straker and the two servants."

"No, I'm not forgetting them, but their absence tells us almost nothing. They may have accompanied him in the first case or been bribed to keep their mouths shut in the second—or they also may have been taken away by force. There are too many possibilities there for the present. But to return to Professor Woodridge. There is still the possibility of an accident following immediately upon a voluntary disappearance. Mr. Drawford's inquiries make it less likely, but it cannot be entirely overlooked.

"Now, from the questions put to Mrs. Shiffer at Golders Green, it seems that his absence, voluntary or involuntary, was caused by certain discoveries he had made, or was suspected of having made."

"Or was liable to make," Derek put in.

"Yes, that also is a possibility, but the questions asked of Mrs. Shiffer rather suggest that whatever the discovery may be, it was already accomplished. Now, has any one of you any idea as to its probable nature?"

They all shook their heads. He continued:

"Then I would like you all to try to find out upon what lines he was working. You, Mrs. Shiffer, might start by approaching Sir Seymour Franks and the German gentleman—"

"Dr. Fessler?"

"Yes, and anyone else whom you think may be likely to help. A clue to its nature might give us a starting point. You see, everything seems to hang round it. First a mysterious burglary at the Grange when the entry was made by someone who obviously knew what he wanted. Then all the rest, not forgetting the burglary at your office, Mr. Allbright."

The solicitor looked astonished.

"You don't mean to say——?"

"I do. It is too much in the picture to be regarded as entirely a coincidence. I understand it took you a long time to clear up the confusion. In fact, there was much more of a mess than would have been made by ordinary thieves after cash. I would be willing to bet that Professor Woodridge's deed box was opened."

"So were quite a number of others."

"Quite, but might that not be to make their object less obvious? No, I think that Mr. Drawford's disappearance so soon afterward clinches the point. That and this morning's attempt on Mrs. Shiffer tell us one thing: whatever it is that they are after, it was not in your office.

"As I see it, the position last night was this. They require some property belonging to Professor Woodridge—it may be a document, a model or something in a bottle, we cannot tell. They have not found it at the Grange, nor at your office. They cannot get the information they want from Professor Woodridge himself. Where then, are they to look next? What are the available sources of information? Mr. Drawford may know where it is, and they are not yet completely convinced that Mrs. Shiffer cannot help them. Therefore they decide to get hold of these two persons and question them. Luckily in Mrs. Shiffer's case they failed."

"You don't think," Barry put in, "that the second attempt on Mrs. Shiffer may have been self-defense on their part?"

"I don't. They know quite well that her unsupported word is no danger to them. Moreover, they were aware from your visit yesterday that she had already told her story. No, quite clearly, despite the words of the man she calls Number 2, there is still an idea in their minds that she can help. And because of this I should like to impress on Mrs. Shiffer the need for caution. I should advise that she does not go out unaccompanied and arranges for someone to be within call at all times."

"Oh, I shall be all right now that I am warned," Phyllida assured him. "It was that I didn't expect it this morning."

The inspector looked at her seriously and shook his head.

"Please don't take this lightly, Mrs. Shiffer. I appreciate that you showed great resource in your escape, but it does not do to underestimate one's opponents. There are so many tricks, old and new, which succeed again and again. These people are unscrupulous and not frightened of bold moves, so let me warn you for your own sake that it may be dangerous for you to go about alone—for a few days, at any rate."

"Why the qualification?" Derek asked.

"Because of Mr. Drawford. If he has the information they want, and if they can force him to disclose it, we might be justified in relaxing our care of Mrs. Shiffer—until then we are not."

"But he seemed as puzzled as we were."

"It is part of a solicitor's job to keep secrets," Jordan replied, his eyes on Mr. Allbright. "It may well be that it was something less of a mystery to him than you thought."

"But I can't believe that he would be so cruel as not to tell me if he knew that Daddy was all right," Phyllida protested.

"No, I don't think he knew that. I was thinking rather of the cause of the whole thing."

Derek had foretold that it would be a long sitting, and the event bore him out. St. Pancras church clock had already struck two before the inspector rose to leave. He repeated his final instructions. They were to find out as much as possible about the professor's recent work. Phyllida must be escorted for her own protection. Derek nodded.

"We obey. Now, one final beer."

They raised their glasses.

"Here's destruction to our friends at 'The Laurels,'" wished Barry.

"Be they never so hardy," Derek agreed.

Barry grasped a bottle by the neck.

"You make just one more like that—" he threatened.

XI

VARIED INQUIRIES

A knock on his door caused Superintendent Warmbrook to pause in his dictation. He glanced at the clock which hung above one of the several photographs of police athletic groups which decorated the walls. He frowned. Finally he loudly ordered his visitor to come in.

Detective-Inspector Jordan entering, received only the barest nod. He stood patiently waiting while his chief finished his correspondence and dismissed the shorthand writer with instructions. The superintendent swung his chair so that his circular form became tangent to the flat-topped desk. He looked at Jordan and permitted his gaze to travel thence to the clock again. His expression was less genial than was his habit.

"Half an hour," he remarked shortly.

"Yes, sir."

"What happened?"

"I overslept, sir."

The superintendent frowned.

"Jordan, when will you learn wisdom? I don't recall that excuse being offered here before. It is usual—in this department, at any rate—to blame the state of the traffic. What was it? Brighton too much for you?"

"No, sir. I was up late last night. I'd like to speak to you about it after I've made this Brighton report."

"All right. Go ahead. Chair. Now what did the Brighton people have to say about it?"

Jordan sat down, and, with the assistance of a bundle of papers from his pocket, started in. By the end of his recital his superintendent's face had cleared. He seemed to have forgotten the missing half hour, and nodded with satisfaction.

"Smart work, Jordan. Nicely rounded off. Let me have the written report this evening."

"Yes, sir."

"And this other matter?"

"Yes, sir. It's a queer business. Not much to catch hold of, but I shouldn't be surprised if we found a fair amount behind it."

He gave a shortened but concise résumé of the stories he had heard at Derek's flat. The other heard him through without comment: to all appearance he might not have been listening. At the end he lifted his eyes slowly from contemplation of the desk.

"This man, Draymond. Something in the City, you say?"

"He's reached a higher stage, sir. Well known in the City."

"Do you know anything about him?"

"I've heard his name. That's all."

The superintendent grunted, swiveled his chair slightly and reached for the telephone. He gave an extension number and requested any information about Ferris Draymond. After a short pause he turned back.

"Nothing. These people who gave you the tale, you think they're straight?"

"Yes, sir, sure of it."

Warmbrook thought silently for a moment.

"But why didn't they come to us at once? Why wait until this solicitor fellow had disappeared too?"

"You know what people are, sir. They'd no proof at all. Probably thought we should browbeat them and then laugh them out. The public has such queer ideas about us."

"I don't need you to tell me that," Warmbrook put in, shortly.

"But Drawford himself had persuaded the girl to let him bring her round here yesterday afternoon," Jordan went on. "Then he disappeared, and that woke them up. They sent for me in a hurry and I went round as soon as I got back from Brighton."

"H'm. Well, if it's all true, there's certainly been some pretty high-handed work going on. What do you think is behind it?"

"No idea, sir. But it seems worth trying to find out."

Superintendent Warmbrook looked thoughtful for a while. He nodded.

"All right, provided nothing urgent comes along. If you do make any headway get these people round here and we'll talk to 'em."

Jordan stood up. "Thank you, sir. I'll get on with it right away if there's nothing else."

"Right you are. Don't forget that report on the Brighton business."

Jordan hurried back to his own office. It looked like being a busy day.

"What's the program? Where do we go first?" asked Derek, across the breakfast table.

"A shop," said Phyllida. "Before we do anything else I must get some clothes."

"But the great detective said—"

"Bother the great detective! Do you two realize that I've got nothing at all but what I stand up in—except my pajamas, which are still down at the Grange. These are the same things in which I spent the whole of last weekend, and now it's Wednesday. I haven't even got a warm coat. I *must* get some things."

"As an escort I look like having an interesting time," Derek observed.

"If you think—" Phyllida began.

"No, I only hoped. You know, it's you, Barry, who ought to be on this expedition. You're an expert on female undies and things."

"Now, look here—" Barry began, indignantly.

"You don't mean to say you're not?"

"Of course I'm not. Don't be such a—"

"Oh, perfidy. Do you mean to sit there and tell me that after advising women what to wear for years you are not an expert at all? That you've been swindling them all the time?"

"That's got nothing to do with advertising: there's no need for an advertising man to—"

Derek lifted his hand.

"Enough. We can't allow your shrinking modesty to lead you deeper into self-accusation." He turned back to Phyllida. "Really he ought to go with you. He can tell you all about the comfort of Joyclad panties as though he never wore anything else, he has every virtue of Siltex stockings at his fingertips, he knows exactly what kinds of corsets do what, and why. Should you require cosmetics, he would be invaluable, he is up to the minute with the fashions in faces—'use Token, the shineless cream, and Get your Man.' You should read his series for the mothers and daughters on 'Preparing for a Beautiful Future.' Poems, every one, bring tears to the eyes. As for shoes, he knows things about them that even Freud—"

"Will you shut up?" Barry demanded. "Breakfast is no time for broadsides of heavy humor."

"Ah! If the mind is sluggish in the morn, take Bruno's Health Crystals, perfectly tasteless on grapefruit—"

"If you don't shut up, I shall invade your profession and give a lecture on the Albert Memorial or Selfridge's clock."

Derek shuddered. "All right, I give in. Let us return to the program. When Barry has gone forth to uplift the taste of the people, you and I will saunter to a shop where—"

"Where you will be left on the mat," Phyllida told him.

"Oh, no. Not—"

"Yes."

"But our instructions. Suppose one of the mannequins should turn out to be Ferris in disguise?"

"I'll risk that. You stay on the mat."

Derek looked depressed.

"For hours and hours, I suppose. I never could see why people want so many clothes. Now, my flannel bags—"

"I shouldn't say too much about them, if I were you," Phyllida advised.

"Why not? They're—"

"If you ever have a son," said Barry, "he'll be born wearing flannel bags—old ones."

"Bourgeois, both of you, very. Let us proceed. After this shopping, we look out old Sir Seymour and see if he can throw any light on the matter. What then?"

"What about Fessler?" asked Barry.

"Oh, yes, I'd forgotten him. We'd better start the telegrams flying. No, wait a minute. Can he speak English, Phyl?"

"About as well as you."

"That's good enough. Let's get him on the phone. Advantages of modern science. Now, how the blazes are we to find out where he's likely to be? It's a quarter-past nine here and now, that means that in Berlin it's a quarter-past eight. If he—"

"No. In Berlin it's a quarter-past ten," said Barry.

"What? Wait a minute."

Derek closed his eyes and drew mystic circles in the air with a forefinger.

"Yes, that's it. A quarter-past ten. And he's an honest German—he'll have been at work for hours. Where does he work?"

"I don't know," said Phyllida.

"Well then we must ask somebody."

Barry rose and sought his bowler.

"Good-bye. I hope to see you both this evening."

"Hope?"

"If you're not both in jail for fooling with the telephone system and maddening the exchange girls. *Au revoir,* Phyl."

The flat door banged behind him. Barry shook his head.

"Now that all is peaceful, we can get on with it. First, how the hell does one get hold of a Berlin Telephone Directory?"

At length, with the helpful solicitude of several Post Office departments and after one false start, Dr. Fessler was run to earth. Derek handed over the instrument.

"Now it's up to you to get something out of him," he told her. He sat down to do a little rueful calculation:

1 call to Frau Fessler to ascertain Dr.'s business number	*12/-*
1 call to Dr. Fessler	*12/-*
Extra for personal call	*4/-*
One minute extra	*4/-*

He paused awhile, listening. Thoughtfully he added to the list:

Another minute extra	*4/-*
and another	*4/-*
still another	*4/-*

Phyllida hung up as his pencil hovered preparatory to another entry.

"Well?"

"Not much good, I'm afraid."

He drew a line under the last four shillings, and added carefully.

"Two pounds four. We ought to have left this part of it to Scotland Yard. Didn't he give any clue at all?"

"He said that the last thing he had heard definitely was that Daddy was trying to immunize rats from something or other I didn't quite catch, by grafting something into some glands."

"You're not very detailed, are you?"

"Well, it was all rather long and involved and, anyhow, Dr. Fessler said he'd finished with that and published the results. So it didn't seem very important if it was finished with, did it?"

"No, perhaps not. Hadn't he any idea what Uncle Henry went on to after that?"

"None, he said. I'm sure he would have told me if he could."

Derek scratched his head reflectively.

"H'm, unless Draymond is a member of the Anti-Rat League and therefore annoyed at them being immunized from anything, we can wash that out—also two pounds four. Fessler knew that he had started on some new work?"

"My dear Derek, did you ever know Daddy to take a holiday? He's always up to his eyes in something."

"True. Well, the next thing is to try Sir Seymour, I suppose."

"After shopping."

"Oh, yes. I'd forgotten that."

Inspector Jordan reached for the telephone.

"Saint Pancras, 4095," he demanded. "Hullo! Georgian Street Station? Detective-Inspector Jordan speaking from Scotland Yard. I understand one of your constables brought in a note for handwriting examination yesterday? Yes, Grayling. Assault in Gordon Square. That's the man. Can you let me have the note and the verified specimen of writing round here? Yes, may be tied up with another case. Thank you."

He put down the receiver and grasped the house phone.

"Nothing yet answering to the description of Drawford?—Yes, Drawford. Posted missing yesterday.—Not yet. Thanks.—No, hold on. I want you to try all the hospitals for a case brought in late Sunday night or early Monday morning.—No, don't know his name. Want to. Description?—About six feet, reddish face, blue eyes, whites a little bloodshot, hair very thin, gray. Eyebrows heavy and dark, nose high-bridged. Large paunch, probably flat feet. Occupation, butler. Extent and nature of injuries unknown, but thought to be severe. Fell from considerable height. Got that?" He listened while the description was read back. "Yes. That's right. Accident occurred at a house in Catalan Road, Golders Green, about nine-thirty Sunday night. Don't know whether he was removed by private car or ambulance. Let me know as soon as you find him."

A moment later he was on to another department.

"Stolen car. Morris. Dark blue saloon, PRT 430. Hold driver. Let me know.—All right." He waited for an impatient half-minute, then: "What? Got it last night. Where?—Oh, the park in St. James's Square—that doesn't help us much. Thanks."

For a time he stared fixedly at the blank wall in front of him before he again picked up the outside phone.

"Winshire Police Headquarters, please."

This time his conversation was longer. It was necessary to explain matters in some detail before he could make his requests. Even then the Winshire police remained dubious. There was, they protested, nothing in the least irregular in Professor Woodridge's decision to close his house and go away for a while. Jordan admitted it.

"By itself it would hardly be likely to arouse any suspicion—in fact, it wouldn't surprise me to learn that that was the intention—but in view of subsequent happenings it begins to look fishy enough to stand a bit of inquiry."

After further persuasion the Winshire authorities grudgingly admitted a slender cause for investigation. They asked what he wanted done.

"For the present I only want you to get on the tracks of three people. The man Tiller and his wife, who looked after Woodridge—I've no description, but you'll be able to get that from the local constable—and a man called Straker, who seems to have been some kind of assistant in Woodridge's work."

He added such particulars as he could and then rang off with the Winshire people's promise that they would do their best.

Once more he took up the house phone. This time his instruction was brief.

"Please send up Sergeant Breen."

Within a short time there was a tap on his door.

"Come in. Sit down, Sergeant," directed Jordan to the man who entered. "Ever heard of a Ferris Draymond?"

"No, sir."

"Well, I want you to see what you can find out about him. Put a man on to watch his house at this address. Times of coming and going, number of persons resident, and all that."

"Yes, sir."

"But before he goes on duty he is to get hold of Constable Pennywise, 'Q' Division, and get as good a description as he can of three men who tried to stop him arresting a girl in Gaydon Road on Sunday night. He is to let you know if any of the inhabitants or visitors to the house tally with these descriptions. Got that?"

"Yes, sir." Jordan waited while Sergeant Breen made notes in his book. When he had finished:

"Now, take down this." He dictated a full description of Miles

Drawford. "It is possible—I don't say it's likely, in fact I think it is most unlikely—but it is just possible that this man is being detained at that house, or that he may be brought there. Your man is to keep a strict look-out for him, and if he does see him, he is to communicate with me direct and at once."

"Yes, sir. Any more, sir?"

"No. That's all for the moment. Wait a minute, though. Yes, I want you to go to one hundred and twelve A, Tolley Street, Paddington, and collect all letters addressed to Henry Woodridge there. They'll let you have them all right—that kind of place doesn't want any fuss. You might find out when he last called and get a description of him. And that's the lot, I think. Sure you've got it right?" At the other's nod, he added: "And be sure to find out all you can about Draymond. The City people may be able to help you a bit."

Sergeant Breen left. Jordan drew a sheet of paper from a drawer and began to compose his report on yesterday's Brighton trip. He had covered half the page when the telephone bell rang.

"Hullo! Yes, Jordan speaking. Who's that?"

A voice informed him that it was Allbright of Drawford and Allbright.

"Yes, Mr. Allbright?"

"Can you come round to my office at five-thirty this afternoon? I think I may be able to throw a little light on the matter."

"Of Mr. Drawford's disappearance, you mean?"

"Yes, *inter alia*."

"In where?"

"What?"

"I said: 'In where?'"

"I know, but why?"

Jordan checked an expletive.

"It doesn't matter. Your office at five-thirty, then."

"Please."

Jordan hung up, and scratched his head during a short period of unproductive thought. With a shrug of his shoulders he turned back to composition of the Brighton report.

"I was wrong about clothes," Derek admitted. "You look so smart that I am almost impelled to buy a new pair of flannel trousers to keep you company."

"All right. I don't mind waiting."

He shied. "It was just a figure of speech—a tribute," he said, hurriedly. "Let's get a bus and we'll have time to see the old boy before lunch."

Ring Road, in common with certain other roads in St. John's Wood, preserves an air of tranquility and detachment. It is in London, but not of it: nor is it of Suburbia, emphatically not. The kind of mind which insists upon categorical classification might, without local disapproval, term it Superbia. Its houses shrink from the communism of the public road; withdrawn into unostentatious individualism behind gates and garden walls, they watch the world change.

A fatherly butler at Number 12 greeted Phyllida and Derek with impressive deference and conducted them to an apartment which could scarcely fail to be called the Morning Room.

He returned to announce that Sir Seymour would join them presently. To occupy the interval, he suggested sherry. Within a few minutes the host himself bustled into the room. Phyllida jumped up and stretched out both hands.

"Good morning, my dear." He deposited a whiskery, avuncular kiss on her cheek. "And there is Derek. You know, I never cease to think of him as a small boy in a sailor suit. Ridiculous, of course. How are you, Derek?"

They shook hands. Sir Seymour turned back to Phyllida.

"Is there any news of your father yet, my dear?"

"Nothing yet, Uncle Seymour."

"Dear me, this really is a most extraordinary state of affairs. And now Miles has gone off, too, I understand. 'Pon my word, I don't know what to make of it. And what were you doing last weekend, young woman? When I rang up on Saturday, it seemed that you had vanished as well."

Phyllida gave him a condensed version of events. He heard her with an expression of growing astonishment.

"But it is preposterous that such a thing can happen in this country; abroad or in America, yes, but in England—You have told the police, of course?"

She explained the situation and gave him Jordan's views as far as she knew them. "You see," she added, "he is not quite sure whether Daddy's work is really at the bottom of it all, but it might give him a line to follow if we could find out what that work was."

The old man frowned. He shook his head.

"I don't think I can help you much, my dear. You know how it is with your father when he is on a piece of research. An oyster. Nobody can get a word out of him until he has his results."

"But you had been writing to one another?"

"Yes, indeed, but that correspondence was over questions arising out of the paper he read before the Royal Biochemical Society last April. You see, he stated that by a certain treatment of a pair of rats he had so affected the genes as to produce hermaphroditic offspring. This was less surprising to me than it may have been to some, but his statement that a regulated increase in the pituitary secretion exaggerated the female characteristics, while a diminution emphasized the male in this second generation, and, furthermore, his claim that if two such artificially stimulated individuals were to reach maturity and mate their offspring would be fixedly hermaphroditic so that quantitative variations in pituitary would equally effect both sets of sexual characteristics, is the sheerest nonsense. It is obvious, even to a child, that variations of quantity in the pituitary secretions, containing as they do the same hormone in both male and female, cannot possibly be the determining factor in the case of the first hermaphroditic generation. If they were (and, of course, this is in itself a supremely comic supposition), why should they fail to determine in the case of the second hermaphroditic generation?"

There was a pause of some length.

"Quite—er—quite," said Derek, noncommittally.

"Of course," Sir Seymour admitted, "it was quite a minor issue, but one did not expect such a slip from a man of Henry's attainments. I felt that the absurdity of the claim should be pointed out."

Derek seized on the opportunity.

"Then this hermaph—, this experiment was not the main subject of the paper?"

"Oh, dear me, no. Quite a side-issue. It arose out of a series of experiments he had been making with a view to influencing the genes. A sound piece of work for the most part, but weakened, in my opinion, by this trivial nonsense about determination by pituitary. Why, every schoolboy knows—"

"Yes. Of course," Derek hastened to put in. "Then you don't think, sir, that it can be the results of his work on genes that these people are after?"

The old man stared.

"No. Why should it be? He read his paper before the Society. Afterward, it was published in the ordinary way. I can get you a copy of it if you care for it."

"I would very much like to have one," Derek told him, mendaciously. "Then you can suggest no reason for these people's activities?"

Sir Seymour shook his head.

"None at all. Perhaps Fessler—"

"No. We telephoned him this morning. He only said something about immunizing rats."

"Oh, that was some time ago—I fancy it led him on to this gene business."

Some twenty minutes later Phyllida and Derek were walking down the drive. They reached the gate in silence, then:

"Go on. Say it," she advised.

"No, I won't. I like the old boy; but hermaphroditic rats—oh, hell!"

On the way back they called in at the flat. A slip of paper had been propped up against the telephone. Derek picked it up and read a couple of penciled lines:

> *Mister Allbrite rung up at 12. Wants to know if you and Mrs. Shiffer can go to his office at 5.30. Will you please ring him. Mrs. Roberts.*

XII

MR. ALLBRIGHT ASSISTS

Mr. Allbright fidgeted with the pen on his desk. He picked it up, began to scribble senseless designs on his blotting-pad, put it down again and for the third time in five minutes pulled his watch from its pocket. Derek watched him with some amusement. Mr. Allbright was not ordinarily a fiddler with trifles; something quite unusual was needed to breach the wall of correct precision with which he habitually surrounded himself. His present state was in ill accord with the aspect of rigid reliability he liked to present.

"H'm," he remarked, and returned his watch to its lair.

"Is he late?" Phyllida asked.

"He has still two minutes," the solicitor admitted, with seeming reluctance.

Close on his words came a knock. Inspector Jordan was shown in. He was welcomed unenthusiastically and waved to a chair. If he was surprised to find the others present, he contrived not to show it. Mr. Allbright set the pitch of the meeting by turning upon each in turn a serious and penetrating gaze. He cleared his throat.

"The step which I am about to take," he began, "might be called by some unorthodox, but having given the matter my most earnest consideration in the light of the unusual circumstances, I have come to the conclusion that it is justifiable. There is no longer any doubt in my mind but that the mysterious absence of Professor Woodridge is in some way connected with the disappearance of my partner. It seems to me, therefore, to be my plain duty to make known to you certain facts. I have asked Mrs. Shiffer to be present as Mr. Woodridge's nearest relative. Mr. Jameson because he is the only surviving male relative and is also intimately concerned. And you, Inspector, for reasons which will, I think, become obvious."

Having unburdened himself of his preamble, he cleared his throat again. He continued:

"As you know, Professor Woodridge and my partner are very old friends. This has frequently resulted in Mr. Drawford having a more detailed knowledge of his affairs than a purely professional association might be expected to produce."

Derek suppressed a yawn. Mr. Allbright's method of address was heavily soporific. However, it would have to be endured patiently. Too much to expect him to come to the point at once. The voice lumbered on through several sentences. At last:

". . . so I think you will agree when you have read it that I am not betraying a trust when I read you a copy of a letter written by the professor to my partner."

He took up a pair of gold-rimmed pince-nez, adjusted them carefully, drew a file closer, opened it at a marked page, peered over the tops of his glasses to assure himself of his audience's attention, and, in his own time, began:

"The letter is headed: The Grange, West Heading, Winshire, and is dated the fourteenth of June of this year. It runs:

"'My dear Miles,

"'I am enclosing with this letter a sealed envelope which I want you to take great care of. Please put it in the safest place you know and deliver it to me only when I make a personal application for it.

*You see that I have emphasized the word "personal." In the event of
my death occurring before I am able to collect it, you are to hand it
over to the War Office for examination.*

*"'To tell you the truth, I have more than a suspicion that I have
let myself in for trouble by an ill-advised remark I chanced to make
before the R.B.S. when I addressed them in April. By mentioning
in passing that as an entirely accidental side-issue of my work, I
had stumbled upon a gas (or, to be more accurate, a highly volatile
liquid) allied to the Yellow Cross group, I seem to have aroused an
undesirable degree of interest in some quarters. I see now, of course,
that it was rash to make such a statement in semi-public, but at the
time this did not strike me; I mentioned it only as an item by the way.
However, it seems to have proved of more interest to some than did
the main subject.*

*"'Between that time and this I have already been approached by no
less than three firms of large-scale chemical manufacturers. The first
was Amalgamated Chemicals, Ltd. Their representative was pained
and astonished by my reluctance to do business with them. He pointed
out that theirs was the largest chemical manufacturing combine in
the country and therefore the best fitted to handle my discovery.
Furthermore, they would be able to pay me a higher royalty than any
competitors. I told him truthfully that the gas needed research and
development; at present the cost of manufacturing it in any great
quantity would be exorbitant, moreover, modifications would be
necessary for safe handling in bulk; in fact, that undeveloped as it
was, it would be practically useless to them. I added that I was busy
on other work at present. But he was not discouraged. Amalgamated
Chemicals, he told me, had plenty of men competent to work out
the details if I would supply the original formula. He was very
persistent. He began to talk about my duty to my country, so I asked
him whether his Company was under State control. He had to admit
that it was not, though, of course, it had "close connections" with the
Government. You know my views upon the private manufacture of
war materials. I told him frankly that in my opinion anyone who*

wished to assist his country would not do so by selling secret weapons to private interests, and I finished by telling him that when I had had time to work out the details I should hand the results, not to his firm or to any other, but to the Government Research Laboratories.

"'That was the first. Following it, came the next two largest firms in the country, United Chemical Engineers, Ltd., and Chemical Enterprises, Ltd. Neither of them made any reference to Amalgamated Chemicals, nor to one another, and their surprise on hearing that I had already been approached was ingenuous. I made a few inquiries. Amalgamated Chemicals does not control either of the others; oh, no, but there is a curiously family party appearance about the three boards of directors.

"'Finally, A.C. sent another man to interview me. His manner was overbearing and his tone coercive: when he reached the point of plain threats, I lost my temper. We were both rather abusive at parting, but I thought that would be the end of the matter.

"'Last night, my house—or, rather, the laboratory—was broken into. A curious burglary: nothing was taken—it may happen again. . . .

*"'Therefore, I repeat, please take the **utmost care** of this envelope; give it up only to me, **personally,** and to no one else.'"*

Mr. Allbright stopped reading. After removing his glasses and laying them on the desk with a nice precision, he looked up at the three faces before him.

"The final paragraph in this letter does not concern us," he said. "It has no bearing on the rest. But I think you will agree that the part I have read opens a possible avenue of investigation."

Inspector Jordan was the first to speak.

"Mr. Allbright, did you know of this letter when we were talking last night?"

The solicitor hesitated. His brows approached one another a little more closely.

"Strictly speaking, yes," he admitted. "That is to say, I remembered my partner once mentioning to me that there had been a letter concerning some important discovery. But until I could look it up in his private file and satisfy myself that it might have some bearing on the matter in hand, I hardly considered myself justified in mentioning it."

Jordan nodded. Mr. Allbright was right, of course. He suspected that he was one of those who are always right. First thing in the morning he had looked up the letter, made his decision and arranged for them to call. It was doubtful in the sketchy state of their knowledge whether the delay was of any importance. . . .

Blame, if there were any, attached to the missing Drawford for not revealing his knowledge—though possibly he had intended to reveal it on his visit to the Yard. . . . No, blame was not the right word, Jordan decided, endeavoring to put himself in the solicitor's place. Just as the circumstances of Woodridge's absence had been insufficient to warrant a police investigation: so the letter was too indefinite for evidence. Seen in the light of recent events, he inclined to thinking it important. But had it been coupled only with Woodridge's absence it might easily have been regarded only as evidence of his decision to avoid interference by going away for a while. On the whole, Jordan decided, it was probable that Drawford had intended to cap Phyllida Shiffer's remarkable story by producing the letter. But why had Drawford himself disappeared . . . ?

"You said that you read from a copy?" he asked.

"Yes?"

"And where is the original?"

The solicitor shrugged apologetically.

"Unfortunately, we have been unable to find it. We have searched, but with all this disorganization . . ." For once he left a sentence unfinished. "We shall, of course, try again," he added.

"When you say 'disorganization' you refer, I take it, to the burglary?"

"Yes. And my partner's absence following it so closely. There was scarcely time to put things straight again."

"Then it is possible that the burglars may have removed the original letter?"

"Possibly, yes."

"But you think it unlikely."

"Not very likely. It was not an important document. If the people mentioned in it were concerned in the robbery it would tell them what they already knew, and an outsider would not have been interested at all."

The inspector was silent for a time. He saw now two possible motives for the kidnapping of Drawford: (*a*) to prevent him laying information before the police, or (*b*) to obtain information on the present whereabouts of the sealed envelope which had been enclosed with the letter.

Motive "a" was not strong in itself or they would have been more careful to ensure that no copy of the letter remained (moreover, they could not be certain that Drawford had not already informed his partner), from which it resolved naturally that "b" must be the motive and "a" an accidental side-issue. Jordan erected a kind of mental notice-board.

"They want the formula—Drawford knows where it is."

Having fixed it firmly, he began to scout round about. He looked again at Allbright.

"You have no idea where your partner put this envelope for safety?"

"No," said the solicitor, achieving the brevity of a monosyllabic reply for the second time in the interview.

"In that case"—Jordan spoke half to himself—"we are probably justified in assuming that no one else knew."

But, the thought struck him, where did Woodridge stand? Suppose Drawford had told him where the formula had been deposited? If that were so, Woodridge might be hiding in safety, or he might be a stubborn captive. And, if it were not so, the situation would be much the same, save that he would be a useless prisoner. That left Jordan much where he had been before, save that he had not overmuch faith in the stubborn captive theory. From what they already knew, it was clear that these people were not fainthearted; a variety of ways could be found to make a silent prisoner either repeat his formula or disclose its hiding-place. The balance showed a slight tilt in favor of a voluntary disappearance. He said as much.

Derek spoke for the first time since he had greeted Jordan's arrival.

"Drawford told Phyllida that he had not seen my uncle since March, but that he had written him several letters in the meantime. Perhaps, if Mr. Allbright were to look through copies of those . . . ?"

Another file was brought, and the solicitor bent over it. For a time the only sound in the room was the crackling of the sheets as he turned them. At last:

"Ah!" he said.

"What is it?" Phyllida demanded.

Mr. Allbright chose this aggravating moment to polish his glasses. When that was accomplished:

"A paragraph," he said, "from a letter written to Professor Woodridge by my partner on June the sixteenth.

"You will be glad to hear that the sealed envelope you entrusted to me has been placed safely under lock and key. I shall, of course,

obey your instructions to the letter, though I must admit that your
insistence that only your personal application for it is to be recognized
savors somewhat of the melodramatic.'

"He then goes on to speak of other matters."

"Thank you," Derek nodded. "I think that entitles us to assume that Drawford did not tell my uncle where the envelope had been 'placed safely.'"

Inspector Jordan amended his mental notice-board to read: *"Drawford alone knows where it is."*

"Now, how much farther does Mr. Allbright's contribution really get us?" Derek continued. "We know, for one thing, that it is a sealed envelope, not a bottle of something, nor a model, that they are after."

Phyllida broke in. "We don't *know* that; it only seems probable."

"But surely—?"

"What I mean is that when they questioned me at Golders Green they said nothing about gas—they only spoke of notes and results. I think we ought to be quite sure we aren't muddling up two different things. I mean, suppose these are not the people who want the gas—suppose they are after something else altogether."

Derek shook his head.

"I grant you the bare possibility, Phyl, but it's very thin, very thin indeed. I think we'll do better to go on the theory that it is the gas they want. After all, it would be too much of a coincidence—"

"I think," Jordan interrupted, "that I can clinch that."

They turned to him expectantly.

"I have put through a number of inquiries today in several directions, and one of my first reports concerned Ferris Draymond."

"Well?"

"He seems to be well planted in a lot of things which do not concern us at the moment, but one of his more important and more interesting capacities is that of a director of Amalgamated Chemicals, Limited."

XIII

MISUNDERSTANDING AND A JOLT

The three in the Gordon Square flat began the evening with the feeling that the world was a slightly brighter place than it had been this time yesterday. Their very mild optimism was due in part to the fact that "things had begun to link up a bit," as Derek expressed it, and in part to Gustave's cooking and his white chianti. Derek was relieved to find threads, apparently unattached, beginning to show their connections, They were slender, but a number of them knit. He had a vision of a great cobweb with Ferris Draymond, spiderly alert, in the middle. He liked his vision; the others seemed unimpressed.

"Trite," said Barry, "I thought you could do better than that."

"If a simile is apt—" Derek began, but Phyllida broke in impatiently,

"Did you ring up Sir Seymour again?"

"I did."

"And was Ferris Draymond at that R.B.S. meeting?"

"He was not. In fact, the old boy seems never to have heard of him—despite all this well-known-in-the-City business. However, he knows that a Dennis Draymond was there, and I found out from Jordan that Ferris has a son, Dennis. So there you are."

"This Dennis is a member of the Biochemical Society?"
"Quite."

Barry frowned. "But it's absurd, you know. A director of a

well-known firm like Amalgamated Chemicals to be mixed up in a thing like this. It's so unlikely."

Derek waved a showman's hand.

"Behold Barry Long. The stuff our juries are made of. The question is, 'Is Mammon a Dirty Dog?' 'No,' says Juryman Barry, 'Mammon is wearing a silk hat, so he can't be a Dirty Dog; besides, he's Mammon.' That, Phyl, is just what your word is worth. It is only through you that we know of Ferris Draymond's connection with it at all. And Barry, who has known you for years, doubts you. What will the man in the street—?"

"No, damn it all, that's not fair. I never said I doubted Phyl's word."

"My dear chap, you doubt whether he is implicated. Phyl's word alone implicates him; therefore, you doubt Phyl's word. Q.E.D."

"I certainly do not. I only meant that there must be a mistake somewhere."

Derek regarded him solemnly for a moment.

"Isn't lucre wonderful! Gold-plate a devil and you make a saint."

Barry stuck to it doggedly.

"It just isn't reasonable that a man of his standing should be mixed up in a thing like this. He's got money and he's got position. It wouldn't be worth his while."

"And yet when we went to see him, knowing nothing about him, you were ready to paste him on the jaw."

"That's just the point—I didn't know his position then."

"And what is position but power? There have, I admit, been a few eccentrics who confessed to having too much money, but I have never heard of the man who bewailed the possession of too much power."

"But this kind of thing—kidnapping Phyl, for instance: it's

not worth the risk. Look at what he would stand to lose if it be-came known. There *must* be a misunderstanding."

"The thing we don't know about that, is what he stands to gain if he gets the information he wants. Besides, you're wrong about his standing to lose—it's known already to ourselves and to the police, and what can we do about it? Damn all. Furthermore, the world is full of chaps like you who will just refuse to believe it. Quite obviously it was intended that Phyl should vanish entirely, but even when he makes a slip like he did, we can't touch him."

Phyllida interposed to check the wrangle.

"Did Sir Seymour say anything else?"

"Not much," said Derek. "He has dug out a copy of Uncle Henry's paper, and he read me the bit about the gas. There wasn't much to it—just what the letter said: that he had discovered a corrosive volatile liquid allied to the Yellow Cross group, and how it was far more drastic than any of the successors of the old mustard gas."

They received this without comment. It was odd, Phyllida thought, that so much trouble could arise from a passing refer-ence. Surely, much more information would be necessary before they would commit themselves to such violent action. Who could have given it? What kind of a man was her father's assis-tant, Straker? Could he, she suggested aloud, have been in with Draymond?

Derek thought not. "For one thing," he said, "I know him fairly well, and I should be very surprised if he is that type. And for another, he came to the job with a genuine enthusiasm and admiration for Uncle Henry, and since then it has increased. Even when Uncle had a touch of temperament and became 'dif-ficult' they understood one another. No, I'm as sure as one can be of anything that Straker would stick by him through thick and thin."

"But he is missing . . . ?"

"That tells us nothing. Old Drawford is missing, too, but we don't suspect him."

"The inspector's heard nothing yet?" put in Barry.

"Not a thing. Hasn't had time. Until Allbright said his piece, there was nothing to catch hold of, and even now there are a lot of forks and cross-roads without any finger-posts at all—excuse the metaphors. Even yet we can't be sure whether Uncle Henry went voluntarily or involuntarily, though . . ." He stopped abruptly. Phyllida took him up.

"Though you think it was involuntarily?"

Derek nodded. "We'd as well face it now as later. In spite of Jordan, I never had much faith in the idea of Uncle Henry going into hiding." He watched Phyllida a little anxiously as he spoke. She did not meet his eyes. She had an unhappy frown on her forehead as she agreed.

"Yes, I've felt like that the last day or two. Just at first I tried to believe he might have hidden himself—it was such a shock to find him gone. But that's not really like him. He would have stayed there and defied them if he could. I think that's what he meant to do when he wrote that letter to Uncle Miles. Why should he go, once the formula was safely put away?"

Her question left an awkward silence. To continue on the present lines would lead inevitably to the problem of whether or not Professor Woodridge was likely to be still alive. It was Barry who turned the conversation.

"The servants; the inspector's heard nothing of them?"

"He's not had much time," Derek repeated. "After all, he only started this morning, and on the whole, I don't think he's done a bad day's work. On Monday evening we knew no more than that Draymond was in it somewhere. Now, two evenings later, we know (*a*) what he was after, and (*b*) who had it. In addition, his expert has proved that the note to Phyl yesterday morning really was a forgery. He has restored Phyl's car and he has discovered that Draymond is a director of Amalgamated Chemicals. To that we can add our contribution that young Draymond is a member of the R.B.S. It doesn't add up to a great deal, I grant you, but it's not bad for one day. We do, at least, begin to know what it is all about."

Barry looked skeptical. He was not at all sure that they did begin to know what it was all about. If Amalgamated Chemicals were indeed behind it, what on earth were they up to? Still rankling was the notion of an insufficient cause for such gangsterish activity on the part of a prominent firm.

"You see, what I mean is this," he explained earnestly. "Here are we supposing that a great firm will use thugs with violence to secure its own ends, but we'll let the thugs and violence pass for the moment and consider the ends. Now, what are these ends?"

The question was intended rhetorically, but Derek slipped in: "To manufacture this gas."

"But your uncle's letter said that he intended to perfect the gas. He must have meant that."

"I gather that when he had time he intended to perfect it and hand it over to the War Office."

"Well, there you are!"

Derek looked bewildered.

"There you may be, but I'm not," he protested.

"Don't you see? Why should they be expending all this effort to obtain what he is going to hand over, anyhow?"

"But he isn't; he expressly said he would not."

"But, hang it all—"

"Wait a minute, there's a tangle here. We are assuming that Uncle Henry did intend later to hand it over to the War Office. All right; but Amalgamated Chemicals is not a part of the War Office."

"Quite, but it makes things for the War Office."

"Certainly, and that alters the whole thing."

"I don't see—"

Derek checked him.

"Now, look here. Amalgamated Chemicals is a private firm. It makes chemicals just as other firms make motor-cars or toffee-apples; and when it's made its chemicals, what does it do? Sells them, of course—wherever it can get a good price. Why should it be satisfied with selling only to the British War Office when all War Offices will be only too anxious to buy?"

"But are they allowed to export gas?"

"It doesn't matter two hoots to a firm like A.G. whether they are allowed to or not. They are allied with the Basic Products Corporation of America; they can manufacture there. They have large holdings in Dubrin-Pique in France, and Kranko in Jugo-Slavia manufactures under royalty from them. In Poland they can make and sell through a company which is under the thumb of Dubrin-Pique. Now do you see why my uncle did not sell to them?"

"You mean to say that they might sell to enemies as well as friends?"

Derek regarded him thoughtfully.

"My dear Barry, where were you educated? Did they never tell you that we English are the world's greatest altruists? Such is our unbounded generosity that we supply anybody with any-thing. When the next war comes, my dear chap, you and I and such children as we may have accumulated by that time will probably be gassed by a bomb dropped from a British-built air-plane. Possibly British capital will have made the bomb. There will be a slight, if transient, satisfaction in the knowledge that the weapons were well made. Everybody knows they are well made, that is why we do nearly a third of the world's trade in exporting arms. Did you never see the slogan which David Low gave to the armament manufacturers—'For King and Country—Any King, Any Country'?"

"And Amalgamated Chemicals?"

"Are well in it. After all, gas is now a most important branch of armament. I've no doubt that you could find their gases in a number of countries—though they haven't yet equaled the bare-faced audacity of Vickers in advertising tanks for sale in Germany, nor the nerve of the Bethlehem Steel Corporation in sending the man Shearer to cause trouble at the Disarmament Conference."

"But the man who approached your uncle made a point of patriotism," Barry objected.

"Naturally. His business depends on patriotism—everybody's patriotism. The more of the flag-wagging kind of patriotism there is, the better for him. I should have liked to hear Uncle Henry telling him what he thought of him." Derek smiled a little bitterly.

There was a silence in the room for some minutes. Phyllida said:

"Then you really mean that Amalgamated Chemicals are out to stop the War Office getting it, so that they can exploit it themselves?"

"Exactly. It boils down to that. They can make it and sell it at a comfortable profit to this and other Governments, whereas if the State makes it itself, there is no profit for anyone."

Phyllida shuddered a little.

"It's all horrible."

"You must take the broad view, my dear," Derek advised. "Take the big view. It makes all the difference, I assure you. Size lends nobility. A tradesman who sells a pistol to a child is a villain; a tradesman who sells whole arsenals to backward nations is a good businessman. One man who kills one man is a murderer;

a million men who kill a million men are heroes. To bear false witness against a neighbor is immoral; to bear false witness against a neighboring nation is praiseworthy—if it leads to good sales. The maker of gas may weep over his one dead son; ten thousand dead sons of other people are a good day's work. To—"

"Oh, shut up," Phyllida broke out surprisingly. "How can you joke about it?"

Derek, cut off in mid-speech, sat staring at her. She jumped to her feet and faced him, as though about to add something more. Instead, there was a queer sound in her throat. She turned suddenly and ran from the room. Derek turned a bewildered face to Barry.

"Joking? Did she say joking?"

Barry nodded without speaking.

"Joking! God!" He stared at the closed door in a puzzled fashion. "Why . . . ? I never thought she was one of those," he murmured half to himself.

"One of what?" asked Barry.

"Ostriches."

"What the hell are you talking about?"

"The ostrich. Interesting bird—traditionally hides its head in the sand. The question is, why should Phyl do that?"

Barry snorted. "Not much question about that. Phyl's lost her father—he may be in considerable danger. And you take it for a suitable time to show off witticisms and wisecracks. If I had been in her place, I should certainly have walked out."

Derek frowned.

"Not good enough. You might, but she wouldn't. And yet she has."

Barry snorted again. "I never knew such a man for missing the obvious. Any girl in her circumstances has cause enough to fling off when you will go on talking facetious rot."

"But Phyl is not 'any girl.'"

"Oh, go to hell."

Barry got up and made for the door. Derek grinned as, with a final exclamation of impatience, he slammed the door behind him, but the grin vanished immediately. There were times when they irritated one another, but it was always Barry who retired....

Derek lit a cigarette and reached for the half-empty glass of beer beside him. Quite likely, Phyl would come back, he thought, gazing into the fire. She was in an edgy state—who wouldn't be, in the circumstances?—as likely to run from her own company as from his. His thoughts ran on unguided. He did not seem to understand her any longer. She was so different from his memory of her. That was to be expected, of course, in a way.... Didn't one always have to get to know again women who had married? Only a few remained the same. Many changed utterly, beyond recognition, almost. Hidden qualities were released, sides they had enhanced, allowed to deteriorate. Quite a large number seemed to feel that "sweet surrender" implied putrefaction of intellect.... Yes, he had known that when he should see her again there would be a change. It would need a slight mental readjustment on his part, adaptation to dominants which had been recessives, and all would be as before. But the thing had become so infernally complicated. So many stresses. Husband had been a rotter, the rotter had died, her father was missing.... He shook his head. Too many permutations; no one could tell offhand what kind of a character all that would build. She couldn't herself; one minute she was up, the next down. And what would marriage with Barry do for her? Good fellow, Barry, honest, if a little dull.... It occurred to him that they had scarcely seen anything of one another as yet. It should have been Barry's job, not his, to act as protective escort. But Barry had to attend his office. Still, if they were never to see one another alone.... Uneasily he wondered: Ought he not to have pushed off somewhere this evening and left them to it? Faced by the straight question, he was in no doubt of the answer. What a fool! Why hadn't he thought of that before? Of course, neither of them had wanted him hanging around. No wonder they had got a bit peevish.

"You poor B.F., why didn't you have the sense to clear out this evening?" he asked himself. "Oh, damn."

He threw his cigarette end into the fire and drained off the remains of his beer. Halfway down the passage he stopped to rap on Phyllida's door.

"Who's that?" asked her muffled voice.

"Me."

"Go away, Derek."

"Nonsense." He opened the door and went in.

Phyllida was in bed. She had raised herself on one elbow and was looking at him from pink-edged eyes.

"I said 'go away.'"

He closed the door, crossed the room and seated himself on the side of the bed.

"You've been crying," he began, rather badly.

"Is that all you have to say?" She stared at him savagely and then dropped her eyes. Her fingers began to twist a small, damp handkerchief into a hard cord.

"No, I wanted to say that I'm sorry I was such a fool. I didn't understand."

Her hands tightened on the twisted handkerchief. She leaned forward. The bed lamp behind her made a halo of the dark red hair. The pale green satin on her shoulders shone with a brilliant highlight. Her face was in shadow, its expression hidden from him. Her eyes were invisibly dark.

"Derek, how could you not understand?"

He scarcely noticed the tone of her voice. He had set himself to explain, and he meant to go through with it.

"Barry told me. He—"

"Barry?"

"I didn't mean to be flippant, Phyl. It's my defense. If one didn't try to laugh, it would—"

"What are you talking about, Derek?"

He stared. Her face was still in shadow; he could not see if her expression were as hard as her tone.

"Why, about Uncle Henry—and about Barry. You ought to know that just because I *seem* to be flippant, it doesn't mean—"

Phyllida leaned back. The light fell on her face. Its expression stopped him suddenly.

"What's the matter?"

"Nothing. Go on."

He went on, haltingly, with a feeling that she did not hear a word he was saying. At length her unresponsiveness pricked him.

"What's the matter with you, Phyl? Anyone would think you didn't care—?"

Quite suddenly she began to laugh. A strident, unpleasant, overwrought laugh. He stood up and came closer.

"Stop it."

The words had no effect. He gripped her arms and shook her violently.

"Stop it. Do you hear?"

She stopped as abruptly as she had begun. She pulled her arms from his grasp and buried her face in the pillow.

"Phyl, what is it?"

Her head shook. There emerged a muffled instruction to go away.

"But, Phyl, I can't leave you like this."

She raised her face. He was horrified by its expression.

"Go away. Get out, damn you. Can't you leave me alone?"

Derek got out.

. . .

Following an interval spent in useless hesitation outside her door, he drifted back to the sitting-room. Fate seemed to be having fun at his expense this evening. Why had it all gone wrong?— "it" being the atmosphere. He had, quite clearly, put his foot well into something. It was difficult to recall exactly what he had said, but evidently it had been the wrong thing—unless, of course, Barry was up the pole, which was not unlikely. However, whether Barry were right or not about the cause of it, there was certainly a wrongness somewhere. And then this hysterics business. . . . Phyl, of all people. You weren't surprised by it in some girls, you definitely expected it in others, but Phyl. . . .

Oh, well, hang it all, he'd have it out tomorrow when everything and everyone would be calmer. Or wouldn't he? It might be wiser to forget it altogether. Oh, damn everything. Why did people have to be so complex about things, why couldn't they just—?

The sudden jangle of the telephone bell caused him to jump. It did not improve his temper. He snatched at the receiver.

"Well?"

"Mr. Jameson?"

"Yes."

"Mr. Derek Jameson?"

"Yes, of course. What do you want?"

"Sergeant Breen speaking, sir. Message from Detective-Inspector Jordan. He asked me to tell you that Mr. Drawford's body was found in the river this evening."

XIV

THE OTHER END

Detective-Inspector Jordan, having shaved with complete absence of mind but entire precision, thrust his razor under the hot-water tap. Simultaneously he reached his decision. There was too little to go on at this end of the affair: that meant that he must have a look at the other. And it would be helpful to have on hand someone who knew the house. Accordingly he made for the telephone.

"What on earth," inquired Derek's voice at the other end, "did the police do before telephones were invented?"

"Good," said Jordan.

"What do you mean—good? It isn't good at all, I was in bed."

"I meant I'm glad I've caught you. Thought you might be out if I left it till I reached the Yard."

"You're dead right. A triumph of detection. After my modest egg I am going to an interview with a man who might know of a man who might have a job to offer."

"Can you put it off?"

"Well, that depends. You see, if I put it off at all, it will be off altogether. Not, between ourselves, that it is very much on."

"You got my message last night?" Jordan asked.

"Yes. Poor old Drawford. I'm damned sorry. Any idea how it happened?"

"I'll tell you about that later. What I want to know at the moment is whether you can come down to West Heading with me later today?"

"You're on to something?"

Jordan hesitated.

"I don't know, but I'd like to have a look round the place, and I thought that you, knowing the house—"

"I see. What time?"

"There's a train from Waterloo about half-past twelve."

"Look here, suppose I borrow Barry's car . . ."

It was decided that he should call for the inspector at New Scotland Yard about noon. It would give Jordan time to polish off some routine work and enable Derek to keep his appointment.

"And what about Mrs. Shiffer?" Derek added. "Oughtn't she to come along, too—it's her home. Besides, I'm supposed to be escorting her everywhere."

Jordan demurred. "I'd rather she didn't, if you can arrange it. Can't Mr. Long take charge of her for today?"

"I'll see. Even if the whole retail trade of the country is slowed up, what does it matter to us? It might be managed. Till twelve o'clock, then."

Jordan hung up the receiver and returned to his dressing. The previous night's discovery had come as a double shock. He was distressed in his private capacity, for though he had not known Miles Drawford intimately, he had formed a liking for him. His official self had been rudely surprised at the sudden intrusion of murder. His case had changed in a twinkling from an inquiry upon very little evidence into a series of dubious events, to an assignment of responsibility for a very definite corpse in the river.

And yet, he asked himself, should it have been a matter for great surprise? Mrs. Shiffer had made it plain enough that this man Draymond was not squeamish. He felt that he ought to have foreseen something of the kind—but he had not. Every disappearance did not lead to a corpse, thank heaven! Had he, indeed, not taken her story seriously enough? Unconsciously discounting some of its sensationalism? He had had no doubt of the facts. She was telling the truth, all right, but she was telling it for the third or fourth time. It was easy enough at that stage for drawn conclusions to overlap with facts. Why, some of the yarns he'd heard since he'd been in the Force! And the people who spun them quite honestly believing that they were telling the truth: that was the devil of it. . . .

Phyllida and Derek would have been astonished to see how pastel-shaded their stories were in the inspector's mind. He was the outside observer. To him it was just another series of odd events; to them it was *the* series of odd events, vividly picked out from all normality. In fact, the finding of Drawford's body had probably shocked them less than it had him. . . .

From the moment he had made the identification in the mortuary, the danger in which Professor Woodridge had stood— might still stand—became ominous. And that might apply to the assistant, Straker, also. Until then he had, as Derek guessed, half thought that Woodridge had taken himself off to avoid being pestered or for some other private purpose. After all, why not? The house had not been casually abandoned; on the contrary, it had been closed in quite a conventional way. For all he could tell, the professor might not wish for his daughter's company; might purposely have refrained from telling her where he was. Inspector Jordan could imagine himself hiding from several women he had met—and they were all somebody's daughters. But, confronted with a corpse, his views changed. What if Woodridge were already dead, had died several weeks or months ago? What would have been the result?

Drawford would immediately have taken a hand. Among other things he would have carried out instructions that a certain sealed envelope be forwarded to the War Office. That would mean that Draymond's game was up. It followed that Draymond's purpose was suited best by Woodridge's remaining alive. Once he was dead, the formula would pass out of reach. But would it? No, there was a loophole there. It would only pass out of reach when Woodridge was *known* to be dead. . . .

On that, Jordan had come to a decision. He had instructed Sergeant Breen to inform Derek of Drawford's death, while he himself had hurried to put through a long call to the Winshire police. This morning had found him more than ever convinced that the solvent of the mystery was to be found at the Grange. If he were right, it would be better that Mrs. Shiffer should not be there. . . .

Derek reached New Scotland Yard a little late and found Jordan already waiting.

"I'm sorry," he explained, "the interview ran on a bit."

"Any luck?" the inspector asked, sympathetically.

"None at all. They're going to 'let me know.'"

"How's Mrs. Shiffer this morning?" Jordan asked, as they ran up Victoria Street. "He was a very old friend of hers, wasn't he?"

Derek shook his head.

"I don't know—as a matter of fact I've not told her yet. It was rather late when I got your message and, well, I haven't seen her this morning."

"Mr. Long is looking after her?"

"Yes. The profession is having to spare him for today." He hesitated for a moment, then: "I say, Jordan, you wouldn't put her down as a hysterical subject, would you?" he added.

The inspector glanced at him curiously.

"From the little I have seen of Mrs. Shiffer, I should think she is very level-headed."

"The same with me—until last night. She went right off the

deep end—never thought such a thing of her. I'm really very glad you rang up this morning," he added, with apparent inconsequence.

"Oh?" Jordan was noncommittal.

"Yes. Gives them a chance."

The inspector seemed a little confused.

"Gives who a chance?" he asked.

"Why, Phyllida—Mrs. Shiffer and Barry. Oh, of course, you don't know. You see, she and Barry were nearly engaged at one time—before she married Shiffer, but Barry, like a fool, made a mess of it. Now she's come back, and—well, you must have noticed?"

Derek was engaged in avoiding a bus. He did not see Jordan's expression.

"I can't say I did," was all he heard.

"Good Lord, and I thought you detectives noticed everything. Anyway, if Barry goes and messes it up again, I'll brain him and let you arrest me."

"Thanks, it might help my promotion."

Derek returned to the subject of Phyllida's hysteria. It was evident that the unaccountable behavior had shaken him. It was not, he pointed out several times, in character for her to behave in such a fashion. Normally she was self-controlled and, as Jordan had said, level-headed.

"Don't let it worry you," the inspector advised. "She has had enough worry to account for it, hasn't she? It's probably the strain of the last few days. She gave in for a moment. Anyhow, people don't always behave 'in character,' as you put it. Think what it would mean if they did. All the good would be impeccably good, and all the villains would never pause from villainy. Everyone would be able to spot a criminal on sight, and then where would my job be? No, thank heaven, most of us have the power of being one of two or three people at will. Haven't you ever suffered from the funny man who can't do that, who must go on being funny all the time? I have."

Jordan was successful. Derek dashed off in full cry on the trail of the red herring.

"No. You don't see what I mean. You said villainy. Villainy isn't a character; it's a part of character sometimes dominant. If a murderer doesn't murder everybody he meets, it doesn't mean that he is acting out of character, it simply shows . . ."

Kensington and Hammersmith fell behind. With the dual occupation of driving and arguing, Derek had no thought to spare this time for the desecration of the countryside, though his subconscious was strong enough to send him along the Kingston Road in preference to the bypass. The inspector sat back comfortably and waited for him to exhaust the subject. In the neighborhood of Ripley, Derek became aware that he had conducted a considerable monologue.

"I'm sorry," he apologized. "I think it must be the effect of living in Bloomsbury. Tell me, why this sudden decision to visit West Heading?"

Jordan explained. The Winshire police, he said, were conducting investigations at the Grange. It was possible that they might have made some discoveries already. Derek darted a glance at him.

"You've made up your mind that my uncle is dead?"

But Jordan refused to go as far as that yet, though his conclusions undoubtedly pointed that way.

"Well, then, let's say you think that he has been killed and his body hidden in the Grange?"

"It's not impossible."

Derek considered in silence for a while.

"You may be right—though I hope you're not. But I don't see how you get there."

"Well, to begin with, you must understand that Mr. Drawford was murdered."

"So I gathered."

"Oh, did you?"

"Well, your message—"

"My message only said that his body had been found in the river. I did not suggest how it came to be there." He paused so lengthily that Derek began to feel uneasy.

"I say, you don't think that I—?"

Jordan, who had been ordering his thoughts, laughed.

"No, you needn't get the wind up. I'm not suspecting you of having a hand in it. For one thing, I have an exact record of your movements yesterday, and, for another, where is your motive? If you were after that formula you would, having Drawford's confidence, have gone to work in an entirely different way. And you would have stood to gain nothing by his death."

"Who has? I can't see that killing him gets anyone any nearer to the formula."

"We can come back to that later. Let's consider his death. Now, he was dead before his body was put into the river—several hours before, and from a blow on the back of the head."

"Then might it not have been an accident, and this just a way of disposing of the body?"

The inspector shook his head.

"No, that is too unlikely. There were finger marks on his throat. Without committing myself too strongly, I should suggest that one man held him while another delivered the blow."

His words called up an unpleasant picture. Derek had a vision of the elderly solicitor getting red and then purple in the face, clawing at the hands which choked him, and a club rising ominously over his head. He tried to wipe the scene out.

"But why the river? Surely, if he were dead already—?"

"For exactly the same reason that American gangsters take

their victims 'for a ride.' So that when the body is found it shall be at a good safe distance from the murderers. We have no means of telling where the murder was done, nor even where the body was put into the river. All we know is that they wanted it found."

"Why?"

"Because Drawford was dressed in his own clothes and there was no attempt at disfiguration."

"No, I meant why should they want it to be found? You'd think they'd do their best to keep it quiet."

"Exactly. So it follows that it must be important to them that his body should be found, or they needn't have taken the risk."

"But how could it be important?"

Jordan shrugged his shoulders.

"Candidly, I don't know at present. That's one of the things we have got to find out." He showed signs of drifting off into thought.

"All the same, I don't quite see why it sends us dashing off to West Heading," Derek prompted. "Surely the position regarding my uncle is just the same as it was?"

"Not quite," Jordan corrected. "Yesterday we knew we were up against persons who were guilty of illegal actions, that is all. Today we know that they are capable of a gruesome murder— not only do they commit it, but they publish the fact that it has been committed. That puts the whole thing on a different level. To put it quite plainly, if they don't mind murdering once, why should they mind murdering twice?"

"In other words we have been under-estimating them?"

"If you like to put it that way." Obviously Jordan himself did not like to put it that way. "I should prefer to say that this gives us a measure of their determination. Before, we had no measure—none, that is, but Mrs. Shiffer's experience, and it was impossible for her or for us to tell how much of that was bluff. You must admit that it was melodramatic enough to have been a bluff."

"Yesterday you thought they were bluffing Mrs. Shiffer—today you think they meant it," Derek said, accusingly.

Jordan admitted as much.

"But that makes no difference," he said. "I was no less keen to get them yesterday. Bluff or not, they were guilty of several offenses, and, bluff or not, I had no more to go on."

"It makes this much difference," Derek pointed out, "if you had believed that they were in earnest we should have been making this journey yesterday instead of today."

"Possibly. Do you mind if I point out that you, yourself, are now attaching more weight than you did to Mrs. Shiffer's experience?"

Derek was forced in fairness to admit that this was true. Since he had heard of Drawford's death he had been wondering how he had managed to take Phyllida's adventure so lightly.

"As I said before," Jordan went on. "Murder alters the aspect. Hunting plain lawbreakers you may be able to take your time, but hunting murderers you must hurry. One murder has a trick of leading to another. Everything quickens up."

"Implying that they may have murdered my uncle and may be after someone else too?"

"Quite. Now, if they did murder your uncle, or even if he met with a fatal accident last June, it would be essential for them to hush it up, to hide the body and to allay all suspicion. Suppose that a man suddenly disappears, takes none of his possessions, leaves his house wide open and has told no one that he intends going away. Pretty soon somebody will get suspicious, and we are called in. There will be an investigation and, if the circumstances are sufficient, leave may be given to presume death. In fact, applying it to this case, everything gained by hiding the body would be lost. Therefore it would pay the criminals to give an air of normality to the proceedings from the beginning. The house is shut up in the conventional way as though the owner might have gone for a long holiday. It may be thought a little odd in its suddenness, but people do odd things sometimes; it will not seem odd enough to raise suspicions for some time. Quite certainly there will be nothing like enough grounds for leave to be given to presume death. Every ordinary citizen is at perfect liberty to vanish if he wants to—provided it is not for an unlawful purpose."

"Then you suggest that the shutting of the Grange is just a blind?"

"If it is not, then there is no mystery about your uncle which need concern the police."

"A pretty risky game to play."

"But safe enough for a few weeks. They were fortunate in their victim, remember. He had few relations." He ticked them off on his fingers. "His sister, Mrs. Tragg, whom he avoided and who avoided him. Yourself, whom he saw very seldom. Mrs. Shiffer, well out of the way in India. They could count with perfect safety on a few weeks before any alarm would be raised. They could not, however, foresee Mrs. Shiffer's return. Had she not come back when she did, they might have had several more weeks undisturbed. It was a mistake to leave those letters uncollected. If they had read her cables they might have prevented her from reaching home at all."

"I see," Derek said, thoughtfully. "And you think they only wanted a few weeks?"

"It would have needed a more elaborate scheme to last longer. For instance, they seem to have made no plans to lull suspicions once they were started. They concentrated on not arousing them for a while. Luckily, as they had no idea of Mrs. Shiffer's return before she actually got here, she was able to spread the alarm before they were on to her. That made them speed up. First they went to Drawford's office and then, not finding what they wanted there, they went for Drawford himself."

Derek drove in silence for a time. When he spoke again they had left the Portsmouth Road and come within a few miles of West Heading.

"Yes, that seems to work out all right, but I must say I don't quite get the implication of the last part. You are really suggesting that Drawford was kidnapped for the sake of the information, aren't you?"—Jordan nodded.—"I thought so, but how does that fit in with your idea that we were intended to find the body? I mean, it seems so much more reasonable to do it all quietly."

"Nevertheless, I'm sticking to it," Jordan maintained. "I still think that unless there was a purpose we should not have found that body—at least, not in a recognizable condition. After all, it stands to sense that if you commit a murder you try not to leave clues—these people have a first-class chance of wiping out a primary clue, the man's identity, and they don't attempt to take it. I ask myself why."

A policeman held up the car at the end of the Grange drive. Jordan gave his name, the man saluted and waved them on. Three cars already stood on the gravel before the house. Derek drew up behind them and looked round with some surprise. The scene was different from that which had oppressed him on his last visit. The Grange had become a center of activity. Several small groups of men were to be seen about the front garden, congregated mostly in the vicinity of flower beds. The front door of the house stood wide open and many of the windows showed raised blinds. As Jordan stepped out of the car a man in uniform emerged from the hall and descended the front steps. He introduced himself.

"Detective-Inspector Jordan? I am Inspector Ruman, Winshire police." They shook hands. Jordan presented Derek.

"Mr. Woodridge's nephew? Yes, I think we have met before." Derek looked surprised.

"You have forgotten leaving a car for five hours in Paulsacre High Street?" asked the inspector.

"What a memory! That must be four years ago," said Derek.

"A long memory's part of the stock-in-trade," the inspector replied, with a smile. He turned back to Jordan.

"You want to look over the house, I understand?"

Jordan nodded.

"You've found nothing yet?"

"Not yet."

The inspector was a large man whose breadth of shoulder gave a deceptive idea of his height. His manner was pleasantly free from exaggerated conceptions of his own importance, though an air of efficiency and moderated bustle seemed to hang about him. He spoke for the most part in short sentences, as if he distrusted conjunctions.

"One or two more beds to dig. A few likely patches. If there's nothing there, looks like having to dig the whole place. It's difficult. June, you know." He shook his head. "Four months'll cover a lot. Come in."

He led the way into the hall. Derek noticed that the floor was covered with dirt and that a number of the tiles were loose.

"Had a few of 'em up. Haven't gone back very well," explained the inspector.

They followed him into the front living-room. Save that the gate-leg table no longer bore the remains of Phyllida's interrupted meal, the place looked much as Derek had last seen it. Jordan's gaze went to the bureau which stood against the wall between the windows.

"You've been through that, of course?"

Inspector Ruman nodded.

"Yes. So had someone else."

"Forced it?"

The inspector nodded again. "After trying to pick it," he added.

"And the rest of the house?"

"Every drawer, every cupboard picked or forced."

"H'm." Jordan considered. "I think perhaps we'd better go over it again, Inspector, if you don't mind."

Ruman agreed. "Not a bit. Don't think you're likely to find anything. If you aren't wanting me, I'll see how they're getting on outside."

He had spoken only the truth. None of the old bills, paid and unpaid, old letters, circulars, out-of-date invitations and general litter which had accumulated in the bureau could be considered to have even the slightest bearing on the professor's absence. Jordan was not surprised. It would need a very slender chance for anything to have escaped the double search.

"Where now?" asked Derek, as they restored the last bundle to its pigeon-hole.

Jordan suggested the laboratory, and Derek led the way to the wing which he had himself designed. The wall shelves there upon which Professor Woodridge had been wont to keep his volumes of notes were empty. Jordan was not surprised.

"First thing they would go for if they couldn't find the formula. The notes might give them a line to work on."

Apart from showing them that the search here had been even more thorough, the laboratory yielded no more information. As they had been told, every drawer and cupboard was open. Not a single sheet of paper, save for a blank scribbling pad, was to be found. They had not been taking any chances, Jordan reflected. Every observation that Woodridge had noted for years back had been seized for examination.

They left the laboratory and started on a systematic search of the house. The first floor, the second, the attics, the lofts were inspected by Jordan, followed by a bored Derek, who had begun to consider the whole expedition a waste of time. He was leaning out of an attic window, watching the countryside recede gradually into twilight, when the sound of a hail traveled up from below. It was followed by a noise of running feet and an excited hubbub of voices on the drive. He craned farther out, but found the disturbance to be still beyond his line of vision.

"What is it?" Jordan inquired, behind him.

"Don't know, but it sounds as though they'd found something."

Together they made for the door and clattered noisily down flights of uncarpeted stairs. As they reached the hall Inspector Ruman entered by the front door.

"What is it?" Jordan asked again.

"A damn fool," snapped the inspector. "He came across one bone; thought he'd found a body, of course. Idiot! Remains of an old sheep. Been there a score of years by the look of it."

"Well, that settles it. It's not in the house." Jordan wiped his forehead and leaned his pick against the cellar wall. Derek dropped the shovel and sought his cigarette-case.

"Yes, if it's about here at all, it must be outside," he agreed, as he struck a match and held it for the other.

He glanced about him. The cellar looked as if it had suffered a bombardment. Who, he wondered vaguely, replaces the police's divots? Jordan was saying:

"This was the last hope of finding it indoors—and not much of a hope, at that. It would have taken a genius at the job to have buried him here without leaving some trace. What's the time?"

Derek looked at his wristwatch.

"Half-past eight."

"I think we might knock off for the night. Can't do much now."

Derek agreed heartily. He found the Grange depressing, and with the departure of Inspector Ruman and his men soon after dark, more than its usual gloom had settled over it. Moreover, he was feeling uncomfortably hungry. Save for a sandwich spared to him by a kindly constable he had had nothing to eat since breakfast, and until now Jordan had shown no inclination to leave. He was bent on establishing to his own satisfaction that the body had not been hidden, inside the house, and he would not be moved until he had done so. Derek, faced with the alternatives of leaving him to it and lending a hand with the pick and shovel work in the cellar, had felt constrained to choose the latter.

"Is there anywhere round here where we can sleep tonight?" Jordan went on. Derek brightened.

"*The Hand in Hand*'s not at all a bad pub," he suggested.

This was a better program than he had expected. The thought of driving back to London tonight had not been welcome. Old Hawkins at *The Hand in Hand* was capable of putting up a good meal with good beer even if he did only provide feather beds of the most engulfing type for his visitors to sleep in. He felt that Jordan should be congratulated.

"Well, we don't want to have to come all the way down here again tomorrow," the inspector pointed out. "If it isn't found then, it won't be found at all. They've finished half the garden already."

"Finished is the word," Derek agreed, thinking of his last sight of the devastated areas.

"Well, they're bound to make pretty much of a mess," Jordan said, pulling on his coat. "If it had only been a week or two since he disappeared it would have been easy enough to spot whether any of the ground had been disturbed, but as it is—well, as Ruman said, four months will cover a lot."

Barry's was the only car remaining on the drive. One of the two constables left on duty to protect the house and grounds unchained the gate and passed them out with a cheerful "Good night, sir," to Jordan. Derek did not envy him his job. There could be many pleasanter ways of spending a night than in hanging about the Grange.

Old Hawkins was pleased to see them. During the negotiations he kept his eyes fixed on Jordan as though he feared he might at any moment vanish into the empty air. In his view a Scotland Yard man was akin to the giants of legend, he had heard a great deal of such, but had hitherto had doubts of their actual existence. Yes, they could have rooms. Yes, he could provide dinner if they didn't mind waiting a bit. Yes, his beer was as good as of old—and God and the Chancellor of the Exchequer being willing, it always would be. They might even have baths while they were waiting—it being Thursday. Though the significance of the qualification escaped them, they welcomed the idea.

An hour later they had drawn chairs before the sitting-room fire and were feeling that sense of comfort which follows a much-needed meal. The continuous murmur of voices in the public bar, which was in the throes of a trade boom stimulated by local excitement, reached them faintly. The tendency of unauthorized persons to open their door, stare fixedly at Jordan and then retire with a mumbled apology had been checked by old Hawkins as soon as he discovered this new diversion. He had come in person to explain.

"There's been a rare lot o' talk about the doin's up at the Grange, and some of 'em do be so impatient like that there ain't no holdin' 'em. But I'll see as they don't disturb 'ee again." And, to judge by the results, he had discovered a method of holding them.

The inspector drew a pipe and pouch from his pocket. Derek lit a cigarette.

"Do you honestly think they'll find anything tomorrow?" he asked.

Jordan paused in the act of pressing tobacco into the bowl.

"To be quite frank," he admitted, at length, "I'm doubtful."

"You thought it would be in the house itself?"

"I did, but there's not a corner of it we haven't searched."

He paused to light his pipe, puffing out great smoke clouds.

"But that doesn't shake your idea that my uncle is dead, and not just being kept a prisoner?" Derek put in.

"No." He threw the match in the fire. "I'm sorry, but one might as well be honest in this. I could raise hopes, but they would be very false. If he were kept prisoner, it would be with hopes of making him disclose the formula. Well, we know they've not got it, and if they could, they'd have had it out of him long before this. People who can treat Drawford as they did are not going to stop short at inflicting pain for a purpose. That's only one of my reasons, and I think it is enough in itself. If your uncle died in June, he was far better off than if they kept him prisoner."

"You mean they would have tortured him?"

"Exactly."

Derek moved uneasily in his chair.

"But in these days—the twentieth century—"

"The twentieth century," said Jordan, "looks like being the bloodiest century on record before it is finished—and I'm not thinking of the war. The system's rotting. It's like a city of great buildings. Up in the turrets, on the roof gardens there is clean air in which thrives a clean culture of magnificent possibilities; down below is the accumulated filth and stench of centuries with the foundations rotting among it."

Derek was taken by surprise. He looked at him oddly. Jordan caught the look and smiled.

"Speaking out of character for a policeman, eh? Mustn't use similes—plain, blunt, honest fellows with a two-foot field of vision." He chuckled, then his voice lost its note of amusement. "But it's true, nevertheless. You nicely comfortable people like to think of the bad old days, you pat yourselves on the back because there is more freedom, less cruelty, less meanness in high places than there was a couple of centuries ago. There isn't. But you're shut off from it all—you don't see it. We do. It's there, and it's growing. Right under the noses of the really educated class—who, I grant you, aim at a high standard—there is a moral rot spreading like a slow disease. Don't ask me where it comes from, I don't know, but it's there. A callousness, a careless, unnecessary cruelty, a return to Nature. The barriers which civilized, educated men have tried to raise against the raw, the savage and the cruel have never been consolidated, and now they're giving way. You don't see quite so much of it in this country yet, but before the end of the century people in your circumstances will be brought face to face with it. You'll put up shutters on your houses; you'll go in twos at night."

Derek fidgeted. "Oh, come. You can't really mean that. Look at the advances, the refinements, the growth of knowledge, the sciences and all the rest of it. You can't really think that all that is going to be swamped by a few people who are suffering from what you call a moral rot."

"I do think it. You can see the signs of it even in England. More frequent use of firearms, risky audacity of smash-and-grab men, increase in arson, increase in corruption, public admiration for defiance and violence. The papers spread it; the films spread it; it's in the air. The type of education of our middle classes does nothing to check it. Those unemployed who haven't had all the spirit taken out of them are becoming rebellious; the employed hang on to any sort of job at any wage with a determination which weakens the unions. The small man above them is willing to indulge in criminal or semi-criminal activities without a pang, so long as he keeps his head above water. The rot is in the middle classes—I'm not sure that it isn't strongest there—young ruffians who want to scrap; bank clerks and shop assistants with inferiority complexes are running to put on black shirts; soon they will be bullying private citizens in the streets. I've been told by a Regular Army colonel that his subalterns today are the most bloodthirsty youths he has ever commanded. They don't know what war is like any more than these blackshirts know what it feels like to be a citizen under a dictatorship, but that doesn't matter. What does matter is the spirit behind it all. The growing desire for violence; the utter carelessness for the rights of others. Well, they'll get their bellies full of violence soon. . . ."

He paused to relight his pipe.

"But that's to come. What started me on this was speculation on your uncle's fate. You jibbed when I suggested torture; it revolted your civilized mind. Why? You know as well as I do that if there is another war the chemical firms hope to make a great deal of money out of causing people to die agonizing deaths. Why be punctilious with regard to the agony of one old man who can, with persuasion, be made to reveal a very valuable secret?"

"But it's different. In cold blood—"

"The whole thing is cold-blooded. Do you suppose the chemist making his gases works in a trembling fury? Or even that the High Command shakes with rage as it orders the bombing of a city? It's a business."

Derek was reminded of his own words on the previous night—size lends nobility. He had been thinking of the double standard of morals; the failure of personal standards to find a place in great affairs. Suppose that, as Jordan maintained, there was a moral decay; that instead of the citizens' morals converting the nation, the national morals were conquering private life. That deceit, lies, the slaughter of one's opponents was about to become the normal thing. And why not? With the double standard in every man's mind, who could say for certain which would win? Why, in fact, should the potential slaughterers of thousands boggle at one? Derek shook his head. For the time being he was going to emulate that bird he so much despised, and put his head in the sand. He dragged the conversation back to the personal.

"Then we'll assume that as they have not got the formula, my uncle must be dead."

"I have been assuming that for some time," Jordan pointed out, patiently.

"And that he died at the Grange. If we don't find the body there, we've precious little chance of finding it at all, as far as I can see. They may have taken it anywhere. Buried it in the garden of The Laurels, even."

"Too risky if he were already dead." Jordan shook his head. "Suppose the car which took the body were involved in an accident or broke down. Not only would it be pretty difficult to explain a corpse, but the whole plot would promptly go up the spout."

From the bar came the sound of old Hawkins's voice calling "Time, gentlemen, please," the phrase repeated more often than usual, and in slightly louder tones. No harm in showing a gentleman from Scotland Yard that the law was carefully observed in West Heading. Presently he thrust his head into the room.

"Any more for you, gentlemen? Just closing the bar."

Derek looked at Jordan, who shook his head.

"Nothing more for me. I'm going to bed in a few minutes."

Hawkins made to retreat, and then changed his mind. He came into the room, holding a pint silver tankard in one hand. Derek looked at it curiously.

"Isn't that——?"

"Just what I wuz going to ask you, sir," said the old man, nodding.

Derek took the tankard from him and examined it more closely.

"No doubt about that. I've had many a pint out of it in my time. How on earth did it get here?"

"My boy Joe found 'un, sir. 'E was fishin' up by Widderbrook a few days since, an' 'e fetched 'un out. It seemed kind of familiar like, but I didn't know as I'd seen 'un before. Then this evenin' I minded you'd told me of just such a piece. This'd be it, sir?"

"Yes, this is it all right," said Derek. Jordan rose and approached.

"You've cleaned it, of course?" he asked.

"Aye—leastways, my daughter, she cleaned 'un."

Jordan took the tankard in his hand, examined it with interest, and stared into it thoughtfully.

"Your son Joe could show us where he found it?" he said, at length. "I'd like to have a look at the place tomorrow."

"Yes, sir. 'E'd show you."

The inspector set the tankard down on the table.

As they climbed the stairs, Derek said:

"Odd, the old boy remembering my telling him about that pot. Must be more than a year ago."

"Very," Jordan agreed, absentmindedly.

XV

CONSTABLE GREEN FISHES

"Coo!" said young Joe Hawkins.

Constable Green disentangled an ornate teapot from the meshes of his net and added it to the pile of miscellaneous silverware beside him. Joe watched the net intently as it submerged again, keeping his eyes on the spot to catch the first glimpse of the next glittering find.

This was the real thing. A treasure hunt like those you found in books—and like those that people told you you wouldn't find in real life. Only on two counts did it fail to afford him complete satisfaction. One was that everything was going off too quietly, no band of outraged pirates had put in an appearance to defend the ill-gotten hoard; the other, that Mr. Jordan (who was a real detective like you'd read about in the *Clue of the Crimson Cross* and the *Sign of the Sinister Six*) had quite firmly forbidden you to bring along your particular friends, Harry Nobbs and Alfred Wickle, to see the fun. You couldn't enjoy things like this so well by yourself. However, it might have been worse: at least, you had been allowed to stay.

"Coo!" young Joe repeated, as a cigarette-box was dragged from the muddy water.

Detective-Inspector Jordan and Derek Jameson, sitting on the bank, watched with scarcely less interest. That they had not actually said "Coo!" was due merely to a difference in working vocabulary.

A large ladle followed the cigarette-box, and the net was thrust in once more. This time it did not make such an easy catch. The constable waded a little deeper and prodded about a bit.

"Steady, Green. It shelves suddenly there," Derek reminded him.

P.C. Green looked up at them, doubtfully.

"Something 'eavy 'ere, sir," he said. His eyes moved questioningly in the direction of young Joe.

"Do you think it is—?" Jordan left the question unfinished.

"Might be, sir."

Young Joe saw the inspector's gaze fix upon him with an expression which was wont to appear in the eyes of those who considered his presence dispensable. Jordan opened his mouth, hesitated and then changed his mind. Joe was relieved; he was not to miss the climax after all.

His presence perplexed Jordan. One did not wish to expose the boy to gruesome sights, but once let him get back to the village and tell his tale, and half the population of the place would be here in five minutes. For the moment, until they found out the nature of the "something 'eavy," he had better stay.

"Try the hooks," he suggested.

At the third cast the constable succeeded in getting the iron hooks to grip. Whatever he had found, it was stubborn and heavy. The other two rose and laid hold of the rope. Young Joe, eyes bulging, came closer. He could not make up his mind whether he expected a chest containing pieces of eight (whatever they might be) or a box of jewels worth a king's ransom—or could it be the body of the pirate chief himself? It was pretty exciting, anyhow.

The bottom of the stream dropped here to form a hole ten feet or more in depth, and it was with exasperating slowness that the three succeeded in dragging their catch up the steep side. Twice it jammed and had to be lowered a little while the constable, wading as deeply as his thigh boots would allow, poked it free with the butt-end of the net-pole. At last it topped the brink and rolled over into the shallower water.

"Well?" asked Jordan.

The policeman prodded again.

"'Ard, sir. Quite 'ard."

"Let's get it a bit closer." Together he and Derek pulled on the rope once more.

It would be difficult to say which of the four was the most disappointed when a large, slimy log broke the surface.

"Damn!" said Derek.

Only phonetic script could do justice to Joe's remark.

Jordan and the constable looked at it in voluble silence.

"Well," said Jordan, at length, "let's get it out of the way, anyhow."

"You thought—?" Derek inquired, when the log had been rolled aside and Constable Green was back in the water, industriously poking away with the pole. "You thought it might have been—?"

"I did." Jordan glanced cautiously at young Joe, who appeared not to hear.

"Nothing else big, sir," announced Green. He reversed his implement and plunged the netted end back into the water. A moment later he had retrieved a sugar castor. Jordan watched him add it to the jumbled collection of silver on the bank, and then rose suddenly to his feet.

"Keep on with this," he directed. "I'll get a man sent along to give you a hand. Come on," he added to Derek, "it's time we got back to London."

Young Joe watched them go.

"Did they think as you'd found a body?" he inquired, hopefully.

Constable Green paused in the act of disentangling a salt-cellar.

"Course not. What 'orrible ideas you kids do get 'old of," he said, severely. "What would a body be doin' in 'ere? Now, you keep quiet if you want to stay. See?"

"Wish it 'ad been a body," said young Joe, wistfully.

XVI

MR. FISK BREAKS A RULE

"We closed," an aggrieved clerk pointed out, "at three-thirty."

Jordan pushed his card through the half-opened door. The young man read it, and his manner changed abruptly.

"You want to see Mr. Fisk?" he inquired, opening the door more widely.

"If Mr. Fisk is the manager of this branch, I do."

Jordan, Derek and the man for whom they had called at Scotland Yard entered. The young man closed and fastened the door behind them.

"If you will wait here a minute—" he suggested.

A few seconds later they were shown into a private office. The manager, a thin, tall, neatly-dressed man, greeted them with an expression of intense inquiry, which did not altogether hide a touch of uneasiness. Even the scrupulously managed Haymarket Branch of the impeccable Metropolitan and Midland Bank, Limited, was not beyond an indefinite sense of apprehension at the intrusion of a card bearing the initials C.I.D. Behind his façade of interrogation Mr. Fisk was anxiously wondering which of his staff had been doing what and, more particularly, where.

"You are the manager?" asked Jordan.

Mr. Fisk nodded in a reflex manner.

"I am," he admitted.

Jordan introduced his companions. "Mr. Derek Jameson and

Sergeant Jefferson. Mr. Jameson," he added, "is the nephew of your client Professor Woodridge."

Mr. Fisk relaxed slightly. He began to see a gleam of light.

"Ah—yes," he agreed, noncommittally.

"I understand that last Friday—that is, a week ago today—Mrs. Shiffer called on you in company with her father's solicitor, Mr. Drawford, to ask you if you could give her any information as to her father's movements."

"Yes," the manager agreed again.

"And you were unable to help her?"

"That is so," said Mr. Fisk, striving to avoid monotony.

"And still you have had no news of Mr. Woodridge since last June?" persisted Jordan.

"No," said Mr. Fisk. "None," he added, making it completely clear.

"And he has drawn no checks whatever since that time?"

"Not one."

There was a knock on the door. A clerk's head appeared.

"A Mr. Allbright, sir. Says he was to join Inspector Jordan here."

Mr. Fisk looked puzzled. Jordan explained:

"The partner of the late Mr. Drawford. I thought it advisable—"

Mr. Fisk nodded. "Show him in." He turned to Jordan. "The *late* Mr. Drawford? You don't mean to say—?"

"Mr. Drawford's body was found in the river on Wednesday night."

Mr. Fisk was shocked, both by the news and by the abrupt manner of its announcement.

"Dear me! I had no idea. An accident?"

"He was murdered—rather brutally."

"Good gracious!" Mr. Fisk looked more shocked. His intention of asking what the world was coming to was forestalled by the entrance of Mr. Allbright. He rose and held out his hand as Jordan made the introduction.

"The inspector has just told me the sad news. It is inexpressibly shocking."

The solicitor shook the hand and murmured some indistinct reply. He turned at once to Jordan.

"What is all this about, Inspector? I must say it was very inconvenient—very. But you made such a point of my coming here at once, that I have come. May I ask?"

"In a moment, Mr. Allbright. I don't think that you will find I have wasted your time." He looked back to the bank manager. "Would you mind telling us what was the last communication you had from Professor Woodridge?"

"Not at all. As I told Mr. Drawford, we received a letter from him requesting us to store his silver as he expected to be away from home for some months."

"And you are doing that?"

"Yes, of course. The box arrived a day or two later; we sent off a receipt for it in the ordinary way, and that is the last we know."

"You examined the box, Mr. Fisk?"

The manager looked pained.

"The bank knows nothing of the contents of packages left with it by customers for safe keeping, unless the customers themselves volunteer the information. Such contents can scarcely be said to be our business," he explained.

"I see. There is no obligation to declare the contents?"

"Certainly not. We simply issue a receipt for the sealed package and keep it until the customer wants to remove it."

"Then no doubt it will come as a surprise to you to learn that Professor Woodridge's silver has today been dredged from a stream near his house?"

"What's that?" Mr. Allbright broke in. He leaned forward, gazing sharply at Jordan. "Woodridge's silver is not here?"

"That is so. At present it is in the keeping of the Winshire police."

"Then what is in the box?" the solicitor asked, still staring at Jordan.

"Exactly," Jordan agreed. "What is in the box?"

Mr. Fisk caught the drift of matters. He began to look worried.

"Unusual," he admitted. "Most unusual."

"The hiding of valuable silver at the bottom of a stream deserves to be called something stronger than unusual," Derek suggested.

Mr. Fisk glanced at him impatiently.

"I was referring to our situation, not to that of the silver," he said coldly. "Professor Woodridge's statement appears to have been deliberately misleading. It is, of course, entirely his own affair if he wishes to keep the contents of his deposit a secret, but I repeat that it is not only unnecessary, but unusual for our customers so to misinform us."

"And how do you know that?" Derek asked, with a smile.

Mr. Fisk loftily ignored the remark. He addressed himself to the inspector:

"You will understand that our receipt was for one sealed package. The fact that we believed it to contain silver is neither here nor there."

Jordan nodded. "But in the circumstances you will not object to our seeing Mr. Woodridge's last letter?"

"No." Mr. Fisk's hesitation was only momentary. "I think there could be no harm in that," he admitted, cautiously.

He pressed a bell on his desk and sent the answering clerk in search of a file. When it arrived, he carefully detached a single sheet of paper and handed it to Mr. Allbright. The solicitor read it slowly and thoroughly before passing it on to Derek. Derek, in his turn, skimmed through it. It contained, as the manager had said, merely a request that the bank should store his silver for an indefinite length of time. He handed it over to Jordan who, with scarcely a glance at it, passed it on to the last member of the party.

Sergeant Jefferson drew his chair closer to the desk. He laid the letter down and read it through carefully. Then, from an inside pocket, he produced another piece of paper which he unfolded and placed beside the first. From another pocket he drew a large magnifying glass and, leaning over the two documents, began to make minute comparisons. The expressions of astonishment on the faces of the manager and the solicitor brought a slight, quickly hidden smile to Jordan's lips.

"Sergeant Jefferson," he explained, "is one of our authorities on handwriting."

"You don't mean—?" the manager began, but Jordan cut him short.

"We shall know in a minute or two."

Sergeant Jefferson continued his studies, completely unperturbed by their concerted gaze. After three or four minutes he shook his head with decision and looked up at the inspector.

"Fake," he observed, shortly.

Jordan looked round with gratification.

"Puts a different complexion on matters?" he said.

"It does, indeed." Mr. Allbright nodded.

The manager looked more worried, but said nothing.

"Now," Jordan continued, "if Mr. Fisk will allow us to examine the box in question—?"

But Mr. Fisk shook his head. "That is quite impossible. It is against our rules," he said, in tones of surprising firmness.

Jordan looked at him thoughtfully. He knew the type. Mr. Fisk might show uncertainty in his independent actions, but backed by a rule, he knew where he was. Access to a deposit was allowed only to the depositor or to someone expressly authorized by him. That was that. Jordan sighed. It was going to be a troublesome business. He started it by producing his warrant card and that of the sergeant. They ought to dispel any doubts of identity. Mr. Fisk looked at them dully. To say that he was unimpressed would be inaccurate; he was impressed in spite of the fact that he had entertained no doubts of his visitors' integrity, but the cards made not the slightest difference to his intentions. The rules said "No." Nobody would be able to blame him if he kept to them. He meant not only to keep to them, but to cling to them.

"Look here," said Jordan, "on the evidence we have I can get an order tomorrow which will let me look at that box. That must be obvious to you. But I don't want to waste time—I don't want to wait until tomorrow. I want to see it now, and I'm sure that Mr. Allbright will support me in this." The solicitor nodded. "Owing to the death of his partner he is now Professor Woodridge's legal representative, and I have asked him to come here on purpose that there shall be no delay, and—in case questions arise later—that he may be a witness to all that takes place.

"Further, may I remind you that this is bound up with the death of Mr. Drawford. I am trying to find a murderer, you understand, a murderer, and my investigations must not be hindered. Mr. Allbright will tell you that willfully to obstruct the police in the course of their duties is a very serious offense—it becomes aggravated when that obstruction is tantamount to assisting a murderer to escape justice. . . . It would not sound to your credit in court if it should so happen that because of your refusal to use your discretion in this matter the murderer is enabled to carry out yet another crime before he is captured. I can imagine that the court might have some extremely unpleasant things to say concerning your unwillingness to assist the police. . . ."

Mr. Fisk began to feel uneasy. He hated having to make such

decisions. Why could not the makers of the rules have framed one to meet an emergency like this? What was the good of rules, anyhow, if you had to decide when they must be kept and when they should be broken? No, he had never broken a rule of the bank yet, and he did not intend to start now. All the same, if the inspector was right, if a judge did have cause to make bitter comments at his expense, the bank would not be very pleased with that, either. It would back him up in public, of course; but what would the directors really think about it? Might they not consider that he had failed to handle an emergency competently? He knew quite well that emergencies exposed his weakest side; until now, save for one or two painfully remembered incidents, he had contrived to avoid them. Really, it was all very difficult, and the inspector fellow kept on going on and on. . . . "Times when the strict letter of the law must be set aside in the public interest. . . ." Yes, all very well for him, but it was he, Fisk, who had to do the setting aside. Still, there was something in it; sometimes it was possible to disobey with honor. There had been that chap Evans—and Nelson and the telescope business. . . .

The rock upon which Mr. Fisk had taken his stand showed signs of cracking. Jordan, watching him, noticed symptoms of a little less certainty, and pressed home his advantage. The manager came at last to a point where he asked:

"But what do you expect to find in this box? It may be of no assistance whatever."

"It may not," Jordan agreed, "but the circumstances are sufficiently serious for us to ask ourselves: 'If the silver did not go into the box, what did?' and to require a quick answer."

"Besides," Derek put in, "your rule applies to deposits made by the customers of the bank. Sergeant Jefferson has just told us that the letter making the arrangement was not written by my uncle at all, so where does the rule come in?"

But the manager preferred still to demur.

"But you have told me that the only things missing are Professor Woodridge's notes. I can quite understand that his work is extremely valuable, but I do not see the necessity for such precipitate action. Surely tomorrow . . . ?"

In the end, however, Jordan's way prevailed. Mr. Fisk, still a little uncertain whether he was rising to an emergency or betraying a trust, agreed. He led them out of the office, and on the way through the bank co-opted two senior members of his staff—one because he held the second key necessary to open the strong-room, the other to give moral support. In the concreted passage outside the steel door of the strong-room he turned to Jordan.

"If you will wait here a minute, Inspector, we will bring out the package."

The two combinations were set, the two keys turned. The heavy door moved slowly open and the three men disappeared within.

The "package" took the form of a wooden box reinforced by strips of iron; the whole, Derek thought, looking not unlike an enlarged specimen of the "play-box" of prep school days. It was heavy. The strength of all three was necessary to push and drag it into the corridor.

Mr. Fisk and his second-in-command carefully re-locked the strong-room door and pocketed their keys.

"You have no key for the box?" he asked, somewhat fatuously.

The lesser subordinate was dismissed with instructions to "find Jevons and tell him to bring a case-opener."

The group waited impatiently round the box. Mr. Fisk fidgeted, flicking nervous glances at it from time to time as though he feared it might contain an infernal machine. Mr. Allbright took advantage of the pause to extract his glasses from their case and adjust them after careful polishing. Sergeant Jefferson saw fit to relieve the silence by trumpeting loudly into his handkerchief. A clatter of boots on the concrete stairs was followed by the entry of a burly individual in shirt-sleeves. He held a businesslike rod of steel in his right hand.

"Ah, Jevons," said Mr. Fisk, "we want you to open this."

The man grunted. He inserted the narrow, clawed end of his rod in the crack close above the lock, and bore upon it. There was a sound of splintering and wrenching. The whole group moved closer. Another cracking, a final sharp snap and the lock gave. He pushed up the lid. Murmurs of exasperation arose all round. A sheet of metal still hid the contents. Jevons examined it.

"Another box. Iron one inside the wooden one," he said.

Derek was reminded of early fairy stories: "in the iron box was a silver box; in the silver box, a gold box; in the gold box . . ."

"Well, go on," said the manager, irritably. "Open it."

Jevons gave it further attention.

"Have to get a blow-lamp. It's all sealed up."

"Well, get it, and for heaven's sake be quick. We don't want to be here all night," snapped Mr. Fisk.

The group relapsed once more into silence as he clumped away. Partly to relieve it, Jordan said:

"It will be easier to get at if we pull it out of the wooden case. Can you give me a hand, Sergeant?"

Jevons returned to find the metal box free of its covering. Everyone watched with deep attention as he started and warmed up his blow-lamp.

The lid of the inner box was a shallow affair with turned-down edges which overlapped the sides by no more than an inch and a half. There were no hinges. It had been fitted on after the manner of a biscuit-tin lid and the edges afterward sealed down for their entire length. When his lamp had attained enough heat Jevons proceeded to work systematically round them with small gouts of molten metal trickling away before the flame. Then, protecting his hands from the heated surface with pieces of rag, he laid hold of the lid and wrenched it aside.

A nauseating stench swept across the passage. Involuntarily the whole group gave way before it.

"Good God!" Jordan muttered, snatching for his handkerchief.

Derek, recovering from the shock of the first fetid wave, pressed forward. He had one glimpse of the contents of the iron box before he was violently and unpleasantly sick.

XVII

WARMBROOK MAKES SUGGESTIONS

"—And, of course, the body in that box was Professor Wood-ridge's?" said Superintendent Warmbrook.

"Yes, sir. Mr. Jameson identified it as far as possible—when he'd got over the first shock," Jordan told him.

Warmbrook nodded. "Pretty nasty business," he said, sympathetically. "I suppose it was—er—?"

"Yes, it was—very," Jordan assured him. "It's been in the bank for just over four months."

"Ingenious," said the superintendent. "Most ingenious. Bit of a knock for the bank people."

"Yes, sir. I'm afraid that manager is in for some trouble—that letter ought to have been spotted for a forgery—even though it was a good one."

"So, I understand, was the note intended to decoy Mrs. Shiffer. They've got hold of a good man with a pen. Any idea who it can be?"

"No, sir. I asked Sergeant Jefferson about that. He said at first that it reminded him of Bright Hughes' style, but Bright's up for seven years and only done three of 'em, so that's out. Now he's inclined to think it's a new man altogether."

"So there's no lead that way. Awkward. What line are you working on now, Jordan?"

Jordan allowed his face to show some of the worry he was feeling.

"Honestly, sir, I think I'm stumped. We know plenty about it now, but we can't prove one thing against anyone."

Again the superintendent nodded sympathetically.

"The same old cry," he agreed. "It's a standing wonder to me that anybody ever does get put away in this country. If it weren't for the knarks—" He broke off. "Well, let's see what we do know." He began to tick off the points on his fingers. "That the solicitor, Drawford, was murdered. That Woodridge's death was concealed (he may have been murdered too, but we can't be sure of that yet). That the assistant, Straker, is still missing—and the two servants. That two attempts have been made to get Mrs. Shiffer. That the moving spirit behind it all appears to be Ferris Draymond—and that we can't touch him."

"And aren't likely to touch him," Jordan put in, bitterly.

"Not so fast. Some of his men might be persuaded to squeal."

"But none of those who go to his house are known to us. I've had men watching."

"Hang it all, Jordan. The man's not a fool. He must know we're watching. But some of the people who do visit him must be acting as go-betweens."

"You suggest following one or two of the more regular ones?"

The superintendent thought for a minute. "You might do that, but I doubt whether it would be much good. Knowing the place to be watched, he'll be bound to have warned his men that they may be followed. No, I doubt if that would get us far."

"Well, what would, sir?" Jordan said, a little desperately. "It's the only lead we've got. The Paddington place was a washout. The description of the man who called once or twice for letters there was hopelessly vague—no good at all, except to tell us that it couldn't have been Woodridge himself. We must start from that house somehow."

"And they know that we know about it, so you can bet your

shirt they're pretty careful. No, they'll be quite ready for us there. We've just got to find another line."

"Well, if you can think of one—"

The superintendent stared fixedly at one of the much-faded athletic groups. At last he said:

"Doesn't it strike you, Jordan, that we are rather overlooking the main cause of all this? We're getting tangled up in the side-issues. Murder is serious enough, God knows, but in this case it is very much the means and, I should say, not at all the end."

"You mean this formula—?"

"I do. That's been the object all the time—and they've not got it yet."

"Unless Drawford was carrying it on him."

Superintendent Warmbrook snorted.

"Jordan, there are times when I wonder how you come to be in the force at all. Would you, if you were given a highly important document to guard, go 'carrying it on you'? Do show some sense."

The inspector shifted uneasily.

"I was trying not to overlook a possibility," he explained.

"That's not a possibility—it's a fantasy. It's about as probable as finding a bearer-check for a million. Besides, didn't you yourself tell me that you thought we were meant to find Drawford's body? What would be the point in that if they already had the formula?"

"What point is there in it at all?" Jordan countered.

"But I think you were right there. There must be a point somewhere."

"Well?" Jordan was still smarting under reproof for a remark he had regretted the moment it slipped out.

"It's obvious enough that Draymond collared Drawford for the sake of information. Now, did he, or did he not, succeed? If he didn't, then we're all square: neither of us knows where it is. But if he did, what then?"

"Just that he is a jump ahead of us, as usual," Jordan said bitterly.

But the superintendent smiled again.

"I shouldn't let that worry you. I'm prepared to bet that the formula is in the obvious place—Drawford's own bank."

"Or a safe deposit."

"Or a safe deposit, as you say. But I doubt that. Why should a man go to the expense of renting a safe in one of those places when he can use his own bank? Anyhow, it should be easy enough to find out if he has. Let's assume for the moment that it is in the bank. What can Draymond do? He wants to get it out, but he can't say to Drawford: 'Go and fetch it for me.' He can force Drawford to write a letter to the bank authorizing the bearer to obtain it. But what will the bank think of that? Drawford has disappeared suspiciously. Are they going to hand over his property to a stranger merely on the strength of a note? They are not: they're far more likely to hand the stranger over to us.

"Is Draymond going to burgle the bank? He is not; and for a dozen good reasons; even one—the difficulty of tackling a bank's strong-room—being enough to stop him. 'All right,' he says to himself, 'if we can't get the formula out of there ourselves, we must get someone else to do it for us.' Now do you see?"

Jordan was not at all sure that he did.

"Then perhaps you will ring up Mr. Allbright," Warmbrook suggested.

Jordan obeyed. He gave Mr. Allbright's private number, for the shock of the discovery in the bank had left the solicitor in no condition to return to his office.

"And ask him," continued the superintendent, "when he is thinking of fetching Mr. Drawford's effects from his bank."

A sudden light broke over Jordan. He began to see what his superior was getting at.

"He says on Monday morning."

"Good! That's what I expected. Let me talk to him for a bit."

Jordan waited until the superintendent had finished and hung up.

"I see," he said, thoughtfully. "To get his things out of the bank, Drawford's body must be found. If not, they would have had to wait until he was presumed dead."

"Quite. And among those things will be found an envelope to be forwarded to the War Office in case of Woodridge's death. We know now that Woodridge certainly is dead—so what happens?"

"I don't know," admitted Jordan. "But whatever it is, it happens on Monday."

The superintendent's brows came down in a thoughtful frown.

"Yes. We'd better think a little about Monday," he said.

XVIII

DEREK BUYS FLOWERS

Derek finished his second glass of beer, waved a hand in vague farewell to Letty behind the bar, pushed open the saloon door of *The Friend of All,* and emerged via a narrow passage into Southampton Row. There, scowling at passersby, at the street itself, at things in general, he paused indecisively. The problem perplexing him was, in essence, simple. It amounted to his asking, "Do I go home to a lunch which, this being Saturday, Mrs. Roberts is even now preparing, or do I honor a restaurant?" But questions do not exist in such complete detachment: the tapes tied to alternatives are the stuff of problems.

Phyllida would be up and about. . . . Furthermore, Barry would be home by now. Should he not leave the coast clear? If he should join them, he reflected, he would be a gooseberry—and not only a plain, ordinary gooseberry, but the kind which had put its foot into it. He had not seen Phyllida since the inauspicious events of Wednesday evening. The last words he had heard her say were "Get out, damn you. Can't you leave me alone?" On the whole, not very encouraging.

And Barry had seemed a bit queer, too, last night. Not himself, as it were. And all because, after that nasty affair at the bank, he had rung up Barry and asked him to break the news to Phyl. Not a nice job, of course. No one could pretend it was a nice job, but he had been unnecessarily curt about it later on. After all, somebody had to tell her. And what with the row on Wednesday night and everything, he hadn't liked to go barging in himself.... Anyhow, it ought to have come better from Barry....

By the time he had put away the car and got home, she had gone early to bed and he hadn't liked to intrude—apart from other considerations he had been afraid that she might demand details—ugh! He had sent Mrs. Roberts in to her with a note. Barry, after a spell of uncommunicative gloom, had taken himself off to address his usual Friday evening class, this time upon the dubious subject of "Advertising Morals." Derek, left to himself, had retired disconsolately to bed, and, in spite of the events of the day, to sleep.

First thing this morning there had been that fellow Jordan on the telephone again. The man seemed to have a passion for ringing up at the crack of dawn.

"Glad I've caught you," he had said, brightly.

"Caught me!" Derek echoed, in bitter sleepiness. "What the deuce is it now?"

But Jordan had been in a politer mood.

"How's Mrs. Shiffer this morning?"

"Sleeping, I hope. Like everyone else ought to be."

"Oh. Well, look here, I want to make an arrangement for Monday. Can you and Mrs. Shiffer meet me at Scotland Yard at ten-thirty that morning? It's rather important."

"To go on from there to the inquest?"

"No, that's fixed for Tuesday. Quite another matter."

"All right. Be mysterious, if you like. Yes, I can come, and I expect Mrs. Shiffer will be able to. I'll let you know if she can't."

"We should be very grateful if she can manage it."

"Right you are."

That seemed to finish the conversation—at least, Derek had hoped so, but it appeared that Jordan had further news to impart.

He was, in his listener's opinion, infernally chatty for such an hour.

"About that butler," he began.

"About what butler?" Derek snapped.

"The man from The Laurels, of course."

"Oh, yes, I'd forgotten him. What about him?"

"We've found him. He's in the Home Counties' Hospital. Pretty badly smashed up, but they think he'll mend all right."

"Good. Phyl'll be glad about that. I fancy he was a bit on her conscience. Have you got anything out of him?"

"Can't see him yet, but he's told the hospital people it was an accident. Says he was loosening a jammed window and his feet slipped on the polished floor. It satisfied them and he's sticking to it. However, we'll have a go at him as soon as they'll let us."

"I see. Anything else?"

"No—only don't forget ten-thirty on Monday."

"All right."

On that he had hung up, written a note for Phyllida, giving Jordan's message, and decided to get away before either she or Barry put in an appearance. Mrs. Roberts arrived as he was leaving, and with her assurance that she would "look after Miss Phyllida like she was me own daughter," he had hurried down the stairs.

Standing now, with his gaze fixed unwaveringly upon an embarrassed seller of matches, he wondered at his behavior, trying to recapture his earlier attitude of mind. It was all so damn silly and, as far as he could see, about nothing at all. Undoubtedly something was wrong somewhere—quite apart from Uncle Henry's death—but this tramping about London all morning until one picked up the familiar moorings in *The Friend of All,* did not help to explain anything.

"A fool," he said, suddenly. "That's what you are." The match-seller who had drawn wheedlingly closer, sheered off. "Have it out. That's the only thing. Have it out," Derek told himself.

As a prelude he stopped on the way home to buy a large bunch of flowers.

"Hullo," said Derek.

Barry grunted morosely from the depths of the best chair. Not a very encouraging start. However:

"Where's Phyl," he added.

"Gone." Barry showed no increase of amiability.

Derek laid his flowers carefully on the table. He frowned.

"What do you mean, 'gone'?"

"Just what I say. You can ask Mrs. Roberts, if you don't believe me."

Barry was no fount of eloquence. Derek decided to take him at his word, and made his way to the kitchen.

"What's all this about Mrs. Shiffer?" he demanded.

Mrs. Roberts looked up from the stove.

"She's gorn, sir. A Mrs. Tragg come and took 'er with 'er."

So that was it. Aunt Malvina had swooped. He inquired after further details. It would seem that Mrs. Tragg, a lady (if you liked to call her that) whom Mrs. Roberts had never seen before, had arrived at the flat full of disapproval and determination. Her remarks, Derek gathered, had been generally disparaging. A flat belonging to two young men was no place for a girl, even if she did happen to be a married woman now, and particularly when she had just learned of the death of her father. What was needed at such times was a woman's care and sympathy ("and me a-treatin' of 'er like she was me own daughter," Mrs. Roberts complained aggrievedly). Aunt Malvina had no idea what things were coming to. It was a preposterous state of affairs. Phyllida must come with her at once to the purer purlieus of Kensington.

"And Mrs. Shiffer didn't object?" Derek asked.

"No, sir." Mrs. Roberts shook her head. "She didn't seem as she cared much one way or the other, poor thing. She just let 'er 'ave 'er own way and then they went off in the big car what was waiting outside. Real 'igh an' mighty, that Mrs. Tragg was."

Derek nodded sympathetically. There was no putting off Aunt Malvina once her mind was made up. Undoubtedly there would come a day when she would bully her way past Saint Peter himself.

He wandered out of the kitchen, drifting back toward the sitting-room. The flat suddenly seemed very empty. He turned aside into her bedroom. The few possessions she had acquired during the last day or two had been stripped from it. They had been meager trifles, bought only to tide over, but their going had left the room bare, impersonal. She might never have been there. . . .

Queer, that blank sensation one felt. Everything looking so abruptly faded. He'd felt like that once before. When was it? Yes, three years ago when the end of the boat train had dwindled down the line: when it had taken away Phyl and Ronald. . . .

He left the room and wandered on along the passage. Barry appeared not to have moved. Derek dropped into the opposite chair. The bunch of flowers, forlorn on the table, caught his eye. He looked across at Barry.

"I say, old man, you might take those along with you when you go." His air was not quite as casual as he could have wished.

"When I go where?" Barry said, harshly.

"When you go to see Phyl. Aren't you going to take her out in the car or something tomorrow? Take her mind off it, you know."

"I'm not going to see her tomorrow."

Derek stared. A worried frown slowly materialized.

"I say, there's nothing wrong—between you two, I mean? You didn't mess it up again on Thursday, did you?"

Barry looked at him for some time without speaking. At last:

"You know, Derek, there are times when you are a complete fool," he said.

"Undoubtedly," Derek agreed, without rancor. "But what I want to know is whether you've been a fool again. I thought—"

"You thought!" Barry jumped up and came closer. He stood beside Derek's chair, looking down. "Well, suppose you think again. Or, better still, stop thinking and try feeling instead. You know so damn much about what's good for other people, don't you? Why not try looking after your own affairs for a change? Try seeing what's in front of your nose. You've got some eyes— well, use them, blast you, and take the damn flowers yourself."

Derek stared up in bewilderment.

"What the—?" he began, but Barry had left, slamming the door behind him. He looked at it with an expression still frozen into clownish vacuity.

A glimmer of suspicion began to invade his mental blackout. It grew rapidly until it burst like a sudden star-shell into a white blaze of comprehension. He looked stupidly at the bunch of flowers. Unconsciously he put out a hand to take them up.

XIX

MISCARRIAGE OF A PLAN

A taxi set Phyllida and Derek down at the Embankment entrance to New Scotland Yard within five minutes of the appointed time. A uniformed constable inquired their business. A few minutes later, after traveling a series of shabby corridors and stairs, they were shown into Detective-Inspector Jordan's office. He rose to greet them and to express condolences on Phyllida's bereavement. A little later, he added:

"I'd like you to come along at once to Superintendent Warmbrook's office. He will explain why we were so anxious for you to come here this morning."

He led the way by more passages and ushered them into his superior's room. Thomas Warmbrook was in a genial mood this morning; he beamed on them paternally.

"Please sit here, Mrs. Shiffer; and you, here, Mr. Jameson. Be careful of that chair, Inspector, it's not quite itself."

He sank once more into the round-backed desk chair which fitted his form so well. Like Jordan, he extended his sympathy concerning the shocking discovery of Professor Woodridge's body.

Phyllida thanked him quietly. She looked a trifle pale, but she was quite calm. The first frenzy of grief had quickly spent itself—more quickly, Aunt Malvina had privately considered, than was becoming in a niece of hers. But their views were from different angles. Malvina Tragg, genuinely startled and very properly shocked by the news that her brother was dead, though she had cared for him so little in life. To Phyllida, most of the shock had come in the manner of the body's discovery. Unconsciously she had allowed her slight hope that he might still be alive to dwindle away during the last week. Friday's news had come as a confirmation of her fears rather than as a surprise. The conventional grief of her aunt (scarcely, she thought to herself, to be distinguished from hypocrisy) had had not a little to do with her determination to put on a brave front.

"I hope," the superintendent was continuing, "that you will not think too hardly of us for bringing you round here at this time, but it is possible that you may be able to give us some help."

"If I can do anything—?" Phyllida said.

Superintendent Warmbrook leaned back and interlocked his fingers across his bulging stomach.

"I will try to explain, Mrs. Shiffer. Please stop me if there is anything you do not understand." He paused, searching for the best opening. "You are aware, of course, that the focus of the entire affair is this formula discovered by your father? And that the formula, in a sealed envelope, was entrusted to Mr. Drawford?" Phyllida nodded. "Good. Now we have reason to think that these men have not yet got that envelope, and that it is still safely held in the strong-room of Mr. Drawford's bank."

"But are you sure of that?" Derek put in.

"Not absolutely *sure*," Warmbrook admitted. "But far enough convinced to make it a working hypothesis. We might have made certain on Saturday, but we preferred to wait until today. Now, if these men cannot get hold of the envelope, all the trouble they have taken will be so much waste. You see what I am getting at? They must make their attempt after it has left the bank, but before it is delivered at the War Office."

"Yes, that's clear enough," Derek agreed, "but where does Mrs. Shiffer come in?"

"Mrs. Shiffer is the only one of us who has seen any of these men face to face and will know them again. (I expect Draymond himself, because obviously he cannot afford to appear in the active part of the proceedings.) It is not unlikely that some of those she saw at the house in Golders Green will be employed on the job of getting hold of the letter. We intend to keep our eyes on this envelope until it is safely delivered—not only to ensure its safety, but to use it as a bait. Mrs. Shiffer may be able to help us a great deal if there are any of these people hanging about. We shall be at a great advantage if our adversaries can be pointed out before they make their first move."

"I'll do all I can," Phyllida assured him.

The superintendent glanced up at the clock.

"Almost eleven. Mr. Allbright is to be at the bank at twelve-thirty. If you don't mind, I'd like you to get there about twelve—it might be better not to have a whole crowd of us arriving there at the same time. The inspector and I will be there about twenty-past."

He scribbled a few words on the back of a card, and handed it to Derek.

"Here's the address. Just give your names: the manager is expecting you."

Once more Derek found himself being shown into a bank manager's office, but Mr. Goosehen of the All Counties Bank, Holborn Circus Branch, did not in the least resemble Mr. Fisk of the Metropolitan and Midland. One might well have been puzzled to know how Mr. Fisk had attained his position, whereas it must always have been obvious that Mr. Goosehen's personality and capability would inevitably lead to a managership sooner or later, and he had contrived that it should be sooner. He was, quite evidently, a busy man.

"Good morning," Derek began. "Superintendent Warmbrook—"

"Quite. Yes. Extraordinary business," said Mr. Goosehen. "Mr. Allbright will be here at twelve-thirty. Would you mind waiting in here?"

He opened a door leading to a smaller office, showed them in, and closed it behind them. They looked at one another. Derek smiled.

"A most efficient magnate," he murmured.

He procured two of the uncomfortable chairs with which the room was furnished, and placed them neatly side by side.

"Derek," said Phyllida. "You've forgotten something."

"Oh, no, I haven't. I've been saving up. Biding my time. And now we're alone. Phyl, darling . . ."

Derek raised his head after a lengthy interval. His arms were still round her.

"Why, oh why, was I ever such a fool?"

"You were rather, weren't you, darling? But so was I, for not seeing that you were. If I had . . ."

"If you had?"

"If I had seen it, Derek, there might have been no Ronald."

"Even then?"

"Yes, even then, my poor dear."

"But I thought—What about Barry?"

"Oh, I liked Barry, all right—I still like him. But, oh, you were so blind, Derek. I didn't think anyone could be so blind: I thought you just didn't . . . If I'd only known then just how big a fool you are, darling . . ."

"And all the time I thought it was Barry. . . . And then there was Ronald . . . I knew you didn't really love him, and I let you go. Phyl, I can still see the back of that train, getting smaller and smaller. . . . Oh, Phyl, your terrible three years. They were all my fault, really. I made you go through . . ."

Fingers were on his lips.

"Hush. They're over now. They've never been. There was a

Phyllida Woodridge: there's going to be a Phyllida Jameson. Somewhere in between them will be a thin, pale ghost, Phyllida Shiffer, rather lost, very unhappy. I'm afraid she can never quite die, but she never really lived. . . . And now she'll grow thinner and paler until we can't see her."

"She's faded now. Phyllida Jameson was born on Saturday afternoon."

"When you came and brought those flowers. . . ."

"And you cried."

"Well, darling, you did look so funny and miserable. And the poor flowers—all crushed and bruised. . . ."

"Stress of emotion, darling. I was scared to death."

"Darling . . ."

Given propitious circumstances, this kind of thing is capable of continuing indefinitely. A certain flushed dishevelment was noticeable when the superintendent and the inspector were shown into the office.

"Oh, er, hullo," said Derek. He took an involuntary glance at the clock. Its hands stood at five-and-twenty-past twelve. The superintendent noticed his look with faint amusement.

"Yes. We're a little late," he said.

"Oh, so you are. Quite," was the best Derek could manage.

"Switching to another subject," remarked Warmbrook, "I'll tell you both the general idea. Now, Mrs. Shiffer, I want you to contrive to be near one or other of us all the time from the moment we leave the bank. Keep your eyes well open and if you recognize, or even think you recognize anyone who may be hanging about, tell us at once. You're not to wait for the man to do something suspicious, or anything like that. The moment you see him, point him out to us. . . ."

A few minutes after half-past twelve the door leading to the manager's office was opened again and a clerk asked them to come in. Mr. Allbright was already present. He seemed nervous, and a weekend spent in the country appeared to have done him little good. He nodded to the rest and was introduced to the superintendent.

"We have just sent a man down for Mr. Drawford's box," explained the manager. "He should be back in a few minutes."

"I suppose you can give us no idea of what form this attempt may take, Superintendent?" Mr. Allbright inquired.

Warmbrook admitted that he could not, but that he had laid preparations to counter all the possibilities which had occurred to him. The solicitor shook an unhappy head.

"I don't like it. I must say, I do not like it."

There was no direct reply to make to this, but Warmbrook did his best to be reassuring. He was thankful to be interrupted by the return of a clerk carrying a japanned tin box. It was dented by long use and at several spots had broken out into sores of rust. On the front and on the top, in letters which had yellowed considerably from their original whiteness, appeared the name of Miles Drawford. Mr. Allbright, fumbling for his key, watched anxiously as it was placed on the desk. After an exasperating interval he secured the key and jabbed it into the lock with a nervousness justifiable only if the contents had been rattlesnakes. It came as something of an anti-climax to see the lid raised from commonplace bundles of papers. Mr. Allbright, relieved that an armed gang did not immediately materialize to demand the envelope, and that the course of normality was in no other way deflected, sloughed a part of his agitation. He began to extract the packets of documents one by one, subjecting each to a close examination before he laid it on the desk beside him. At the seventh or eighth dip an "Ah!" of mingled satisfaction and apprehension escaped him.

With deliberation he loosened that pink tape which lawyers call red and spread out the released papers.

One envelope caught all eyes.

"Ah!" repeated everyone. Everyone, that is, except Mr. Goosehen, who remained somewhat in the dark.

Mr. Allbright extracted the envelope from its position between a lease and an insurance policy, and laid it down in splendid isolation. The rest leaned over to read:

In the event of my death, to be forwarded immediately to the proper authorities at the War Office.

Henry Woodridge.

and below, the date, the fourteenth of June of the current year.

There was a sudden knocking at the door. Mr. Allbright started violently, all but dislodging his pince-nez. His and all other heads in the room jerked round questioningly.

"Come in," said Mr. Goosehen.

The knob was turned with hesitation. A youth, his arms full of newspapers, stood on the threshold. He advanced into the room, something of his load falling by the wayside.

"What the devil," demanded Mr. Goosehen, "do you think you're doing?"

"'E told me I was to bring 'em 'ere," said the youth, aggrievedly.

His effort to jerk a thumb in the superintendent's direction set a fresh flood of newsprint cascading.

"That's right," agreed Warmbrook, as Jordan bent down to gather the scattered sheets. "It had slipped my memory for the moment."

They waited while the youth set down his burden and retired. Mr. Goosehen inquired testily the purpose for which his office was thus filled with rubbish.

"It occurred to me," the superintendent explained in mild tones, "that an attempt might be made to seize this box. Of course, we shall do all in our power to prevent it, but in order to take no risks, it will be safer if all documents are removed, and a new contents provided to give it the necessary weight. If you wouldn't mind taking charge of the present contents for a few hours . . . ?" he suggested.

Mr. Goosehen hesitated and then agreed. Messrs. Drawford and Allbright were good customers. It was irregular that their papers should be left in his private safe, but this was a time when such details might be waived. While he and the solicitor transferred the bundles of documents to the safe, Jordan replaced them with folded newspapers. The substitution took only a few minutes. A single envelope now lay on the desk. Mr. Allbright looked at it thoughtfully. "—*to be forwarded immediately*—" He picked it up and placed it with care and precision in the inside pocket of his coat.

Inspector Jordan, with a slight smile, caught his superior's eye, but the latter seemed conveniently to have forgotten his earlier remarks on the improbability of such a resting-place for an important document.

"Now," said Warmbrook, "I think we are ready. It has seemed to us that the most likely place for the attempt is outside your office in Bedford Row, Mr. Allbright. If the box should be snatched, I want you to put up no resistance. Just let them take it, you understand?"

"Yes, indeed. Yes." Mr. Allbright gave melancholy agreement. The idea of putting up any resistance had not even entered his head. All his battles had been fought with words and he had no desire at all to exchange the weapons of a lifetime. "Yes. Just let them take it," he repeated.

"Exactly." The superintendent turned to the others. "Will you, Mrs. Shiffer and Mr. Jameson, leave first with Inspector Jordan, who will call a taxi. If you recognize anyone out there, you know what to do."

Phyllida nodded and picked up her handbag. The three left the office together and passed out into the street. Phyllida, mindful of instructions, looked about her carefully. The pavement was full of pedestrians hurrying to or from their luncheons. The only loiterers in sight were two paper-sellers gifted with every mark and sound of authenticity and an aged optimist holding in one outstretched hand a single matchbox. In answer to Jordan's look of inquiry she shook her head. He left the pair standing beside the bank door while he went to hail a taxi.

"Do you think they'll really try to do anything?" she asked, with just a trace of nervousness.

"Well, not here, at any rate. Too many people," Derek encouraged her, glancing at the passing crowd.

Within a minute or two Jordan was back with a taxi. The space directly in front of the door was occupied by a small black saloon car with obscured rear windows—a semi-commercial type of vehicle such as dress salesmen use on their travels, so that it was necessary for the taxi to halt a few yards to one side. The inspector beckoned them over.

"Get in," he directed. "I'll fetch the others." He dodged across the pavement and vanished through the swing doors.

A moment later they parted again to show him in company with the superintendent and an apprehensive-looking Mr. Allbright, who gingerly carried the black box. They had scarcely set foot on the pavement when it happened.

The door of the innocent-looking traveler's car was flung open and a man sprang out. Simultaneously, an apparently innocent passerby turned and flung himself at the three. The sudden double attack took them by surprise. Two bewildered citizens falling headlong before the men's rush added to the confusion. Derek saw the superintendent abruptly double up and caught a glimpse of Mr. Allbright's top hat falling to one side. In a flash the man was running back across the pavement, clutching the tin box. He dived back headfirst through the open door of the already moving saloon. There was a roar as it accelerated and shot away up Hatton Garden. On the windscreen of a gray car which had been loitering inconspicuously there appeared as if by magic a crown and the letters, M.P. With a deafening blast of exhaust it flung itself in pursuit.

Derek jumped out of the taxi, pulling Phyllida after him. He shouldered his way toward the center of a growing crowd where somebody was blowing shrilly on a police whistle. By the time he had reached the front rank all the persons within earshot were rushing to swell the mob behind him. He could see the superintendent sitting on the ground, both hands clasped over his expansive stomach. He was trying to speak, but no words would come; evidently he had been thoroughly winded. Jordan's hands were full with a twisting, squirming prisoner, while Mr. Allbright, his silk hat trampled somewhere underfoot, lay bareheaded close by.

They had a rear view of a tall figure bending over the solicitor, resting his hand above the heart. He raised his head and spoke to a uniformed constable who came plowing through the crowd like an ice-breaker.

"He'll be all right. Better get him inside."

Derek heard Phyllida gasp. She tugged at his sleeve.

"That's the man I saw at that house."

"That tall fellow?"

"Yes. Yes."

Derek glanced round. The superintendent was still out of action; Jordan was out of reach and still busy with his captive. There was only one thing for it.

"You stick close to Jordan," he told her. "I'll be back soon." He turned and fought his way back through the indignant crowd.

Several constables were by now advising sensation seekers to move along. In the consequent flux Phyllida lost sight of the tall man and her efforts to approach Jordan brought her up against a large and solid policeman. By the time she had convinced him of her right to be present both Derek and the other had vanished utterly. Jordan had handed over his prisoner and was assisting the superintendent, while another policeman was carrying Mr. Allbright back into the bank.

"Better come inside out of this crowd," the inspector greeted her, ruefully.

With Warmbrook still making strange sounds and looking suggestively green, they regained the manager's office to find that Mr. Allbright, although still dazed, was now conscious. Mr. Goosehen hastened to produce a bottle of brandy. Under its influence, Warmbrook's face began to present a less exotic appearance, and the solicitor's faculties to reassemble themselves.

"There seems," said Mr. Goosehen, chattily, "to have been some miscalculation. Did they get the box?"

"They did—but there ought to be a squad car on their tail," growled Warmbrook. He looked at his inspector for confirmation.

"Yes, sir. I saw it get away."

They turned to look with some concern at the solicitor. Mere apologies are not strong charms to allay the wrath of one who has been knocked out. Both suffered a lively fear of unpleasantness to come. Mr. Allbright, fingering his chin thoughtfully, was well into his second strong brandy.

"It hasn't felt like this since I was at school," he remarked reminiscently.

"Very lucky thing you removed those papers," put in the bank manager.

Mr. Allbright nodded. "And the envelope," he said.

His hand slid to his inside pocket. It stayed there. An expression of horrified amazement crossed his face.

"It's gone!"

They all stared at him.

"It's gone—and my pocket-book."

"That man," Phyllida said, suddenly.

"The doctor!" Jordan exclaimed.

The superintendent looked bewildered.

"What man?" he demanded.

Phyllida explained.

As they approached more populous streets he decided to close the distance between them. It was well he did, for at his former range he would have been out of sight when his man decided to enter a post-office.

Derek hesitated. Should he wait until the man came out, or should he risk recognition by following him in? He had not yet showed the slightest sign of suspicion, and there might be some information to be gained.

A quick glance round showed the tall man writing at the telegram desk. Passing close behind, Derek contrived to look past his arm. He was surprised to see, not a telegraph form, but an envelope already half-addressed. The man wrote the last word and underlined it with a dash; he laid down his pen and reached into his inner pocket. It took all Derek's self-control to repress an exclamation as he saw another envelope drawn out. He could see only the back, but the blob of blue wax which sealed it was unmistakable. He had last seen it sliding into Allbright's pocket. They'd got it then, after all. How . . . ? Of course, the man had been bending over Allbright. At that moment Derek, like the rest, had taken him for a doctor. . . . But what could he do? The man evidently considered the safety of the post greater than his own personal care. Very wisely he was going to carry the evidence no farther. Derek watched him slip the one envelope inside the other, lick the flap and press it down. He stowed his fountain-pen, picked up the envelope and crossed to the counter. Derek stiffened. It was a case of now or never. In a few seconds it would be out of his reach. The envelope was laid on the counter.

"I want to register—" the man began.

But he got no farther. A hand snatched the envelope from beneath his own. Before he could even turn, Derek was halfway across the room, racing for the street door. The tall man took a step after him, then he hesitated and turned back.

XX

WHO LAUGHS LAST

Derek dragged himself free of the crowd and looked round. For a desperate moment he was afraid he had lost his man. Then, with relief, he caught a glimpse of a bowler hat at more than average height approaching as its owner pushed his way through the crush. He drew to one side, watched the other emerge and, without a glance behind him, set off briskly in the direction of Ludgate Circus. Derek followed down St. Andrew Street, keeping well to the rear on the opposite side of the road, but the other did not pause. Only once did he turn his head to look behind him, and that in an entirely unsuspicious manner. The advantage lay with the shadower for the lunch-hour crowd was still thick enough to render him inconspicuous to the casual observer, while the height of the other made him easy to keep in view.

For the moment when Phyllida had said: "the man I saw at that house," he had thought she meant Draymond. Then, with a glimpse of the face beneath the bowler, he realized that it must be the one she had referred to as Number 2—the man who had questioned her in the bedroom at The Laurels.

Derek had no more than a vague notion of why he had engaged on the chase. It had been on impulse, with the sparest reasoning behind it; just a nebulous idea that perhaps something might be gained by following. Possibly it would only lead him back to Golders Green, but there was at least the chance of a new line opening....

"It's all right," he assured the astonished girl behind the counter.

The expression of amazement was still on her face as she watched him walk, frowning thoughtfully, to the telephone booths.

Derek fled along Fleet Street, turned up an alley and dodged round a number of corners before he paused. There was no sign of pursuit. Now he came to think of it, there wouldn't be. If he were caught it would become necessary for the tall man to explain how he had come by the letter in the first place—not, considering everything, an easy explanation to make.

He took the letter from the pocket into which he had crammed it. Straightening out the creases, he read:

Dennis Draymond, Esq.,
22 Drivers Road,
St. Albans.

Dennis, the son! Yes, of course, Ferris Draymond would not want it delivered to him, nor to have it on his premises.

He returned it to his pocket, lit a cigarette and made his way back to Fleet Street. What next? Go back and find Jordan or make for Scotland Yard? Or should he go to the War Office itself?

He looked up at the narrow sky above him. Between occasional hurrying clouds it was a soft, shining blue. A golden October sun, now past its zenith, still made a joyful thing of the day. God in His heaven, all right with the world . . . superficially. He looked again at the crowds hurrying along on unknown business. They were not joyful. Mostly they looked tense or worried. Things were sadly awry with most of their worlds. But at least they were alive—their bodies were mostly whole and clean. He pictured a gas bomb bursting in this street. A cloud of dull mist rolling up this chasm between the buildings, like November fog from the river. He pictured the crowds fleeing before it, and the plight of those who could not flee. . . .

The formula for a very horrible death lay here in his pocket. "Allied to the Yellow Cross group," his uncle had written. . . . The most loathsome, the most agonizing of all the types. . . .

Derek strolled thoughtfully down to Ludgate Circus and caught a number eighteen bus.

There was somebody else on the stairs to the flat. A heavy-footed visitor descending. Derek, on his way up, stood aside for the other to pass. He came on down, a bulky, dimly-seen form on the poorly-lit stairs, but he did not pass. Something hit Derek a vicious blow on the chin. A hand fumbled in his clothes. He struggled feebly and tried to call out. The envelope. . . .

"Stay quiet, damn yer," muttered a voice. The man followed it up with a crashing blow on the temple.

Derek gave no more trouble.

XXI

THE UNEXPECTED

A man emerged from the gates of the Royal Central Hospital into the misty grayness of a mid-November day. For a few indecisive minutes he stood on the curb, shivering a little and pulling his scanty clothes more closely about him. His age was problematic. His body, save for the inconsistency of its weary stoop, might have belonged to a man of twenty-six. The face, too, held contradictions. At a distance it looked young, seen more closely it was lined, almost middle-aged. The dark brown hair above it was streaked with gray. The head was held forward and the eyes screwed up, as though their owner peered into a dimly-seen world.

At length he made up his mind. He waved a taxi out of the passing traffic and gave the driver an address. At his destination he paid the man off and, turning into the house beside him, began to climb the long flights of stairs in a slow, uncertain manner. He was badly out of breath when he reached the top and pressed the bell-push.

Derek himself opened the door.

"What—?" he began. Then his expression changed. He looked more closely at his visitor.

"Good God! Straker?"

The other nodded. Derek opened the door wide.

"Come in, man. Come in."

He led the way into the sitting-room. Straker sank thankfully into an easy-chair.

"Whisky? You look all in," Derek offered.

"Thanks. It'll help. Make it weak, though."

Derek glanced at him surreptitiously as he mixed the drink. Straker! Yes, it undoubtedly was Straker. But the difference. It had been more than the absence of the glasses which had put him off at first. His whole face, manner, bearing had changed. What on earth had been happening to the man?

Straker took the glass. The very first few sips seemed to do him good. "Have to go easy," he murmured, noticing the effect. "Haven't had a drink since the summer."

"Where the deuce have you been?" Derek asked. "There's been a hue and cry for you all over the country. Police and everything."

"Hospital, the last three weeks or so. Before that, I don't know."

"Don't know?" Derek looked incredulous.

Straker shook his head. "I'll tell you about it later. First, I want to know what's happened. Your uncle, he's dead?" At Derek's nod, he added: "Then they did kill him, the swine."

"Look here," said Derek, "suppose you tell me—"

"No. I must know what's been happening first. The police have been on it, you say?"

"Yes. C.I.D. and all. The first thing we knew was when Phyllida came home and found—"

He told the story from the time of Phyllida's return until the moment he had been knocked out on his own staircase. Straker, sipping occasionally at his weak whisky and smoking a number of cigarettes, listened almost without interruption. At the end he nodded comprehendingly. He shifted his position slightly, bringing the intense gaze of his dark, short-sighted eyes on Derek's face.

"And why," he asked, "why, when you had actually got that formula, did you come back here? Why was it you didn't take it straight to the police?"

Derek hesitated only a moment. He looked squarely at Straker as he spoke:

"Because I did not want the police or anybody else to get it. I was going to burn it in that fire."

There was a touch of defiance in his tone; a preparation against criticism, but no outburst followed, no sign of the anger and indignation he had expected.

"I'm sorry you didn't," said the other. "I don't know what your motives were, but I'm damned sorry you didn't."

There was a pause. Derek made no attempt to explain. His intention had owed more to impulse and emotion than to reasoning. It was a long time before Straker spoke again. At last:

"If I believed in a devil," he said, "I'd say that that gas came directly from him. God, you've no idea what a filthy stuff it is. You know what mustard gas is like—the old original Yellow Cross stuff? It's spread in a fine spray. It gets on everything, clothes, boots, hands. When it gets warm it vaporizes, it gets into your skin, in your eyes, you breathe it. It eats open sores into your body—and if it can do that to your outer skin, think what it does to your lungs and your eyes. If it gets you properly they begin to decay inside you—you rot before you're dead. They were using that back in the war. They've been improving their gases ever since. Things like this one your uncle stumbled across have been worked on, but I think—I hope—they've perfected nothing quite so foul.

"One part of the old mustard gas in five million of air could cause almost incurable disease. We knew this stuff was far stronger. We tried it on a rabbit—one part to ten million of air. It was blind in a couple of seconds, it coughed up its lungs in nine or ten; in a minute it was rotting, falling to bits before our eyes. We tried another with one of gas to twenty million of air. It was a bit slower and therefore more painful, that's all."

He paused and looked at Derek doubtfully.

"You think I'm exaggerating? I'm not. It's the plain truth. Why, even in 1918 a gas was tried out, an arsenical gas that time, which in a proportion of one to ten million of air would put a man out of action in less than a minute. The point about the stuff we found is that it is capable of working at a greater dilution than any known vesicant gas, and it might be improved still further. I wanted your uncle to get rid of it there and then and to destroy all records, but he wouldn't. For one thing he had a scientific interest in it—he wanted to make further experiments at leisure— and, for another, he had an idea of duty to the country."

He looked reflectively into the fire.

"We argued about that for weeks. He talking about his duty to his country, and I about his duty to mankind. Does that sound priggish? But try to see it as I did—as I do. This gas business has grown too big—it menaces the whole world. In the old days a scientific worker who assisted the military was working not to destroy a nation, but its army. It is the business of armies to destroy or to be destroyed: they're a parasitic class kept for that purpose, and taken in the mass it doesn't matter much what happens to them—in fact, if they all wiped one another out, the world would be free to get on with the things which really matter.

"But nowadays things have got to such a pitch that the army, the servant paid by the people for the people's own protection, is so incompetent that the moment a war starts it declares martial law. You see what I mean? During peace we support an unnecessary army; when a job of war arises, we have to do it for them. Apparently the whole profession is so incapable that we are all dragged in. Whether we like it or not, we too are put in the position to destroy or be destroyed. In another war what will happen? The two armies will sit down with such a spread of gases in between them that neither can do a damned thing: the 'front' will be a farce. The ruined areas will be inside each country. Our populations will probably be disease-ridden, and even if bacteria bombs are not used, most of those who survive the gases will become tuberculous. We might manage to survive one such war, perhaps two, but where should we be a generation later? A nation bred from the neurotic and the tuberculous—a C3 nation struggling to rebuild the ruins. Great God, haven't we seen the effect of the last war—where are those who should be leading us now? A little more of that sort of thing, and we shall be too weak even to struggle with our problems.

"The weapons are reaching a point where they are capable of destroying humanity itself.

"It is almost within one nation's power now to *wipe out* another nation. By revealing the secret of this gas your uncle was facilitating not just the defeat of troops, but the extermination of peoples.

"He argued. He said that I exaggerated; that gas could not be used on such a scale. I pointed out that all the time people were inventing gases capable of greater dilution and therefore of greater diffusion, he had done it himself; it was only a question of time—the longer another war was postponed, the deadlier the gases. He called me an alarmist and I admitted it. I am an alarmist, just as Cassandra was an alarmist—but I am not a false-alarmist. He suggested that since other nations had these pernicious gases, we ought to outstrip them—the same old race—and that many a better man than himself had not been ashamed to associate his name with a gas. Professor Lewis of Chicago obviously considered that his invention of Lewisite was an act of the greatest patriotism. I pointed out that if the war had not ended when it did, Professor Lewis stood a good chance of becoming the supreme slaughterer in history, and asked if that were his ambition.

"We went on, ding-dong, for weeks, and then he went and referred to it in that paper before the R.B.S. I think it gave him a bit of a shock to find how soon Amalgamated Chemicals and the rest were on the scent. He certainly had a jolt that night the house was burgled. We had no doubt what they were after; luckily they missed it. Then we argued again, all over the same old ground. Still I couldn't get him to destroy the records altogether, but he did go as far as to send them away for safe keeping.

"A few days—less than a week, I think—after that, I woke up about two in the morning and heard a commotion going on somewhere in the house. I was just getting out of bed to investigate when there was a sound of footsteps right outside my room and the door was flung wide open. Two men I had never seen before told me that I was wanted below. When I asked them who the devil they were, they simply took me by the arms and marched me out.

"Professor Woodridge lay sprawling on the tiles in the hall. A tall man who seemed to be in charge of things told me that he had slipped on the stairs and broken his neck in the fall. It may have been the truth, but it was their fault that he died. I was marched into the laboratory. The tall man asked me if I knew the formula for the gas. I told him that I did not and that it was none of his damned business, anyway. The man on the right gave me a clout with his free hand and told me to keep a civil tongue. I was not feeling in a civil mood. To be manhandled, to be shown the body of a man to whom you are attached as I was to your uncle, by men who may have murdered him and to know that you are up against a ruthless organization (oh, yes, I knew a thing or two before about A.C.'s methods) does not induce civility—not in me, at any rate. It was the first taste I had had of their treatment.

It made me lose my temper, so the man followed up that first punch with a lot more. My head was singing and bruised, but I could still hear the tall man persistently repeating his question: Where had the notes and the formula been hidden? After a while I told him that they had been sent away for safety; and it gave me some pleasure to add that when your uncle's death was discovered they would be handed over to the War Office.

"He didn't know whether to believe me or not, but he wasn't taking any chances. His men collected all the notebooks, the work of years and none of them even touching on the subject, and went through every desk and drawer and cupboard in the place. They were so unhurried and efficient that I began to feel pretty hopeless. They were perfectly sure of themselves.

"Since I had been brought downstairs, I hadn't seen either Tiller, the manservant, or his wife. I had a hope that one of them, perhaps both, had got away to fetch the police, but these men went on so calmly that the hope withered a bit. It finally died when I saw Tiller enter the lab, with an armful of papers which he dumped down in front of the tall man. I watched him closely, but he avoided meeting my eyes."

"So that was it," Derek exclaimed. "We've been hunting high and low for them, too."

"You'll be lucky if you find them. They've not only been paid well, but silenced by threats of trouble over your uncle's death."

Straker paused again, reflectively.

"I'm afraid that if you dig down to the roots, I'm responsible for what followed. If I hadn't blurted out your uncle's arrangement in case of his death, they wouldn't have gone to such lengths to conceal it. If they hadn't known that, Drawford would have been able to pass the envelope over to the War Office in safety. Mind you, I didn't actually tell them he'd got it, but once they knew the plan, it was pretty simple for them to guess who had. But they were not overlooking the chance that there had been a copy—hence their treatment of me and, later, the kidnapping of Mrs. Shiffer. Their real trouble was too much disbelief all round.

"Well, it took them a long time to convince themselves that there was no copy in the Grange—if they really are convinced yet, which I doubt. But in the morning they decided to remove me and the collection of notebooks. Until you told me just now, I didn't know how they intended to avoid raising an alarm over the professor's absence, but it was clear that they had some scheme. They put me into a car with my hands tied, a bit of cloth over my mouth and a man to see that I didn't remove it, and we came up to London.

"Somewhere in the northern suburbs we stopped to unload the notebooks, and then we went on. As I told you, I don't really know where we went, but from what the hospital people told me, I gather it must have been somewhere around Hackney. And there I stayed until about three weeks ago."

"You mean they kept you a prisoner all that time?" Derek stared, incredulously.

Straker set his teeth in an ugly fashion.

"They did. And, by God, you don't know how long it was to me."

Derek shook his head. "I don't quite understand. They weren't squeamish with the others. Why didn't they—?"

Straker interrupted with a queer laugh.

"Squeamish! No, they weren't squeamish. They tried starvation first, and then when they got afraid of losing me, they stopped that and went on to other things, the swine. There were four of them living in that house. One of them a red-headed devil. He enjoyed it. By heaven, if I ever meet him again . . ."

It was Derek's turn to interrupt.

"A red-headed man? Fellow with a squint? Had an anchor tattooed on the back of one hand?"

"That's the brute. How on earth——?"

"You won't meet him for a while. He was one of the gang who snatched the box at the bank. The flying squad collared them, and they're all doing a few years."

Straker thought for a moment. "That probably explains why I'm here now," he said, nodding as though a puzzling point were cleared up.

"The only thing that saved me from going the same way as your uncle and Drawford," he went on, "was that they couldn't make up their minds about me. I told them heaven knows how many times that I knew nothing of the gas formula and that it was your uncle's secret, but they were never absolutely sure that I wasn't lying. If they had been, I think they'd have bumped me off there and then—you see, I was a potential source of danger to them all the time I was alive. So they scratched their heads and came to the conclusion that if they made life hell for me, something might come of it: and they set out to do that pretty efficiently. . . .

"I couldn't keep any count of time. They had me cooped up in a top room ventilated only by a skylight which I couldn't reach. I didn't know how many weeks or months had passed, but it felt like years. Then one day, at the time that they usually brought me my food, no one turned up. I thought it was another starvation dodge at first, but when nobody even came to look at me, I began to guess that something had gone wrong somewhere. Of course, I see now what had happened—the whole four of them must have got roped in over that bank business, and there was nobody left to look after me; but I only knew then that I was being left alone longer than I ever had been before. After a while I decided to take a risk. I couldn't hear anybody moving in the house, and it seemed worth having a try, even if they did take it out of me afterward.

"I began battering at the door with a chair, and when nobody came to see what was happening, I got bolder and went at it harder. It must have taken me a good long time to break it, for it was a strong door, and I was pretty nearly all in. Very little food for months, a back that's raw from beatings and a body that's aching all over doesn't make you a Sandow, but the door gave way in the end. I remember crossing a landing, staggering down steep flights of filthy stairs and unlatching the front door. I've a vague recollection of wandering along a slummy street or two—then nothing else till I woke up in hospital."

He stopped. Derek got up to fill his empty glass. As he poured out the whisky, he asked:

"What are we going to do? It seems to me we've lost all round, unless . . . I say, you can't give any evidence to implicate Ferris Draymond, can you?"

Straker shook his head. "No. I've known all along that he was at the back of it, of course, but as for evidence. . . ." He shrugged his shoulders. "You could get nothing out of the men who were in the bank business—the red-headed man and his pals?"

"Nothing. They were only up for smash-and-grab and assault—there was nothing in the way of evidence to connect them with Uncle Henry and Drawford, and very naturally they weren't going to implicate themselves. The sentences were a bit heavier than they expected, owing to the way the superintendent and old Allbright were knocked about, but we couldn't hang anything else on them. I think the best thing we can do is to go and see Jordan about it at once."

But Straker did not jump at the idea. What good, he wanted to know, was that likely to do? The small fry were in prison already. The man they really wanted was Draymond, and still there was no evidence to take him.

"He's a well-known man, almost a public figure, a director of a huge business and immensely rich. He simply can't be touched unless we've got a cast-iron case. And look at us; the case we've

got wouldn't hold as much water as a sieve. No, it's no good trying to tackle it that way."

"But look here," Derek told him, "it's your duty to tell Jordan
all you know, even if he can't do anything at the moment. It'll all
go down in his notes and tell against Draymond in the long run."

"The long run! Who the hell cares about the long run? Do you
mean to wait until Draymond puts his foot in it over some other
dirty business?" Straker's voice grew bitter. "He's caused the
death of your uncle, he's murdered Drawford, he'd have got rid
of Mrs. Shiffer if he could and he's got hold of that formula in
spite of everything. And all you can do is to bleat about 'the long
run.' Hasn't he had a long enough run?"

"Yes, but—" Derek began, hopelessly.

"Why the devil didn't you destroy that envelope instead of
letting him get it back? Why not tear it up?"

"I did think of it, but I wanted to burn it—to make dead sure
it was destroyed."

"But—oh, well, it's gone now, blast it. Buller and the rest will
be working on it—oh, damnation."

"Who's Buller?" Derek asked, bewildered.

"Their big man on gases—the man they're sure to have turned
it over to. I know a bit about A.C."

"It wouldn't be possible—?" Derek began, but Straker's
thoughts had run on ahead of him.

"Steal it back from Buller? No, it would not. For one thing
Buller is part of a great organization, and for another, he's no
fool. There'll be copies, filed away in case of an accident. It's too
late to stop them making the filthy stuff, but—" He stopped
short. For some moments he glared into the fire with a savage
intensity. At last he broke out: "No, by God, they shan't get away
with it."

Derek stared at him. His face had become transformed. It was
angry and vicious. His eyes glittered venomously and the skin

seemed to be stretched tight across his cheekbones. Suddenly he snatched open his shirt: the thin, bony chest beneath was criss-crossed with scars.

"You see those. They're just a bit of what I went through in that house and, by heaven, I'm not forgetting it. They wanted that filthy gas, and they've got it. But, by God, I'll make them sorry they ever wanted it."

Derek faced him nervously. The unaccustomed whisky per-haps . . . ?

"What do you mean?" he said. Then with a sudden flash of understanding he added:

"Do you know how to make it, Straker?"

Straker jumped from his chair. He threw back his head and laughed.

"Do I know? Of course I know. I made the stuff we used on the rabbits. They thought your uncle made it: I told them he did. But it was I who made it up from his formula—and the formula's here." He tapped his forehead. "I made it once, and I can damn well make it again. And, by God, I will . . . I will. . . ."

Straker had run from the room, slamming the door behind him before Derek could interfere or even reply. Derek stared after him for an astonished moment, made a move to follow, and then checked himself. For a few minutes he stood in thought, irresolute. The sudden change in Straker had bewildered him. He had looked ill, very ill and worn when he came, but he had spoken normally enough to begin with. There had been nothing to suggest more than a physical breakdown in his health. And then he had changed. His whole face, expression, voice. . . .

Had the months of imprisonment and ill-treatment unbal-anced him mentally? It would not be surprising. Or was it all due to the unaccustomed whisky? Not had a drink since the summer, he had said. Or had the two things together combined to drive him into that wild-eyed frenzy which was undoubtedly over the brink of normality?

What ought one to do? He reached a conclusion at last and sought for the telephone. Jordan had better know. Under his fingers the dial spelt out once more the familiar:

"W-H-I—1-2-1-2."

XXII

POST SCRIPTUM

Phyllida sorted the mail.

"Two for me. They're bills. One for you, darling." She handed the envelope across the breakfast-table.

"Disgusting how the world intrudes," said Derek. "No sense of fitness. I expect it's a final notice."

He slit the envelope open. Its contents consisted of a folded newspaper clipping and, fastened to it by a paper clip, a note in a handwriting only faintly familiar. He glanced down at the signature.

"Jordan," he said. Phyllida frowned. "What does he want?" she inquired apprehensively.

"It's all right, dear. Not sudden orders to go home or anything like that." He began to read Detective-Inspector Jordan's communication aloud:

At the risk of making myself unpopular, I think you ought to know of the enclosed. Foreign newspapers can be unreliable for home news, and I am told that newspapers of any kind are not much read on honeymoons. As you know, we failed to pick up Straker's tracks after he left your flat, and we have heard nothing of him since. In the circumstances (i.e. his condition and the whisky on top of it) we felt justified in supposing it to be no more than a momentary mental instability, but—well, what do you make of this cutting?

My regards to Mrs. Jameson and yourself.

Derek detached the note and unfolded the cutting to its full extent.

"What is it?" Phyllida came round the table and looked over his shoulder. A black headline caught her eye:

CHEMICAL WORKS DISASTER

and in slightly smaller type:

Lives Lost in Mystery Tragedy

Derek was already reading the column of print below:

"A grave disaster, involving the loss of several lives, occurred at the Amalgamated Chemicals Research Station at Leabrook, Norfolk, yesterday afternoon. While it is still impossible to determine the full extent of the tragedy, there can be little doubt that all the workers trapped in the building are beyond help. Mystery continues to surround the cause of the accident, as noxious fumes which have not yet dispersed still prevent close approach to the scene. The police have drawn a cordon round the danger area and are diverting all traffic.

"Among those known to be in the building at the time of the accident was Mr. Ferris Draymond, who is well known as a director of Amalgamated Chemicals, Ltd. He was on a visit to Mr. Frederick Buller, who is in charge of the research station.

"Dr. Dennis Draymond, interviewed by our representative early today, said: 'I know that my father intended to pay a visit to the Research Station yesterday. He was very anxious to inspect some of the results which Mr. Buller had obtained. The fact that he did not return home last night as we expected, leaves very little doubt that he must have been in the building at the time of the accident.' Asked if he could reveal the nature of Mr. Buller's researches, Dr. Draymond expressed regret that he was not at liberty to throw any light on the matter. The tragedy of Mr. Ferris Draymond's death is made more poignant by the fact that this was his first visit to the station for several months."

(Someone, presumably Jordan, had underlined the last half of the sentence and put an exclamation mark in the margin. Derek nodded concurringly.)

"From another source it has been learned that Mr. Buller was interested in the development of gases for use in warfare. There is reason to suppose that the accident was due to certain experiments in this direction. It is thought that no less than twenty persons were inside the building at the time. Three outside employees, who were in the immediate vicinity, have been admitted to hospital in a critical condition, and little hope of their recovery is entertained.

"The state of health of four members of the local fire-brigade who attempted to approach the affected area wearing gas-masks, is also the cause of grave concern. It is understood from a member of the hospital staff that the symptoms of all these men are not unlike those suffered by the victims of mustard gas during the war.

"Operations for clearing the area of gas are now in progress, to enable experts to ascertain the full extent of the tragedy and to investigate the causes of the accident."

"All of which, being translated, means that nobody really has a ghost of an idea what happened, except that some gas got loose," murmured Derek.

An additional note had been penciled by Jordan at the foot of the column:

Stop Press report that after an explosion a fire broke out and destroyed the building before the gas could be cleared.

Phyllida looked up as she finished reading:
"I suppose it was Straker?" she asked.
For answer, he pointed to the underlined words:

—this was his first visit to the station for several months.

"Jordan evidently does."
She nodded comprehendingly: "Yes, it could hardly be a co-incidence."
"It was too thorough—and there was the fire as well. . . . He said to me: 'By God, I'll make them sorry they ever wanted it.' And he has. Yes, Straker did it, all right. And he did his best to burn the records, too."
"It's horrible, horrible." Phyllida shivered a little.
Derek nodded slowly. "It is. But Draymond got just what he was planning for thousands of better men. He is no loss." Absent-mindedly, he folded up the cutting and put it away in his pocket.
He raised his eyes to the window and the scene beyond. A string of little black figures was trudging slowly up the rounded flank of a snow mountain. He drew Phyllida close and kissed her.
"Come along, darling. To our work. God's fresh air is calling. While you go and put on some Glypalm—'Complexion's Concierge,' as Barry would say—I'll go and iron the skis."

ABOUT THE AUTHOR

JOHN WYNDHAM PARKES LUCAS BEYNON HARRIS was born in Knowle, Warwickshire, England, on July 10, 1903. The recent discovery of his personal papers has shed light on the previously unknown life of Wyndham. Until 1911, he lived in Edgbaston, Birmingham, England, and then moved to other parts of the country. After attending several private preparatory schools, he enrolled in Bedales School in Petersfield, England, about an hour's drive from London. He began writing short stories in 1925 after unsuccessful attempts at careers in farming, law, advertising, and commercial art, and through the 1930s made his living by selling his stories to a myriad of periodicals. When England entered World War II, Wyndham joined the English civil service and later the British Army. After leaving the army in 1946, he resumed his writing, turning to novels and publishing under many different pseudonyms. The 1950s brought him great financial and critical success with *The Day of the Triffids* (1951), *The Kraken Wakes* (1953), *The Chrysalids* (1955), and *The Midwich Cuckoos* (1957). He died on March 11, 1969.

ABOUT THE TYPE

The principal text of this Modern Library edition was set in a
digitized version of Janson, a typeface that dates from about
1690 and was cut by Nicholas Kis (1650–1702), a Hungarian
working in Amsterdam. The original matrices have survived
and are held by the Stempel foundry in Germany. Hermann
Zapf (1918–2015) redesigned some of the weights and sizes for
Stempel, basing his revisions on the original design.